MAYORAL MYSTERY: WEB OF LIES

HAVERSHIRE MYSTERY BOOK 2

R. M. SHEPHERD

DEDICATION

To Charles, who has supported my efforts through the years.

CONTENTS

Chapter One

AN INVITATION

With fluid movements, the woman used her dagger to cut flowers in the rose garden. A few strands of Ellene's dark, curly hair escaped her linen coif. The sweet scent of roses teased her nose as her skirt brushed against the bushes. Flitting from one bloom to another, honeybees filled the air with their constant buzzing.

She paused as the sound of hoofbeats in the courtyard echoed off the walls of the residence. Jeremy, the valet, emerged from the house to greet the rider. She attempted to catch their exchange, but their voices did not reach her ears. They conferred briefly, then the rider departed, and Jeremy returned to the house. Ellene hurried to finish gathering the roses, then returned the dagger to her skirt pocket. She wondered about the message's intended recipient and its contents.

Her niece, Avrill, a lively thirteen-year-old, had reached marriageable age. Her brother's previous attempt to match his daughter and the son of a long-time friend ended badly. Still, he continued to search for a suitable match. Perhaps the messenger brought a letter from a wealthy friend with eligible sons.

Inside the house, she made her way to the dining room. Carefully, she arranged the roses in a ceramic vase in the middle of the wooden table.

"Who was that, Jeremy?" Sir William Throck-Morton, Ellene's brother and the owner of Haver Hall, made his way from his office to the dining room. Like his sister, his hair was dark and curly. Ellene tilted her head up to make eye contact with him, as he was a foot taller than her.

"Sir, the messenger brought this for you," Jeremy said. He handed the sealed parchment to William.

Avrill descended the stairs with a lightness in her step. "What is it, Papa? Anything interesting? Or boring business matters as usual?"

William's voice was light and playful. "I'll open it when we have our noonday meal, *ma Cherie.*"

The family sat at the table and Sorcha, their maid, brought out meat, cheese, fruit, and fresh bread. As they ate, William broke the seal and unfolded the paper. He took his time reading it, glancing occasionally at his daughter, who stared at him and wiggled in her chair.

William glanced at Ellene and Avrill, then back at the letter.

"Well, this might interest you both. Your uncle, the Earl de Beauvoir, invites us to his daughter Louisa's wedding at his estate in two months. It will include dances, banquets, and hunting. The earl specifically invited you and Aunt Ellene. He plans to have other young people attend as well."

After he finished reading the letter, William looked up and smiled at Avrill.

"Really, Papa? I can't wait to see my cousins again. Will it be a chance for me to meet single men?" Avrill gasped, her jaw dropping. Avrill's mother, now deceased, was the earl's sister.

Ellene chuckled at the infectious enthusiasm radiating from Avrill. "That is splendid, William. It will be a wonderful opportunity for her."

Avrill's joy evaporated, replaced by a wave of despair. "I have nothing to wear. My clothes make me look like a little girl. I need to have something that will be more, well, womanly." As Avrill entered puberty, her slender body filled out, and her clothes no longer fit properly.

"She needs to be dressed appropriately to attract a wealthy husband." Ellene looked thoughtful, then smiled at Avrill. "We'll arrange for you to have beautiful clothing for the gathering. Your father and I need to have a chat, and then we'll let you know what we've decided."

Ellene paused, then addressed her brother. "Why would the earl ask about me, do you think?"

William's brows drew close together as he pondered her question. "Did I forget to tell you? His wife died six months ago. He may be interested in you as a mate, not just as a chaperon."

"I'm flattered, but this should be Avrill's opportunity. I can wait to find a husband until after she's married." The thought of the much older earl proposing marriage caused Ellene to frown. She had no intention of finding another husband. She had been married to Lord Hunter who died several years ago. Raising Avrill filled the emptiness in her life.

Later, Ellene made her way to William's office. The aromas of ink and sealing wax permeated the space. He sat at a large desk in the center of the room, writing on parchment. Bookshelves lined one wall, and a fireplace dominated another.

"I want to suggest something about Avrill's wardrobe if you have a minute."

"By all means, tell me more." William arched his eyebrows.

"I know the cost of silk and velvet fabrics, plus the cost of trims. And we must hire a seamstress." Ellene paused as William nodded. "So, I propose we alter some gowns that are still in excellent condition."

"Who would these items belong to?" William grasped his pen in both hands, as though preparing to break it.

"Desiree."

William's face reddened in anger. He loved his wife and believed that if he preserved her things just as she left them, it would somehow keep her presence alive. "NO, I won't hear of it."

Ellene took a deep breath. "Take a moment to hear me out before deciding. Avrill has three options. One is to be a spinster and live here until you die. Another is to marry beneath her station. Alternatively, secure suitable attire and a dowry to attract wealthy suitors."

"I know, but—." William let out a sigh and shook his head.

"Think about it. Desiree's beautiful clothes hang in a wardrobe. In time, the fabric will rot, and they'll be nothing but rags. They should go to her daughter. Avrill's complexion is like her mother's. A skilled seamstress altering the skirts and bodices will make Avrill look fashionable and beautiful. If you want your daughter to marry someone at your level of society, you must dress her appropriately."

William's color returned to normal. He was always frugal; he appreciated his sister's conservative approach.

"Well, what you say makes sense. You and Avrill figure out what she needs for the earl's festivities. We can decide later regarding other clothes."

Haver Hall had been in the Throck-Morton family for two generations. The siblings' great-grandfather received his title and land from King Henry

VII. William inherited the estate when their father died. Ellene moved away when she married Lord Hunter. Following his death, she returned to help raise her niece when Desiree had passed away.

Constructed of stone and heavy timber over one hundred years ago, the walls of the primary residence were thick, with openings for windows to let in fresh air and sunlight. It had three levels and two wings, forming a U-shape. An underground cellar, accessed through a kitchen floor opening and a set of stone steps, housed barrels, shelves, and tables for storing food and drinks.

The "U"-shaped ground floor housed the vestibule, Great Hall, and main stairs to the east wing's upper level. The sitting room, library, and William's office were all in the east wing. On the west side were the dining room, kitchen, and pantry. From the kitchen, a narrow staircase meant for the servants ascended to the top floor. A door at the rear of the kitchen led into the garden area and the stable.

On the upper floor, the main stairway led to a long hall with three guest bedrooms and two rooms for the house servants. The west wing held a suite with bedrooms for the master and mistress and dressing areas for both. After Desiree died, William kept her rooms locked. On the east side were bedrooms for Ellene and Avrill, and a storage room containing extra bedding, clothing, shoes, and other items. Ellene returned to the room she had as a child, while Avrill occupied William's former room.

In her bedroom, Avrill sat in front of the mirror, brushing her hair until it shone, when Ellene came to tell her the news.

"I just talked with your papa about clothing. Did you know that your mother's clothes are still in the wardrobe in her room?"

Avrill's eyes darted away, a sheepish look replacing her usual confidence. "I used to go in there after she died until Papa locked the door. I could pretend she was still with me, just in another room in the house. Her clothes were beautiful."

"Your papa has just given permission for you to select a few items. We can hire Pernilla, Simon Gates' daughter, to alter them for you."

Avrill's expression changed as her eyes glowed with excitement. "Oh, can we? I adore the fabrics and colors. How soon can we start?"

"Well, you can select what you need for your cousin's wedding. Then we will go to the fabric shop tomorrow on our way to the Smythe estate and talk to Pernilla. Let's get an accurate count of the garments to negotiate the price."

Ellene unlocked the door to Desiree's bedroom. The room had ample space, with windows lining one wall and a wardrobe on another. A fireplace dominated the third wall. The bed, aligned to the fourth wall, had four posts and fabric draped from the corners. On the same wall as the wardrobe, a door led to a passageway to William's room.

Ellene noticed spider webs in a corner. She made a mental note to tell Sorcha to clean this room.

Avrill skipped as they made their way to the wardrobe. Ellene opened the doors to reveal bodices, gowns, and skirts in brocades, silks, and velvets.

"Aunt Ellene, let me see." Avrill bounced on her tiptoes, her eyes darting around the wardrobe's interior.

"Here they are. Select colors that will make you look beautiful."

"Oh, I like these." Avrill chose silk and velvet bodices and gowns in shades of blues and greens, and skirts in yellow and tan that had a delicate shimmer in the light. They enhanced her medium brown hair, brown eyes, and pale skin.

"Let's take them to a guest bedroom. There you can try on the garments and store them until the alterations are completed."

Ellene felt her heart swell with joy as her niece's tinkling laughter filled the room. Ellene recalled the experience of selecting fabrics for her own trousseau.

"While you try on the garments, I need to find my clothes for the mayor's banquet this week. They should be in the hallway closet." Ellene left Avrill in the guest bedroom.

Eustace Ellingham, mayor of Haver Hamlet, held a sumptuous banquet annually at his estate, Coeur de Lion. He invited the members of the village council, of which William was a member. The banquet provided the ultimate summer celebration, featuring musicians, mouthwatering food, and a joyful ambiance. Known as a miserly man, this was a rare occasion when Eustace was generous with food and drink for his guests.

He expected the women to dress in their finest gowns and the men in their best breeches and doublets. The guests wore a mask of feathers and intricate artwork on the upper part of their face.

Ellene and the mayor's wife, Marguerite, were best friends. Marguerite was not familiar with Haver Hamlet, having married Eustace in London only a few years before. Marguerite's husband restricted her opportunities to meet with other women in the county. Ellene's face contorted as it reminded her of her late husband's control over her social life.

In the hallway closet, she found her bodice, gown, and skirt, but not the mask. Many years ago, she commissioned the mask and wore it annually. She shook her head with annoyance. Where could it be? She would seek the help of the servants in searching for it.

A tall, muscular, auburn-haired man, wearing riding boots and a leather baldric, armed with a firearm, a sword, and several daggers, rode up the narrow lane leading to nearby Haver Manor. The afternoon sun's rays illuminated the dust that clung to his sweat-soaked skin. The rhythmic clatter of hooves on the gravel mingled with the distant chirping of birds, welcoming Sheriff James Asher back to his home. Fatigue gnawed at his muscles, but a deep sense of relief washed over him as he arrived.

The queen awarded Haver Manor, located south of the village, to James for his faithful service in the army. He remained unmarried during his military service due to extensive travel. However, he reached the age when his thoughts turned to a home and family. His father owned a large holding in northern England, but James was the second son and would not inherit. Soon after James moved into Haver Manor the previous year, bandits killed the county sheriff. Eustace persuaded James to assume the role.

Thomas Carter, who served as his steward, met him in the courtyard and took the reins of James' horse as he dismounted. Thomas was his cousin on his mother's side of the family. A dozen men emerged from the barn and barracks to greet him. They were mercenaries on his payroll, but also available to others who needed trained warriors for hire. James was in high demand for training young men in weaponry and combat skills because of his experience as an army officer.

Ellene was foremost in his thoughts. When he departed on his journey to visit his ailing father, their strained relationship weighed on his heart, and he hoped that time would soften her animosity. He was determined to make things right between them.

CHAPTER TWO

THE DRESSMAKER

The next day, Ellene waited in the courtyard while Clive saddled their horses. She shaded her eyes from the bright noonday sun and felt the soft caress of the gentle breeze on her cheeks. To prepare Avrill for a suitable marriage, Ellene resolved Avrill needed to practice her social skills. She regretted that her desire for seclusion contributed to her decision to keep Avrill home. Avrill deserved better, especially now that she was old enough to marry.

First, they would visit the seamstress to arrange alterations. After that, they would spend the afternoon with Molly Smythe and Marguerite Ellingham, two of the most influential women in the county.

Avrill donned her riding clothes and hurried down the stairs, her overskirt swishing around her ankles. She rushed to the courtyard to join her aunt. William followed close behind. He felt the weight of his sword and daggers tugging against the leather of his baldric with each step. The threat of bandits in the area made it imperative to take precautions.

Clive emerged from the stable, leading the horses as they neighed and stamped their hooves, eager to be on the move. William's horse was a large gray gelding. Ellene and Avrill rode brown mares, who were smaller and gentler than William's horse.

"When do ye expect to be back?" Clive said. He always asked about their plans before they left the estate.

"This afternoon, in time for the evening meal." Ellene said.

Clive helped Ellene and Avrill mount their horses, and the family set off at a trot. As the trio traveled down the lane and onto the main road, the horses' hooves created clouds of dust.

When passing the lane leading to Haver Manor, Ellene thought of James. Although he had been living there for a year, they first met just a few months ago. As sheriff, he conducted an inquiry into a theft at Haver Hall. Despite the initial friction caused by his haughty attitude and commanding manner, they eventually found common ground and collaborated to solve the mystery. When they were last together, he revealed his romantic feelings for her.

Ellene took a deep breath and tried to identify the sensations swirling inside her when she thought of him. His military service instilled in him a decisive and uncompromising nature. She found him attractive, but her previous marriage had been overly restrictive, and she valued her freedom. James insisted on having control, expecting her to be submissive. They quarreled several times over the course of their brief relationship. She put him out of her mind while he traveled to the northern borders for a month dealing with family issues. She hoped he had given up on courting her and shifted his interest to another woman.

Simon Gates, a prosperous merchant, kept his shop stocked with fabrics, thread, and an array of trimmings. For those of the servant class, he stocked wool and linen for everyday wear. For the middle-and upper-classes, he kept a variety of imported brocades, jacquards, silks, and velvets. Simon's wife died from smallpox a few years back. Pernilla, his second oldest daughter, worked as a seamstress and helped sell the merchandise.

William, Ellene, and Avrill stopped their horses in front of the shop. Cool air and dim lighting awaited them as they stepped inside. Simon kept the windows covered to prevent the sun from fading the fabrics. Ellene saw Avrill's eyes grow wide with wonder as she gazed at the scene before her.

"Welcome, Sir William, Lady Ellene. How may I serve you today?" Simon greeted them. His lips curled up into a smile, revealing his crooked teeth. About William's age, he had long, straight black hair, and a scraggly goatee. His slender physique included elongated fingers that reminded Ellene of a spider's legs.

"My daughter has need of a seamstress. We thought immediately of Pernilla. Is she here?" William raised his eyebrows as he looked around the shop.

"In the back room. I'll go get her."

Simon disappeared and returned a moment later with a young woman, her hair in a tight braid pinned to her head and concealed by a linen coif.

"My father tells me you need my services." She spoke in a high-pitched, squeaky voice.

Ellene nodded, her voice low and steady. "We own some garments that were made about seven years ago. The fabric is in pristine condition, with no signs of wear. We would like to have the garments altered for Avrill to ensure she looks her best at an upcoming wedding. Primarily shorten the skirts, take in the sides. They need to be finished in a month. Are you interested?"

"Yes, certainly." Pernilla nodded in agreement.

William and Simon negotiated the fee. As Avrill watched and listened, she shifted her weight from one foot to the other, her hands fluttering at her sides. There would be some magnificent outfits for her to wear to her cousin's wedding.

The negotiations finished, Pernilla retreated to the back room. As the trio headed toward the door, Simon asked Ellene to stay a minute. She paused while William and Avrill kept going.

"Are you planning to attend the mayor's banquet?" Simon stood with his arms folded, his eyes fixed on her.

"Yes, William and I plan to be there." It perplexed Ellene as to why he waited for William and Avrill to leave. "Will you and Pernilla be there?"

"I will. Pernilla can't go this year since she just had a baby. What I want to ask is, well, may I have the honor of dancing with you?"

Ellene paused, her fingers fiddling with a loose thread on her skirt as she thought about her answer. The way he looked at her made it clear he desired something more than just a dance. Besides, he could have waited until the evening of the banquet to ask her. "There will be more men than women at the banquet. I'll be happy to dance with you and the other men as well."

"I look forward to the dancing," he responded, his voice filled with anticipation.

CHAPTER THREE

VISITING THE SMYTHES

I n southern England, County Havershire had within its bounds many large estates, some smaller freeholds, and the village of Haver Hamlet. Originating from the east coast, the primary road passed Haver Hall and Haver Manor, then ran through the village before continuing northwards to London. Andrew Smythe, Eustace, and the county justice of the peace, Callum Etchell, owned estates to the north of the village.

A fertile area, the fields flourished with thriving crops, and healthy livestock roamed through the pastures. In the spring, the sound of bleating baby lambs filled the air as they gamboled in the lush fields. Farmers also raised chickens, ducks, and geese for food. Summer brought fruit and fish to the tables. The fields would bustle with activity in the fall as farmers worked to gather the grain harvest. Deer roamed the forest, occasionally accompanied by wild pigs.

William, Ellene, and Avrill chatted as they made their way to the Smythe estate, anticipation building as they drew near. The family turned off the main road onto the lane leading up to the house. Constructed during the same era as Haver Hall, the house appeared smaller compared to others in the area because of its few narrow windows and long, rectangular shape.

In the fields, the tree branches hung low from the weight of the ripening fruit. Sheep dotted the slopes of the green pastures nearby. As they neared the house, William recognized Marguerite's mare, tethered to a post beneath a shade tree.

Avrill's squeal of delight filled the air. "Ooh, I'm excited to see Molly today. She always gives me a big hug."

"Marguerite is here too," William spoke with a warmth in his voice that made Ellene glance at her brother. A broad smile appeared on his face.

"It was gracious of Molly to invite us. William, what do you plan to do while we visit with the ladies?"

"Andrew and I have some things to talk about. We may head to his office or take a stroll around the estate. He appears to have an abundant crop of apples this year."

The stableman met them in the courtyard to take their horses. A servant met them at the door, then led them down the hall to where Molly and Marguerite waited in the sitting room.

When Molly saw Avrill, her face lit up. She leaped up and gave her a warm hug, just as Avrill predicted.

William stopped to greet the women on his way to see Andrew. "Good afternoon, Molly. It's good to see you again, Marguerite."

Ellene noticed his eyes lingered on the mayor's vivacious wife, who blushed in response. The fragrance of the Italian perfume Marguerite wore wafted in their direction.

After the women greeted him, William followed the servant down the hallway to Andrew's office.

Molly gestured for Ellene and Avrill to sit on the upholstered chairs, which formed a semi-circle for conversation. A fireplace dominated one wall. Multi-colored tapestries adorned the remaining walls. Ellene and Avrill took their seats across from their hostess and Marguerite.

"I'm glad you could join us, Avrill. My, my, you are looking more like your mother every day." Molly beamed at the girl, who was about the same age as her granddaughters.

"Mrs. Smythe, your comment means a lot to me." Avrill's cheeks flamed, and she wriggled in her seat, embarrassed by the attention. Hearing others compare her to her mother, a woman known for her beauty, always brought a smile to her face. People were prone to characterize Avrill as plain, noting her almost childlike features.

"Is everything coming together for the banquet this week, Marguerite? Could we be of any help?" Ellene remembered the problems that occurred the previous year because of Marguerite's inexperience.

"No, thank you. Everything is in hand. Everyone on the council will be there. Eustace is so looking forward to having them attend." She smiled and her brown eyes sparkled. "We're waiting for confirmation from Rev. Broun and James, however."

Christopher Broun was the vicar of the Anglican church in Haver Hamlet.

"I have never known the vicar to turn down an invitation to a meal." Ellene's chuckle was contagious, bringing a smile to everyone around her.

"My thoughts as well. Ellene, do you know if James has returned?" Marguerite peered out of the corner of her eyes as she sipped at her beverage.

"I've not heard yet. Thomas expects him back soon, I'm told." Ellene's focus was on Avrill and her social skills, determined to help her improve.

James was a complication that she did not want to consider right now. "If James returns before the banquet, he may decline. He may have to chase criminals." Ellene scrunched up her nose. She moved on to a different topic. "Avrill's uncle, the Earl de Beauvoir, invited her to his daughter's wedding to be held in two months. We hope she will meet some eligible young men." Ellene spoke with pride.

Avrill felt heat rising to her cheeks when Molly and Marguerite turned their gaze towards her.

"Of course you need some beautiful clothes to wear. I hear Simon has some brocades and velvets just arrived from Italy. And lace from France," Marguerite gushed. "Eustace promised me a new gown this fall. He always complains about the cost, but in the end, he buys what I want."

"Eustace is wealthy and you have the means to buy Simon's wares. We have less to spend on such things." Ellene gave her head a shake.

"But William is wealthy, isn't he? He owns the largest estate in the county." Marguerite peered out of the corner of her eye.

"He is devoting as much as possible to Avrill's dowry." Ellene reached over to Avrill and patted her hand.

"We're going to take my mother's clothes to the dressmaker for alterations." Avrill proclaimed with pride. "We already hired Pernilla to do the work."

The women smiled, remembering their own journey into womanhood and how eager they were building their trousseau.

"Speaking of Simon, I hear he is looking for a wife." Molly's voice was a whisper.

"Oh." Ellene uttered the word before she could stop herself.

Three pairs of eyes turned toward her, curious about what she meant by her outburst.

"Well, it explains something. He pulled me aside at the shop and asked to dance with me at the banquet. He could have waited until the event. I felt there was more to his request than just a dance."

"It seems James has a rival." Molly gave a small chuckle. "I can imagine athletic James dueling with skinny Simon. James can certainly best Simon in a fair fight."

"James and I are just friends. My primary concern right now is introducing Avrill to society. My personal life can wait." Ellene's statement was firm, and her smile disappeared.

Molly and Marguerite exchanged glances.

"You must want a husband and children. What would you do if William married again? He would no longer need you to manage the household. Be mindful of your own needs and look out for yourself. I always do." Marguerite spoke with a confident tone.

Annoyed by her comments, Ellene introduced a new topic of discussion.

As the owners of the biggest estates in the county, William and Andrew's interests aligned. Andrew inherited his estate from his uncle. He and Molly were about fifteen years older than William. The men had become friends when Andrew moved to County Havershire. In Andrew's office, they discussed local livestock and produce prices.

Andrew furrowed his brow. "I understand Michael Milner is raising his fees at the mill again."

"I had not heard about that. How much?" William's eyebrows flew up.

"Ten percent over last year."

"It's hard for farmers to make a profit at those prices. We need to see about finding another mill."

"The one in Updyke Chase has better prices, but the transportation costs alone make that prohibitive."

William let out a deep sigh. "I know. But there must be some way to reason with the man. Perhaps if all the estate owners confronted him, he would back off."

"Doubtful. Word has it Eustace raised the mill's taxes to pay for his extravagant spending on his young wife. Michael is just passing the costs on to estate owners and farmers."

"Eustace seems to have his hand in everything that goes on in the county. Someday, somebody will put a stop to his conniving." William shook his head, a hint of exasperation in his voice.

Andrew nodded in agreement. "Eustace tried to pressure me to pay more taxes. I stood up to him and he backed down. He uncovers secrets about people and threatens to make them public knowledge, promising to keep silent if they pay. Despite this, I know a few things about him he doesn't want me to reveal. There will come a time when he crosses paths with the wrong individual, and his threats will backfire."

William acknowledged his agreement with a grunt, but did not reveal his own vulnerability. He and Marguerite met often, always sneaking away from prying eyes. If Eustace were to catch him with Marguerite, he would exact merciless revenge.

After William, Ellene, and Avrill left, Bridgette cornered Sorcha in the downstairs hall.

"Have you tidied up recently?" Bridgette stared at her.

Sorcha squirmed, her body tense and her heart racing. "What do you mean? Of course I have. Tis my job."

"Lady Ellene says the fancy masks for parties have gone missing. The previous maid stored them in the closet with the fancy clothes. They aren't there anymore. Did you move them?"

"What do they look like?" Sorcha's eyes darted, and she cringed as though expecting a blow.

Bridgette watched the girl as she described the masks. Sorcha's eyes grew large, and her hand flew to her mouth.

"Is that what they're for? Nothing I had seen before was so lovely. The thought of them getting damaged made me nervous, so I put them in a trunk to be safe. I'll bring them to you." Sorcha scurried up the stairs. After some commotion, Sorcha appeared again, holding two satin masks with gold trim and feathers.

"I'm ever so sorry. Please don't tell the master. I didn't hurt them any. I wouldn't steal them, I swear." The words tumbled out and tears formed in her eyes.

Bridgette cradled the objects. "I appreciate your honesty. But don't do that again. Do you understand?"

Sorcha nodded. "May I continue cleaning?"

"Go on. I'll give these to Lady Ellene when she returns."

Chapter Four

EUSTACE VISITS THE VILLAGE

E ustace winced as his carriage lurched on the bumpy road. His foot pulsated with pain from his gout flare-up earlier in the day. He would normally have remained in his office with his foot propped up on a stool, but he received a cryptic note about a deal on wine. Because he was always trying to save money, he was intrigued.

It was mid-afternoon when he reached the White Stag Inn in the village. His servants carried him inside on a chair, since walking proved too painful. He pointed to a table in the middle of the room, where they set him down. His stringy gray hair brushed his shoulders, framing his round face and emphasizing his obesity. Food and wine stains marred his velvet doublet and breeches.

While waiting for the note's author to identify himself, Eustace ordered some wine. After the innkeeper's daughter, Bess, served him, a wiry man with a gray beard and hair and wearing shabby clothes approached the table. He carried a tankard of ale.

"Are ye Mayor Ellingham?" The man peered at him as he took a drink from the tankard.

"Who wants to know?" Eustace's voice had a wary edge to it.

"Call me Harry. I've some wine I could sell ye for a reduced price."

"Yes, I'm Ellingham. Sit. And keep your voice low."

The man took the chair opposite Eustace. "I've five barrels of fine wine to sell. The original buyer changed his mind, so I'm looking for another one. It's on my wagon, so I can deliver it right away. I can sell it to ye cheap." Harry took another drink from his tankard and wiped his mouth on his sleeve. "I hear ye are a man who knows his wine."

"What's your price?" Eustace studied him.

"Depends on how soon ye can pay. I need to empty my wagon to pick up another load. I've other buyers, but thought I'd give ye the first chance. Other opportunities might present themselves, if ye know what I mean."

"If you deliver tomorrow, I will pay tomorrow."

Harry stated his price in a level tone.

Eustace shook his head in disbelief. "No, too high. I pay that much now. I have no reason to buy your wine. Besides, I have only the word of a stranger that it's not sour. I insist on tasting it before I'll pay."

They haggled back and forth for several minutes. Bess stopped by the table to see if either man wanted a refill. She noticed a vivid scar resulting from a burn on Harry's wrist, the red color standing out against his pale skin. The men declined, and she left to serve another table. They continued haggling until they settled on their price.

Harry stood up to leave, and they shook hands. "I'll fetch yer wine tomorrow, then." He sauntered to the door, but once outside, he scurried to his wagon and rushed away from the inn.

Eustace gestured to his servants, who waited near the door. They carried Eustace in his chair out of the inn to the waiting carriage.

The county's physician, Zachary Morgan, was passing by when he noticed Eustace climb into his carriage. Seeing Eustace grimace, he stopped. "How is your gout today, Mayor?"

"Bad. I can hardly walk. Need to go home and put my foot up." Eustace snarled and bared his teeth in a threatening display.

"I understand congratulations are in order."

Eustace's eyebrows flew up. "For what?"

"Why, Marguerite is with child. I just confirmed it this week." Zachary's face lit up with a warm smile.

Eustace's eyebrows drew together in a deep frown. "She hasn't told me yet. Keep it to yourself, you hear?"

Zachary nodded, furrowing his brow in confusion. He expected the mayor to be ecstatic about the baby.

Eustace shouted to the driver to head to the estate, and the driver set the horses into motion.

At Coeur de Lion, the peaceful sound of a babbling stream filled the air as it made its way from beyond the village, flowing over moss-covered rocks and meandering through the property. The orchard, set back from the road, was fragrant with the aroma of ripening fruit. In the nearby pasture, a flock of sheep grazed, their fluffy white coats a sharp contrast to the green grass.

Some time ago, Eustace evicted the tenants from his land and tore down their cottages, depriving them of the properties their grandparents and parents had farmed. He agreed to let them keep their sheep in his expansive pastures, receiving some profits generated from the sale of both meat and wool. Many still bore hard feelings about losing their homes and livelihoods. He hired farmhands to come in as needed to plant, harvest, and perform maintenance.

The residence, built with heavy timber, stones, and a slate roof, was older than Haver Hall. The house rose three stories high, the ground floor three feet above the courtyard. Stairs bordered by shrubs ascended from the courtyard to the ground floor. The front door, twice a man's height, was of thick wood planks hung on sturdy metal hinges. A massive tree grew outside the front bedroom, its branches grazing the stone wall.

A servant helped Eustace hobble to his office. His toe throbbed, and he sat in his chair, propping his foot on a stool with a sigh of relief.

"Has my wife returned from her outing?" His voice rumbled.

"I'll inquire, master." The servant exited the room.

A few minutes later, Eustace scrutinized Marguerite, graceful and effortless as she glided in, her expensive perfume wafting in the air. When they met in London, he was smitten by her beauty and innocence. Now, he grew suspicious of her activities.

"Did you enjoy your visit with Molly?" Eustace growled as his eyes narrowed.

"Yes, my love. We enjoyed being in each other's company." She kissed him on the forehead. "Ellene and Avrill were there as well."

He made a grunting sound. "What still needs to be done to prepare for the banquet?"

"I picked up my new gown from Pernilla. Prudence ordered the food, and I hired the musicians. It will be delightful. The entire council is coming. Rev. Broun and the sheriff haven't told me their plans yet." Joy filled Marguerite's face as she beamed her bright smile. "How are you feeling today? I assume you are feeling better since you went to the village?"

"I had business to attend to."

Eustace's face contorted into a fierce scowl and he fixed her with a piercing stare.

"Zachary approached me when I was getting into my carriage. He mentioned that you have something to tell me."

"What—what do you mean?" She felt her face go pale as a wave of icy fear coursed through her.

"He told me you are with child. Is this true?"

"No, he is mistaken. It is merely an upset stomach."

"If I find out you are pregnant, I shall publicly accuse you of adultery. That child cannot possibly be mine. I shall divorce you and leave you and the child without a farthing. When I discover who the father is, I will file charges against him."

Eustace's face flushed as he jabbed his finger in her direction.

Marguerite swallowed hard. "I assure you, I'm not pregnant."

Eustace glowered at her and pointed toward the door. "Get out of my sight."

Marguerite scurried out of the office, her hands trembling as she fled to her bedroom.

CHAPTER FIVE

JAMES VISITS ELLENE

That morning, James spent an hour sparring with his men in the courtyard, then rode into Haver Hamlet to catch up on his work. When he opened the door to his office, he found papers and scrolls piled on his desk. Removing his bonnet and baldric, he sat at the desk ready to work.

He began reading and sorting the papers into piles, then signed those which required his authority. For a small county, there seemed to be a lot of crime, he reflected. Most of these minor infractions resulted in flogging or a day or two in the pillory or stocks. A few hours later, hunger pangs prompted him to head to the White Stag Inn. He noticed the mayor's carriage tied up near the stable.

Inside, his eyebrows lifted in surprise to see the mayor sitting at a table with a wiry man with gray hair, a sharp face, and shabby clothes. Eustace seldom left his house anymore because of his gout. Bess greeted James as he threaded his way around the tables to sit at one in a corner facing the door.

"The usual, Sheriff?" she asked.

Bess chuckled because James ordered stew, bread, and cheese every day, and a cup of ale to wash it down.

At his nod, Bess hustled to the kitchen to assemble the food and drink. James passed the time by scanning the room. Except for the mayor, most of the customers were strangers, traders who were just passing through.

While Bess placed the food on James' table, Eustace and the gray-haired man stood and shook hands. After the stranger left, Eustace gestured to his servants and departed the inn without acknowledging James' presence.

James shrugged before taking a bite of his meal. Eustace normally ignored those he considered lesser social status. While eating, James couldn't help but think of Ellene and their moments together. Picturing her bright eyes and the way her lips curved up in a welcoming smile cheered him up. He planned to stop at Haver Hall on his way home.

Ellene, William, and Avrill were back at Haver Hall after their visit to the Smythes. Ellene heard hooves echoing in the courtyard. It must be another messenger had arrived for William, she thought.

Soon after she heard Sorcha greet a man at the door, the maid appeared in the upstairs hallway. She was twenty, short in stature, with stringy blond hair. Her gray eyes seldom looked up, and her shoulders slumped. Her voice floated down the hallway.

"Lady Ellene. Are you up here?" she asked.

Ellene emerged from the hall closet. "Yes, what do you need?"

"Sheriff Asher is in the Great Hall. He asked if he could speak with you. He wants to let you know he's back from his journey."

No, not today; I'm too busy, Ellene thought. She remembered promising him she would invite him to dine when he returned. She wondered why he did not just send a message, and why he asked for her instead of

William.

"Thank you, Sorcha. Inform him I'll be downstairs to welcome him shortly."

Sorcha curtsied and hurried down the stairway.

Ellene went to her bedroom to tidy her coif and brush the dust off her skirt. She paused at the upstairs landing and looked down. Avrill, who heard the exchange, emerged from her bedroom, but lingered behind her aunt.

James stood in the Great Hall. He looked up and saw Ellene, a wide smile spreading across his face.

Despite her misgivings, she smiled back, then descended the stairs to greet him. Ellene noticed his eyes watched her every move.

"James, it's been a while. Welcome to Haver Hall. Has your father recovered from his illness?"

She strolled toward him. He towered over her petite frame. He grasped her outstretched hand and kissed it, but held on until she pulled it back. As always, a lavender fragrance surrounded her.

"My father has recovered. Thank you for asking. I returned home last night and spent today in my office. How are things with your family? How are you?"

"We are doing well." She gave him a polite smile.

Avrill followed her aunt from a distance. James smiled when he noticed her.

"Ah, Avrill." He pivoted to face her, took her hand, and gave it a courteous kiss. Avrill's cheeks turned a deep shade of pink.

"Come along to the sitting room. William is in his office. Sorcha, notify Sir William of James' visit. Have Jeremy help you bring refreshments to the sitting room. Avrill, you may come with us." Ellene led James past the staircase and down the hallway. Avrill followed close behind.

Sunlight filled part of the sitting room, leaving the rest in shadows. It contained a bench and several chairs arranged for conversation. Woven baskets on the floor contained colorful fabric, thread, needles, and scissors, which Ellene and Avrill used for needlework projects.

Ellene settled on the bench, and Avrill perched near her. Ellene noticed Avrill peeking at James from the corner of her eye. Did she still have a crush on him? James sat in the chair closest to Ellene. His presence filled the room with an electrifying energy.

As he strode into the room, William welcomed James with enthusiasm.

"I returned late yesterday. I regret leaving in a hurry, but my father's sudden illness demanded my presence. Thankfully, he has regained his full health." James shifted his gaze from William to Ellene and Avrill.

"We are relieved you returned safely." Ellene spoke with a cheerful tone.

"I spent today at my office. It appears there were minor crimes that seem to be manageable with little effort. Can you fill me in on any important happenings during my absence?"

"No, nothing came up at the last council meeting," William said.

"The mayor's annual banquet is tomorrow night. According to Marguerite, she's already sent you an invitation." Ellene glanced at him, and he smiled back with a twinkle in his eye.

"I noticed a packet with the mayor's seal but have not opened it yet. I assume you and William are going." James stared at Ellene, which caused a blush to rise from her neck, so she averted her gaze.

Ellene gave a short, affirmative nod. "Yes, we will be there. Marguerite expects all the village council members will be there as well."

Sorcha and Jeremy entered the room with refreshments. Jeremy was of medium height, had brown hair with gray streaks, brown eyes, and enormous ears. He walked with a slight limp. Sorcha passed the cheese and sweetmeats while Jeremy poured the ale. While he chatted with William, James kept glancing at Ellene. She avoided eye contact, seeming to look everywhere but at him.

Soon James announced he needed to leave, and the family and James filed out of the sitting room toward the front door. He fell into step with Ellene.

"When Marguerite asked about you this afternoon, I didn't know you had returned." Ellene's tone was light.

"I need to assess what is happening at my estate and in the county. But I expect I'll be there. They didn't invite me to the banquet last year because I was a new resident. Now I'm the sheriff, so the mayor thinks I'm important enough." He chuckled. "William, would you and your family come for an evening meal next week?"

William glanced at Ellene. James faced away from her. She shook her head, but William responded. "Yes, we look forward to it."

James clapped him on the shoulder. "Splendid." He pivoted to face Ellene, causing her to bump into him. James grasped her so she wouldn't fall. He held her hand and kissed it. He blocked her advance as William and Avrill proceeded to the courtyard.

"Stay a minute. I have a gift for you." James reached into his purse and produced a round silver brooch mounted with small rubies and emeralds. "This belonged to my mother, and she gave it to me before she died. I want you to have it."

Ellene was awestruck, her eyes widening in amazement. "It's beautiful.

But I can't accept it."

"Why not? It is a token of my love." The confusion on James' face was clear.

"I'm pleased to remain in the role of your friend. You know I'm not ready to commit to courtship. This gift is too valuable."

"Wear it daily and think of me when you do. That is all I ask." James took her hand, placed the brooch in the palm, and closed her fingers around it. Then he kissed her fingers.

Ellene stared at her hand, then looked up to meet James' eyes. "I make no promises," she said.

"Come, the others are waiting." They followed the others into the courtyard, with James holding her arm.

Clive tethered James' horse near the door while he was inside. He mounted, waved goodbye, and trotted down the lane toward the main road.

Ellene gazed down at the brooch in her hand, a look of bewilderment crossing her face.

"Aunt Ellene, he gave you that? How romantic." Avrill squealed with delight. "Are you courting now?"

"No, Avrill. I told him there's no romantic involvement between us." Ellene shook her head. "William, I wish you had not committed us to dine with him."

"Now, Ellene, it is his turn to entertain us. Avrill will enjoy the visit." William rubbed the back of his neck.

"I'm curious about James' family, Papa. Maybe he has a brother who would be a suitable husband?"

William chuckled, face lighting up with amusement. "I think his brothers are already married, with children. He has several nephews about your age. Still, I don't want you to move to the northern borders." At her crestfallen look, he chuckled. "Time will tell, *ma Cherie*. You may find a suitable match at your cousin's wedding."

CHAPTER SIX

THE DAY OF THE BANQUET

Upon William's return from his errands, Jeremy handed him a packet delivered by a messenger that morning. He wrinkled his forehead when he recognized the seal, but he resolved to wait to open it.

As the family assembled in the dining room for their noon meal, William produced the packet.

"What is it, William?" Ellene noticed his expression.

"It's from de Beauvoir's secretary. Probably just additional details about the wedding. I'll open it after we eat."

Avrill bounced on the bench. "Please, I want to hear. Open it now? Please, Papa."

William smiled at her enthusiasm. "Just for you, *ma Chérie*," he teased. He opened the envelope, and his grin faded away as he read what was inside.

"Papa, what are you frowning about?"

"Your cousin's fiancé got thrown from a horse while hunting. He broke his leg and must stay in bed for a month. Your uncle regrets to inform you he has postponed the wedding until spring.

"That's not fair. I want to go so much." Avrill's eyes welled up with tears that glistened in the light. "Can't you write to him and tell him to have it, anyway? The fiancé can sit in a chair and watch while we dance."

"You know I can't do that. Since the fiancé is too ill to attend, the only other option is marriage by proxy. Having both bride and groom present is a stronger alliance. He can cancel it altogether if he wants."

"Well, Avrill, I'm disappointed too." Ellene reached out and patted Avrill's forearm. She turned her head and looked at William. "Is it alright if we go ahead with the clothing alterations?" Ellene hoped she would not have to go to Simon's shop and cancel Pernilla's work.

"Yes. Avrill deserves to have new clothes. They will be ready for her should another invitation arrive."

"Papa, can we have a ball here? By the spring I'll be almost fourteen."

"Our house is not large enough for the number of guests one invites to a ball. Maybe we can hold a banquet and invite a few families. I will discuss it with Aunt Ellene. For now, let's finish our meal."

"You stupid woman. Come here. Now." Eustace bellowed from his office. He was reviewing bills for the banquet and found a record of a payment for wine. Because of her limited literacy, Marguerite made a mark on the paper.

"The mistress is in the kitchen, sir," remarked his valet.

Grimacing, he lifted his throbbing foot off the stool. Shaking off his valet, Eustace made his way towards the kitchen, hobbling with each step. His valet followed behind him, ready to assist if necessary.

In the kitchen, Marguerite supervised preparing the food for the banquet that night. When she heard Eustace bellow, she cringed, and her face turned ashen, trembling in fear of another confrontation. As his health worsened, his temper seemed to flare up more frequently. And he grilled her about everything she did. So far, she had soothed him when angry.

Prudence, the cook in charge of the kitchen, looked at her mistress. The servants stopped what they were doing and held their breath, watching to see how Marguerite would react this time.

"Why, if he were my husband—."

The muttered threat trailed off. Marguerite could not identify the speaker. Before she could respond, Eustace hobbled into the kitchen, his face the color of a beet from the exertion. His foot throbbed with every step.

"What is it, my love? What has troubled you so?" Her voice had a calming effect, yet she tactfully positioned herself on the far side of the food preparation table to maintain a safe distance. His enormous body made her look even smaller.

Eustace hobbled over to a stool and plopped on the edge, wheezing from the effort. "You foolish woman. I found this bill for wine for the banquet." He spat out the words as he waved a piece of paper under her nose. "Why did you buy the wine from this merchant?"

"We were low on barrels for the meal." Explaining, her face showed clear signs of confusion.

"You bought it from the wrong merchant."

Surprise made her eyelashes flutter. "I don't understand. We always order wine from him."

"Well, not anymore. I now buy from a different trader, a man called Harry. He's coming this afternoon to deliver it. Cancel this order." He growled as he waved the paper in her direction.

Prudence spoke up. "He delivered the wine yesterday, sir. And there is not enough time to find the merchant, return the wine, and get our money back."

Marguerite nodded in agreement, her head bobbing. "We can buy from Harry next time. Surely he'll understand. Now, would you like a flagon of ale or a goblet of wine? Your valet can assist you to your office, or the sitting room, whichever you prefer. I'll carry it for you."

Eustace glared at her, but his face reverted to its usual color. "Bring me ale."

His rage spent, he allowed the valet to grasp his arm and help him from the kitchen and hobble to his office. Marguerite followed with a flagon of ale. After he settled in his chair, she approached the desk and placed the ale beside him.

He lunged forward and grabbed her by the neck, his fingers tightening around her throat. "Never defy me again," he warned.

"No, my love, I always obey your wishes." The fury she saw in his eyes filled her with fear. Her eyes bulged, and she found it hard to catch her breath.

He released her with a shove. "Get out of my sight."

Her heels clacking, Marguerite scampered from the room. Blinded by tears, she stumbled into the garden, her body shaking from fear. Who did he think he was? How dare he treat her like that, especially in front of the servants? How was she supposed to guess he had changed suppliers the day before their banquet?

She came from a middle-class family in London. Her parents died when she was just a teenager and she had to survive as best she could. She married Eustace because he was rich. Given his age and illness, she had low expectations for a long-lasting marriage. But she did not expect him to attack her. Now she feared he might kill her. If she left him, she would be poverty-stricken again. She must reflect on the hard choices she would have to make to stay alive.

When Marguerite returned to the kitchen, she appeared calm and composed. But the servants could see red marks on her neck.

That afternoon, Harry arrived at Coeur de Lion with his wagon loaded with barrels of wine. Holding a bottle in his hand, he knocked on the door.

The servant recoiled in disgust at seeing the disheveled man in front of him. "If you have a delivery to make, come to the door in the back of the house."

He started to close the door, but Harry stopped him.

"I've wine on my wagon for the mayor."

"Come to the back of the house," he repeated.

"He insisted I speak with him personally. Tell him Harry's here."

The servant hesitated. If the master wanted to speak with this man, he dared not interfere. "Wait here while I talk to the mayor." The servant closed the door, leaving Harry standing on the landing. He returned a moment later. "This way, please."

The servant took Harry down the hall to the office, where Eustace sat with his foot propped up. The valet had placed a jar of honey and slices of fresh bread on his desk.

"I've your wine, sir. Just as we agreed. Here's a sample for you to taste."

Eustace took the bottle and set it on his desk. "I can't take delivery today. It seems my wife has already bought wine. But you shall be my supplier in the future. Come back next week."

Harry's voice went from obsequious to menacing. "We had a deal. What am I supposed to do with it in the meantime? I need to free up the wagon for another load."

"Store it, of course. Where would you put it if I had not agreed to purchase it?"

"I'd have sold it to another buyer." Harry wriggled in discomfort. The urgency of finding a place to deliver it intensified as he realized he had no available place to store it.

Eustace, a shrewd man, suspected something was amiss because Harry seemed anxious. "Well, you could put it in my barn. But I shan't pay you until next week."

"How do I know you'll pay me when you already have it?"

"You don't have any reason to believe me, except for my word. That's the deal. Take it or leave it."

Harry thought for a moment. It would be only three days. Harry concluded it would be better to deliver the wine with the promise of payment than to be caught with it on his wagon.

"Agreed. I'll be back on Monday. I expect payment then, or I'll go to the sheriff."

Eustace sensed that the threat was empty. He called for the valet and told him to escort Harry to the barn and have the stableman unload the barrels. With an expectant smile on his face, he opened the jar of honey, salivating at its rich amber color. He couldn't wait to experience the luscious sweetness as he coated a slice of bread with it.

CHAPTER SEVEN

AT THE BANQUET

E llene's excitement for the banquet grew throughout the day. She looked forward to seeing the women's elegant gowns and glittering jewels. Ellingham's cook always served irresistible treats to the guests. A subtle sense of unease dampened the usual anticipation she felt for a feast. She hoped Simon was not interested in her other than dancing. Would James be there? She had never danced with him, but suspected with his military rank and family history, he knew the more popular dances. His agility was obvious when he sparred with his men.

In the afternoon, the servants carried heated water upstairs so Ellene and William could take baths before dressing in their finest clothes.

William donned a fine white linen shirt embroidered with gold thread, and a dark blue brocade doublet and breeches. His bonnet, made from dark blue velvet, featured feathers and jewels. He finished with heavy gold chains and his favorite rings.

Ellene's burgundy satin bodice, gown, and sleeves complemented her fawn satin skirt. After Sorcha braided her hair, she placed a French hood and veil on her head, and dancing slippers on her feet. She picked up James' brooch from her dressing table and held it up to her bodice. The jewels would be the perfect addition to her clothing. But if she wore it, others at the event would conclude she and James had a formal relationship. It might put Simon off, but she did not want to give James false hope. Carefully, she replaced it on her table. Instead, she wore a double string of pearls given to her by her late husband.

Avrill shifted from one foot to the other in the Great Hall, waiting for them to come down the stairs. She wrinkled her nose as she watched the brother and sister descend the stairway, the scents of lavender and musk wafting up from their movements.

"You look so elegant. And smell divine. I wish I could go too." Avrill had a dreamy look about her.

"Well, I would take you, but the mayor invited adults only. You shall go to many banquets and balls in the future. Never fear." William put his arm around Avrill's shoulders, her hair tickling his cheek. "I think we should have a banquet here and invite some eligible young men, don't you?" he teased.

Avrill nodded. Her face lit up with joy. "I hope so, Papa."

Bridgette gave them the masks, and the pair went out to the waiting carriage.

The Throck-Morton carriage pulled into the courtyard at Coeur de Lion as the setting sun cast a rosy glow on the horizon. They arrived early so Ellene could help Marguerite with her preparations.

The flurry of activity struck the siblings as they entered the Great Hall. The servants scurried around, placing silver candlesticks on tables and torches in wall brackets to light up the Great Hall. In the dining room were two long tables with benches set in place for the meal. Musicians stood in a corner of the Great Hall, strumming their lutes and singing ballads. The tantalizing aroma of roasted meats and sugary-sweet desserts wafted through the room.

Marguerite wore her new gold brocade bodice and gown over a red satin skirt, and a white lace partlet covered the bruises on her neck. Matching gold brocade and pearls decorated her French hood. Eustace lounged in a plush armchair by the crackling fireplace, sipped from a goblet of wine resting on a nearby table, and propped his foot up on a stool. His doublet and breeches of black velvet were free of stains, and a beautiful feather and jewels adorned his bonnet. A heavy gold chain around his neck and gold rings on his fingers completed his attire.

Ellene went to the kitchen to oversee the last of the food preparation, while Marguerite welcomed her guests. Servants circulated carrying trays of sweetmeats and silver goblets of red wine. The kitchen odors and the guests' perfumes created a cloud of competing scents, with Marguerite's Italian perfume dominating.

Soon, the mayor's home was abuzz with the village council of Haver Hamlet and their wives as they gathered for his annual banquet. Those with wealth dressed in brocades, silks, and velvets. They adorned themselves with pearls, gold chains, and gemstones.

Andrew and Molly Smythe strolled in, calling cheerful greetings to their peers. Simon arrived by himself. Without delay, he began scanning the room for Ellene. Widower Jonathon Hooper, the blacksmith, also came by himself. He was from the lower class, and it mystified everyone why he was a council member. Michael Milner and his wife Edith, also from the lower class, looked bewildered. His first year on the council had just begun. Edith, in awe of the finery and self-conscious about her own simple clothes, retreated to stand by the wall. Forest Babbage and his wife Harriet strode in, both wearing gold and jewels. Forest was a prosperous goldsmith. Rev. Broun appeared in a high-quality wool habit, with a gold cross hanging from a gold chain.

The guests formed groups, chatting and laughing together, making it hard to hear individual conversations. The masks did little to conceal the identity of the wearers. Broun circulated among the groups, greeting everyone.

James, wearing black velvet trimmed in gold and a white linen shirt, but without a mask, was the last guest to enter the Great Hall. Attending the banquet for the first time, he stationed himself at the entrance to absorb it all. Although he was not on the village council, he was the county sheriff, a major landowner, and a favorite of the queen. He understood Eustace invited him because his presence enhanced the mayor's importance. Although reluctant to attend, James decided it would be an opportunity to hear gossip about the people in the county and see who seemed to maneuver to become the next mayor. He reserved his greatest anticipation for dancing with Ellene.

As he surveyed the room, James spotted Ellene. Having finished in the kitchen, Ellene joined Harriet, Molly, and Marguerite, gathered in a tight group. How could he not recognize her even though she wore a mask? The way she moved, the tilt of her head. He frowned when he realized she was not wearing the brooch he gave her. Marguerite's lace partlet, hiding her throat and chest, took him by surprise. The other women's low-cut bodices showcased their jeweled necklaces.

While walking towards Ellene, he froze when he saw Simon grasp her hand. Feelings of jealousy overwhelmed him. His jaw clenched as he continued toward the women. Did Simon believe he could court Ellene? James pushed past Simon to stand beside her. Simon scowled at James for the intrusion, but retreated when James glared back. After greeting Marguerite and the other women, he faced Ellene.

"Ellene, may I talk to you in private for a minute?" James put his arm around her waist and guided her to the side of the room. His eyes lit up as he looked at her, and he murmured, "You look so beautiful."

"Thank you, James. You look especially dashing."

"I see you didn't wear the brooch. Tonight is the perfect occasion to wear fine jewelry."

Ellene's face grew pink, and she spoke in a hushed voice. "But I feel uncomfortable wearing it. Your gift is overwhelming, James. It implies a commitment I cannot make."

"Let's not have that conversation now. Will you dance with me later?"

"I will, but I promised others I would dance with them, too."

"Did you promise a dance to Simon?" He spoke his words through gritted teeth.

"Yes, I did. There are more men than women present, so I'm in high demand." She couldn't help but let out a soft, melodic laugh. She saw his face fall into a grim expression. "Don't be jealous, James. I have not encouraged Simon at all."

James gazed into her eyes as he kissed her hand. She cast her eyes downward.

"I will see you later, my love. I need to go greet the mayor." He squeezed her hand and turned away.

Ellene stood gazing at his broad back as he strode across the room. Then she heard Marguerite call her name.

"Ellene, Molly just told the most amusing story. Come join us."

Ellene returned to her friends. After Molly repeated the story, she gave Ellene a sideways look. "Tell us about you and James. Are you going to be betrothed?"

Ellene sighed and rolled her eyes. "No, we are just friends. He's our closest neighbor. William and Avrill also enjoy his company."

"It's hard not to be impressed by his wealth, charm, and physique. What else could you want in a husband? If I were single, I would not hesitate to marry him," Molly said.

"Yes, he has many fine attributes. But I know little about him. He is new to the county, after all."

"You know more about him than you knew about Lord Hunter. It's time you stop grieving and find a new husband. Have some children. Avrill will soon be married and gone. You must see to your own needs."

Ellene responded to Molly with a gentle smile, but kept her thoughts hidden.

James strode over to greet Eustace. He observed that the mayor's face was flushed and guessed he already had too much to drink. Sweat ran down Eustace's forehead, and he winced, rubbing his abdomen. William and Andrew stood before him, their faces tense with frustration. He heard them mention the sudden increase in mill fees.

Eustace waved them away with an angry gesture and called on two male servants to help him stand. Marguerite hastened to his side as the conversations in the room stopped and all eyes turned toward him.

"Thank you, my friends, for coming tonight." Eustace peered around the room. "The county is having a prosperous year, and we look forward to a bountiful harvest. Let us go into the dining room and enjoy the feast."

The servants supported Eustace as he and Marguerite led the way to the dining room. William, Ellene, and the Smythes sat at the head table with Eustace and Marguerite. James sat at the opposite end of the table from William and Ellene. The Babbages, Simon, Jonathon, the Milners, and Broun, sat at the other table.

Servants carried silver platters with boar, fish, fowl, vegetables, fruit, and cheese. The servers kept the wine and ale flowing. James enjoyed the festivities despite his misgivings. Meanwhile, the musicians played their lutes and sang ballads.

The servants helped Eustace stand after the meal was done. All heads turned in his direction.

"It is time to go to the Great Hall for dancing." Eustace waved his arm in that direction, and the servants led the way. Eustace again sat in the chair by the fireplace to watch his guests dance, his foot propped up as before.

The musicians strummed their lutes as the dancers sought their partners. James was quick to react, reaching Ellene's side before Simon caught up. When James' fingers closed around hers, Ellene could feel the rough callouses of his hand.

William asked for Eustace's permission to dance with Marguerite. Eustace nodded his approval, and they took their place on the dance floor. The Babbages, the Milners, and the Smythes also entered the dance floor. Simon stood on the side, his fists clenched and his eyes burning into James.

The couples glided and turned, going through the intricate forms of the popular dances. They switched partners after each dance to allow the men on the side to take part. William danced with Ellene once, then returned to Marguerite. Simon smirked as he claimed Ellene's hand for a dance, while James stood on the side, fuming.

James and Ellene moved around the room, their hands brushing, creating a spellbinding sensation for Ellene. When the music stopped, Ellene's face was flushed.

"Oh, I must sit. I'm exhausted." Ellene protested with a smile.

James escorted her to a bench along the wall and motioned to a servant for wine. He sat beside her, a sign to the other men that he claimed her undivided attention. When Simon approached them, James gave him a menacing glare. Simon spun on his heel and started talking to another guest.

William's eyes followed Marguerite when she danced with the other guests. During a pause in the music, Eustace motioned her over. After a brief conversation, she disappeared into the kitchen. She reappeared with a plate of sliced bread and a full jar of honey and placed it on a table next to his chair. He slathered the honey on the bread and wolfed it down.

A few minutes later, Eustace shouted. James saw Eustace's eyes balloon out as he staggered to his feet. He waved his arms, but he was off balance and fell back into his chair.

"Mayor! The mayor needs help." James shouted over the noise of the gathering. Weaving through the dancers, he reached Eustace, with Ellene close behind.

The vibrant music stopped abruptly, replaced by an unsettling silence. Eustace had everyone's attention, and gasps filled the room.

Marguerite and William hurried over to him. She reached out and grabbed his arm. "What is it, my love? What is the matter?"

Eustace shook away her hand. In a fit of anger, he spat out the words, his voice dripping with hostility, "Leave me alone."

Then Eustace slid to the floor, with spittle coming from the corner of his mouth. His eyes rolled back, showing only the whites. He convulsed twice, then became still.

Marguerite fell to her knees, clasping her husband's hand. "What is the matter with him?" Her voice trembled as she scanned his pale face. Her eyes filled with tears.

Broun rushed over, sank to his knees, and began praying for the unconscious man. The guests and servants stared at his body, stunned.

After failing to find a pulse, James' expression turned solemn, and he shouted to the servants. "Get Zachary. Quickly."

Whispers and murmurs rippled through the room as some guests leaned in to see the mayor. Other guests milled about, uncertain how to help.

Not yet retired for the night, Zachary, who lived close by, rushed to the estate. He had witnessed a multitude of medical issues, from minor ailments to life-threatening injuries, in his lifetime.

Zachary examined Eustace, then closed his eyes and declared, "He's no longer alive."

CHAPTER EIGHT

UNEXPECTED DEATH

"**N**o, no!" Marguerite screamed, her voice full of desperation. "He can't be dead." She broke into sobs.

William put his arm around Marguerite's shoulders as the woman fainted. A servant brought a feather, which they lit and held under her nose to revive her. William took one arm and Ellene the other and together they coaxed Marguerite to stand and helped her climb the stairs to her bedroom.

Zachary directed his attention towards a servant. "Get the undertaker."

He hurried to the kitchen to prepare a sleeping potion, which he took to Marguerite's bedroom. After she drank the potion and climbed into bed, Ellene sat with Marguerite until she stopped weeping and fell asleep.

William and Zachary returned to the Great Hall. Broun insisted on staying beside the mayor to pray for him. The remaining guests huddled in small groups, engaging in muted conversations. The musicians packed up their instruments to leave. They knew there would be no more dancing that evening.

James shifted his gaze towards the physician. "Before the undertaker removes the body, tell me the cause of death."

"It was heart failure," Zachary replied.

"But look how discolored his lips and his fingernails are. There is spittle around his mouth," James pointed out, placing a finger next to Eustace's mouth. "It feels sticky. So do his hands."

"He just ate bread and honey. That is probably why," a servant commented.

"James, what are you suggesting?" William turned his head toward James, a puzzled look on his face.

"It could be poison."

Zachary shook his head. "Let the undertaker take the body to the mortuary. I can examine him tomorrow and make a diagnosis."

After the undertaker arrived, Zachary described the mayor's condition and the whereabouts of Marguerite.

The undertaker's nod signaled his understanding of the circumstances. "I need some men to carry his body outside to my wagon."

Since Eustace weighed over eighteen stone, it took several servants and the undertaker to carry his body. The undertaker owned a building used to store corpses until they could bury them. Zachary left with the undertaker.

"Molly and I will leave now. There is nothing more to be done, it appears."

Forrest nodded. "That goes for us as well."

The others nodded or murmured their agreement. As the guests prepared for departure, a servant handed them their cloaks and capes. Other servants cleared the tables and moved the remnants to the kitchen.

James warned the guests and servants not to talk about what happened until Zachary could give his professional opinion the following day. As the other guests departed, James, William, and Broun remained standing and pondered what had just happened. James' displeasure was clear in the way his jaw muscles flexed and his lips drew together. He had only suspicion. Yes, Eustace was obese and had too much to eat and drink. It was possible he died from heart failure.

Ellene descended the stairs to the Great Hall, her expression solemn. Her eyebrows lifted when she saw the others were gone.

"Ellene, how is Marguerite?" William inquired, his voice trembling.

James narrowed his eyes and scrutinized William as he spoke.

"She's asleep. One of her maids is with her." Ellene wrapped her arms around herself, her body quivering with fear.

James walked over to her and pulled her close. She allowed herself to relax against him, feeling the strength of his arms around her and knowing she was secure. He murmured, "How are you feeling, Ellene?"

"I don't know yet. Eustace's death was so sudden and grotesque. What did Zachary say?"

James spoke after the men exchanged glances. "The cause of death is not determined yet. Tomorrow morning, the physician will examine the body. His initial conclusion is heart failure. I suspect it was poison."

"Poor Marguerite. She's too young to be a widow. I think I should stay with her tonight, William. I can make sure the servants put everything away before I retire for the night."

Ellene bit her lip. She realized James had his arm around her, and she disengaged.

James looked at the siblings. "I don't think you should stay. If it is poison, there may be a murderer in the house."

"But more of the guests would be sick if it were poison. Perhaps Zachary is correct that it was heart failure. After all, Eustace has been in poor health for some time."

"Well, we will know more tomorrow. I'll stay here in case of trouble and visit the undertaker tomorrow."

"James, that is unnecessary," Ellene protested.

"I insist."

"I'm leaving." William pivoted toward Broun. "Vicar, do you want to come with me?"

"I appreciate the offer," Broun responded.

"Let me find my cape and we can be on our way."

While William looked for his garment, James spoke to Ellene. He grasped her hand and raised it to his lips.

"I enjoyed dancing with you tonight."

"You are an excellent dancing partner, James. Perhaps we can dance another time." A brief smile crossed her lips before her face returned to a solemn state.

William appeared with his cape, and he and Broun went out into the night.

After the servants cleared the food and wine, Ellene made sure everything was in order. The maid prepared the guest room with fresh bedding for Ellene to use. James wrapped himself in a blanket and slept in the Great Hall in case someone broke in during the night. One by one, the servants extinguished the candles, lamps, and torches, then left for their rooms or homes. Darkness and silence enshrouded the house, creating an eerie atmosphere.

After stripping down to her chemise, Ellene crawled into bed. Although she was exhausted, sleep was slow to come. She smiled when she remembered James and Simon vying for her. But she had no feelings for Simon and he was beneath her class. He would be better off married to one of the village girls who could help him in his shop. She felt a spark of excitement when James embraced her or kissed her hand. Still, she could not bring herself to open her heart to him.

Ellene sympathized with Marguerite. She experienced the reality of becoming a widow at a young age. People expected a widow to wear drab clothes and stay in seclusion. Marguerite enjoyed socializing and her clothes were colorful. The one positive thing was Eustace could no longer bully her.

When Ellene's father arranged her marriage to Lord Hunter, she was fourteen. Until then, she had friends in Haver Hamlet. She rode her horse, climbed into the haymow, picked apples and berries, and delighted in running through the fields with her brother and other children.

Hunter owned a large house in Cheapside. In the town, houses jostled for space, the air was thick with unpleasant odors, and pickpockets lurked on every street corner. The fields and streams were too far for her to explore by herself, and Hunter had no interest in going there. He refused to let her visit her family. She missed her father's funeral, Avrill's birth, and Desiree's funeral. A trusted maid helped her smuggle messages to and from William.

The women and girls of her class spent much of their time visiting each other and shopping. Hunter was wealthy, but miserly. She felt ashamed to shop with her friends, as the money she had to spend was so limited. He seldom allowed her to invite her friends for a social gathering. He corrected her posture, her pronunciation, her grammar, and anything else he thought of. The clothing he chose for her was appropriate for a woman in her fifties. At first, she thought they would come to love each other.

Instead, she learned to avoid him.

His touch was cold and lifeless, his embrace stiff and awkward. He hesitated before touching her, as if he would rather do anything else.

When Hunter grew ill, she became his nursemaid. She felt the chill of exclusion as the other women no longer invited her to gatherings. She slept on a cot in his room so she could be available to cater to his needs. His diseased body emitted a foul odor. After he died, she thought she would never get the smell out of her hair and clothes.

One night, he ranted about seeing his dead parents at the foot of his bed. His eyes bulged and arms flailed. She summoned the physician, who informed her that her husband's death was imminent. The physician gave him laudanum to calm him. They watched his chest rise and fall in shallow breaths as he lay still. At midnight, he drew a long shuddering breath, and he was gone.

Ellene rolled onto her side and cried into her pillow. He broke her spirit, but that girl, with a zest for life, struggled to re-emerge. Would marriage to James result in the same heartbreak? How could she risk it again? Better to live alone in a cottage on her brother's estate.

CHAPTER NINE

THE DIAGNOSIS

The next morning, James rose early while Ellene and Marguerite slept. Prudence served him bread and cheese before he rode to the village to talk to Zachary. He ruminated about Eustace's death and its likely causes. Despite the physician diagnosing it as heart failure, James had doubts. He had seen someone die from heart failure before, and Eustace showed no signs of chest pain. He was, however, foaming from his mouth.

The road teemed with people going to the market. Some waved, others ducked their heads and hurried by. He slowed his horse to keep from trampling any unsuspecting pedestrians. Word had not spread yet about the mayor's death. He hoped things would remain calm for some time so he could find out if anyone saw anything suspicious.

A plain cottage housed the undertaker's office, with a living area in the front. In the back stood the small building serving as a mortuary.

When James knocked, the undertaker's wife answered the door. She informed James her husband was still at breakfast, but gestured for him to follow her to the kitchen. There the undertaker sat eating his breakfast. Sunlight penetrated the room through the open windows. She bustled around the kitchen, preparing a stew for their lunch. Odors of garlic, onion, and bread just out of the oven vied for dominance.

The undertaker was a short man with a bald spot on top of his head. Wavy gray hair brushed his shoulders. He chose black clothing to convey an aura of authority and solemnity.

"Come in. Would you like something to eat?" He looked up from his porridge.

"No, thank you. I've eaten. I came about Eustace." James noticed a faint stench of decaying flesh.

The undertaker furrowed his brow. "Let me finish my breakfast before starting. Zachary is coming back this morning for another look at the body. I'll let you know when we're ready. Eustace isn't going anywhere, after all."

"Of course. I'll be in my office, then. Send a servant to let me know when you're ready."

James left, somewhat impatient. He searched for an answer to explain why Eustace's death was so sudden. If foul play was involved, he had to take action to preserve evidence and apprehend the culprit. Several people greeted him as he rode to the stable where he kept his horse when in the village. After leaving his horse, he strolled to his office. He removed his doublet and bonnet, then cleared the accumulated papers from the center of his desk into a neat stack on the side. Seated at his desk, he stared out the window.

James reviewed the facts, and several possibilities came to him. He pulled out a sheet of paper and a pen and began writing possibilities and courses of action.

If the mayor died of natural causes, then James could continue with his normal job. The simplest path would be for him to accept the physician's diagnosis of heart failure.

If the cause of his death was poison, that raised many questions. Was it something he ate, or something he drank? What kind and was it slow or fast acting? Did Eustace consume it before, during, or after the banquet? The mayor ate and drank the same things as everyone else, except the bread and honey he ate during the dancing. Did anyone else become ill after last night? Was Eustace the intended victim, or did he eat it by accident?

He resolved to speak to Marguerite and the servants, then the guests. The musicians had been in a corner playing their instruments and did not approach Eustace. He looked up when he heard knocking at the door.

"Come in."

The undertaker's servant opened the door, his body blocking the light from outside. "My master sent me. He bids you to come."

"I'll be there shortly." James rose from his desk, put on his doublet and bonnet, and followed the servant.

When they arrived at the undertaker's cottage, the servant escorted him to the mortuary, where Zachary and the undertaker waited. Eustace's body lay on a wooden table. The undertaker had removed his boots and hose, revealing his swollen and discolored big toe and sores on his bloated legs. The corpse gave off a foul stench. Candles and incense burned on tables placed near the body to mask the smell.

Zachary, with the sleeves of his shirt rolled up and a book open on a table, stood beside the body.

"Ah, Sheriff. It seems we have some interesting results here." He formed a tight pucker with his lips.

"I'm listening." James' eyebrows raised in anticipation.

"Well, it seems your suspicions were correct. Eustace consumed some substance that, at the minimum, caused illness. At worst, it may even have killed him. I recorded the symptoms."

"So, I should treat this as a suspicious death, at least?"

The physician nodded his agreement. "I believe the poison that killed Eustace was wolfsbane. It grows along the stream near the woods. Some villagers plant it in their flower gardens. To be deadly, someone must harvest wolfsbane and place it in food or drink.

"Could it get into his food accidentally?"

"Perhaps if someone was careless. But why would anyone take it into their kitchen? It's impossible not to notice it in their food. It's bitter and makes the tongue numb if eaten."

"How long before it takes effect?"

"A few minutes if the dose is large enough."

"Did you notice a sticky substance on the mayor's face and hands? According to a servant, it was honey."

"Yes. I believe it was honey." Zachary responded. "If it was in the honey, that may have disguised the bitter taste."

"Thank you. You have been very helpful."

James held back a groan. Now he could focus on who administered the poison, and how.

CHAPTER TEN

SPEAKING TO WITNESSES

J ames left the mortuary and returned to Coeur de Lion. When the valet opened the door, James' face was grim. The valet tried to block James, but he pushed past him into the Great Hall. He noticed the servants cleared the tables and benches set out the night before.

"Mrs. Ellingham is not receiving visitors today." The valet's voice shook. He knew James was the sheriff, but he had his orders to turn away visitors.

"She will see me. Where is she? I have news about her husband."

Hearing voices, Ellene entered the Great Hall, wearing her clothes from the previous night. He noticed lines of worry etched on her forehead, and dark circles under her eyes suggested a lack of sleep.

"Good morning, Ellene. I need to see Marguerite."

"She's still in her bedroom. Eustace's passing was a dreadful shock. Before Zachary left last night, he told her to rest today."

"I must speak with her. Will you show me to her room?"

Ellene swiveled, her skirt brushing the floor as she crossed the room to the stairs.

James kept pace with her. "How are you feeling? I suspect his death also alarmed you?"

"Any death is distressing. I was present when my late husband died. It brought back those memories. I hope I can offer Marguerite some comfort. Rev. Broun promised he will come by sometime today to pray with her."

James held out his hand and stopped her when they reached the upper floor.

"The physician thinks Eustace may have consumed poison. I need to investigate the circumstances of his death. It's possible that I'll have to reschedule our dinner with you and your family."

"I'm accustomed to you being preoccupied with your duties." Ellene's hand brushed his arm, and he covered it with his, giving it a slight squeeze. His expression was grave, with no hint of a smile.

"This worries you, doesn't it?"

"I need to find out if the poisoning was intentional, and if he was the one the poisoner was after. If not, whoever did this could try again."

Hearing voices in the hallway, a maid emerged from Marguerite's bedroom. James and Ellene stepped apart.

"Sheriff. Mrs. Ellingham is not receiving visitors today." The maid seemed taken aback that he was upstairs.

"I'm here on official business. I just left the mortuary, and I have news for Mrs. Ellingham about her late husband."

The maid's expression changed. "I'll let her know, Sheriff." She spun around and led the way. When Marguerite responded to her knock on the door, she showed them in.

In Marguerite's bedroom, colorful tapestries hung on wood panels on the walls. A large four-poster bed backed up to the far wall. The bed was in a state of disarray, with scattered fluffy down pillows and rumpled sheets. Perfume filled the room with its heady scent. Marguerite sat at a table while the maid brushed her hair before braiding it for the day. She wore a linen chemise, with a silk dressing gown covering her upper body. She shifted her body to face James. Ellene withdrew to the side of the room.

"James? I expected the vicar. We need to plan Eustace's funeral." Tears had left her eyes swollen and red. Her right hand clutched a white handkerchief with flowers embroidered in colorful thread.

James concentrated his attention on Marguerite, noticing the red marks on her neck. "Marguerite, I spoke with Zachary this morning. His examination of Eustace leads him to conclude heart failure did not cause his death." He observed Marguerite gasp in surprise. The maid's mouth dropped open. Ellene's sharp inhalation was audible to him.

"Zachary announced that heart failure was the cause last night." Marguerite shook her head from side to side.

"The cause of death is now believed to have been poison."

"Poison? But who would do such a thing?"

"That is what I need to determine."

"What will you do now, Sheriff?"

"I know your guests, but I need to talk to the servants. I'll start making inquiries. Did you see anything suspicious yesterday, especially near the time we ate? Did your husband eat or drink anything unusual? Or anything that only he consumed?"

"Well, I need to think." Frown lines appeared between her brows. "We were both so busy getting ready for the banquet. I had to make sure the food was prepared, and that we had plates and cups enough for the guests. I didn't see him most of the day." Marguerite wrung her hands.

"What about the bread and honey you brought him while we were dancing? He had a sticky substance on his face and fingers. Did anyone else eat it?"

"Oh, that is his normal fare. Not unusual at all. He doesn't share it with anyone, even me. He always eats from the same jar which the servants or I refill."

"Do you know anyone who might have a grudge against him?"

"No, not at all. I believe he was popular with the villagers."

James pointed at Marguerite's neck. "How did you get those marks on your neck?"

Marguerite's hands flew to her throat. "Oh, I accidentally caught my partlet and almost choked myself. It's nothing." She tilted her head and rolled her shoulders in a careless shrug.

"Do you know who benefits from Eustace's death? Did he have a will?" James took a different approach with a fresh set of questions.

"You would have to ask his solicitor. I assume I'll inherit the estate since I'm his wife. He didn't tell me any details."

"Who is his solicitor?"

"Robert White."

James frowned. He would visit Robert and find out about the will. "I'm ready to talk to the servants now. Send them to the sitting room one by one. Do not discuss the details of his death with anyone. I don't want people to influence each other."

"Of course. Right away. I'll finish dressing and go downstairs immediately to let them know." Marguerite gave a quick nod, acknowledging her agreement.

James bobbed his head and went out the door and down the stairs while the maid resumed helping her mistress dress.

"Oh, Ellene, what will I do? I'm so frightened. Someone fed my husband poison." Marguerite clenched her handkerchief.

"Trust James to discover what happened. I'll follow him and see if I can help." Ellene offered words of reassurance before she left.

By the time Ellene caught up with James, he was in the sitting room. He arranged the chairs and a table so that he could face the people he questioned and record their responses. He nodded when she entered the room.

"Are you certain that it was a murder? Perhaps it was an accident."

"That's why I need to ask questions to find out who might have seen anything."

"How can I help, James? Shall I record the answers for you? Or keep track of who comes in?"

"No. I'll manage. This is an official inquiry. You can stay with Marguerite. I need you to keep anything you learn confidential as well. I'll talk with you and William as a formality."

"But I want to help."

James frowned and shook his head. "You can help by looking after the widow."

Stung by his words, Ellene went to the hallway, where Marguerite and the servants gathered and sat down.

First in line, Prudence entered the sitting room and closed the door. James greeted her and gestured to a chair. He began by asking questions about normal duties and activities, then focused on the preceding few days.

"Oh, the master and missus had a right row the day before the banquet. The master accused her of ordering wine from the wrong trader." She clicked her tongue and shook her head at the memory.

"Did you say the wrong trader?"

"Yes. Well, it was the man we always use. Seems the master agreed to buy wine from a different man, but we already had enough for the banquet. The master was furious. He came into the kitchen and shouted at her."

James perked up. "Had this happened before?"

"Oh, the master had an evil temper since I've worked here. He shouted at everybody, but his behavior towards the missus has never been this bad. His gout was bothering him, and he most likely needed his medicine."

"What medicine?"

"You'd have to ask Zachary. He provides it. The master took it several times a day for his foot."

James made a note. Perhaps Eustace overdosed on his medicine and no third party was involved.

"Do you know anything about his honey jar?"

"Oh, yes. He keeps it to himself. He had a snack in the afternoon, and it was almost full."

"Do you know who filled it last?"

"No, it could have been any of the servants."

"Where is it now?"

"I don't know. It's missing and none of the servants remembers putting it in the pantry."

The valet's turn with James came next. He recounted the attack on Marguerite in the office.

"The mistress and I helped the master to walk from the kitchen to his office. She carried his ale and set it down on the desk. He grabbed her by the neck and threatened her. She ran out of the house into the garden."

"Have you seen him attack her before?"

"No sir. He shouted plenty of times, but I saw nothing like that."

"Did you give him pain medicine that day?"

"Yes, I gave him extra doses of pain medicine."

One by one, the remaining servants entered the sitting room. Several confirmed they saw the argument between Eustace and Marguerite in the kitchen. Two overheard the threats against Eustace by someone in the kitchen, but did not know who made them. He had his usual snack of bread and honey late in the afternoon and again at the banquet. No one remembered filling the honey jar or putting it away after the banquet. The valet who accompanied Harry to the office recalled he left a bottle of wine for Eustace to sample, but the bottle was missing.

James admonished each person not to reveal what they had told him.

Ellene and Marguerite remained in the hallway and watched the servants enter and leave the room, straining to hear the conversations. When someone knocked on the front door, the valet responded, and a minute later, William came down the hallway.

Marguerite and Ellene leaped to their feet.

"How are you faring?" William grasped Marguerite's hand.

"Oh, William, I'm so relieved to see you." She conveyed to him that Eustace's cause of death might be poison. She then explained about James and the interview process.

A worried look crossed William's face.

"But we're not supposed to tell you. James warned us not to talk about the case." Marguerite placed her hand over her mouth.

"I hope he doesn't suspect me in this. I'm his friend." William raised his eyebrows.

As the last servant left, the door opened, and James caught sight of

William.

"Oh, good. You're here. I need to talk to you and Ellene separately."

"I'll go first." Ellene turned sideways as she brushed past James. Taking her seat opposite his chair, she waited for him to sit. "Do you suspect me, James? I had no reason to kill Eustace."

"I just want to know if you saw anything that could help me. Were you aware he tried to choke Marguerite two days ago?"

Ellene's mouth dropped open. "So that's where she got those—." She stopped talking, fearing she would implicate her friend.

"Marks on her neck?" After finishing the sentence, James shifted in his seat.

His desire to embrace and kiss her was strong, but he maintained a collected and professional attitude.

"Ellene." He paused, considering his next words. "Has Marguerite ever told you she wanted to harm her husband? Or that she wanted out of her marriage?"

"No. No. Her marriage was—difficult—but she placated him when he was unhappy. She enjoyed the status of being the mayor's wife. Surely there were others with a motive?"

"That I intend to find out. But those at the banquet had the opportunity."

"Doesn't it depend on when he consumed the poison? If it was slow-acting, it could have been any outsider. Or a servant who was tired of being bullied. Or seeing Marguerite bullied." Ellene furrowed her brow.

James exhaled in frustration. Ellene was too trusting.

"The servants reported you helped in the kitchen while the guests arrived and helped clear up after everyone left."

"Yes, Marguerite needed my help. She's had little experience with entertaining. Eustace didn't feel well enough to greet the guests, so she did. And of course, after he died, the physician gave her something to make her sleep, so I volunteered to help."

"Did you notice any unusual food or beverage at the mayor's place at the table?"

"No, everything was the same as the other guests. But he ate some bread and honey in the Great Hall that was not served to anyone else."

"Do you know where the servants put the honey jar?"

"No, I had gone upstairs with Marguerite when the servants started clearing the dishes and putting away the food. They cleared most of it by the time I returned." She waited while James stared at the wall. "Is there anything else, or can I go now? I must go home to attend to the household."

James resumed gazing at her. "I have nothing further to ask. Let me know if you remember anything relevant. And please don't discuss the case with anyone else."

"Not William? Or you?" Ah, she saw him wince. They complemented each other well when searching for the thief at Haver Hall. And he needed someone to listen to his ideas since he was prone to reaching conclusions without all the facts. Annoyed, Ellene did not wait for an answer as she stood and left the room.

William looked at her with raised eyebrows, but remained silent as he entered the sitting room and closed the door.

James and William had a similar conversation.

"It must have been an accident. While I knew he had enemies, the thought of murder never crossed my mind. He dealt harshly with everyone.

He treated the merchants and servants poorly. There are rumors of corrupt dealing with the merchants."

"Well, right now, all we know for sure is he consumed poison. Whether it was intentional, we must discover. And was he the target, or was it meant for someone else? If we find out what contained the poison, it will help to determine if it was murder. I plan to talk to everyone who was here last night."

William joined Ellene and Marguerite after completing his interview with James.

"Let us know if you need anything. One of us will check on you tomorrow." Ellene hugged her friend.

William took Marguerite's hand and spoke in a gentle tone as he gazed at the young widow. "If it was one of your servants, the sooner we find out, the better."

Astonishment registered on Marguerite's face as her eyebrows arched in surprise. "I find it hard to believe that one of my servants would poison him. They need their jobs."

"Forget I mentioned it. You are probably correct. He was in such poor health. I saw him clenching his stomach and perspiring all evening." William moved his hands to show Eustace's movements.

As the trio strolled to the door, James emerged from the sitting room, clutching his notes.

"It looks like you're on your way out. I'm leaving to talk to last night's guests. Let me walk you to your carriage, Ellene."

James fell into step with Ellene. He put out his hand to help her up into the carriage. "I'll let you know about inviting you and your family next week. I may not be home enough to plan." He again grasped her hand and kissed it.

"I look forward to it whenever you are ready. I know Avrill and William do, too."

William lingered to talk to Marguerite and kissed her hand before he joined them. James mounted his horse, and they set off at a trot. The trio parted at the village.

—*ele*—

When James stopped at Zachary's cottage, he was treating a patient. The physician stepped outside to talk to James.

"I hear you provided a potion to Eustace for his pain. What's in it?"

"The chief ingredient is autumn crocus. I was careful how much I mixed for him. He had dropsy but wouldn't submit to leeches."

"The servants gave him multiple doses the day of the banquet. Could that have killed him if he had too much?"

"No, he would pass out first. He built up a tolerance, so he could consume quite a lot."

"Would his poor health make him more susceptible to poisoning?"

"Yes, indeed, it would."

Chapter Eleven

THE NEWS SPREADS

R ev. Broun rode toward Haver Hamlet, greeting the villagers and farmers who gathered to market their wares. He did not look forward to his meeting with Marguerite. He saw many men die when he was in France with the army before he became a vicar. Still, he could never ignore suffering by friends and family of the deceased. His thoughts turned to James and his doubts about the cause of death. Soon, he spotted James coming his way.

"James, well met." Broun hailed the sheriff.

When they drew next to each other and stopped, their voices dropped to a murmur, ensuring their conversation remained confidential.

"Are you planning to visit Marguerite today?"

"I'm on my way now to see her. Do you have information I should know before I go there?"

"Zachary told me this morning Eustace's death wasn't from heart failure. It may be poison."

"Was it accidental or murder?" Broun's eyebrows shot up in surprise.

"It's too early yet to draw any conclusions. I already talked to the servants. I plan to speak with the guests who were here last night. Several live in the village, so it should not take too long. I would appreciate it if you don't tell anyone about the poison."

"Sheriff, you can trust me to keep it confidential."

"I won't detain you any longer." James bobbed his head and spurred his horse into a trot while the vicar continued his journey.

At Coeur de Lion, a servant ushered Broun to the sitting room, where he found Marguerite staring at the wall, with needlework in her lap. Her eyes were red from crying.

"Vicar, thank you for coming." Sniffle. "James thinks my husband consumed poison. What shall I do now? I'm too young to be a widow." She sobbed into her white linen handkerchief.

Broun's words had a calming effect on her, and her sobs subsided. He prayed, then asked for her thoughts about the burial.

"Eustace told me there is a plot for him in the graveyard next to his parents."

"Yes, there is. I checked this morning before coming here."

"Shall we have the burial in two days?"

"I believe we must wait until Zachary finishes examining his body. In the meantime, I'll verify that there is a casket for him. Because of his size, it might be necessary to have one custom-made."

"Thank you, Vicar. You are most kind." Marguerite gave a slight, weary smile. "I know you will do what you can."

When Ellene and William returned to Haver Hall, Avrill ran from the kitchen to greet them both with a hug. William told her about the mayor's death that morning before he went to Coeur de Lion to pick up Ellene.

"How is Marguerite?" Avrill peered at her aunt's face. "Is she crying?"

Avrill remembered how she cried after her mother died.

"Marguerite is overwhelmed with sorrow." Ellene gave Avrill a quick hug.

"Zachary thinks someone may have poisoned him. James is investigating." William patted her shoulder.

Avrill made a face. "I hope James asks for your help, Aunt Ellene. He needed your help when Papa's dagger disappeared."

"He made it clear he does not want my help. I'm going upstairs to change. What are you doing now?"

"Bridgette and I were planning meals. She suggested it was a worthwhile way to spend my time."

"I like that idea. You can do your embroidery when you finish."

"When are we going to visit James and Thomas?"

"Not yet." Ellene shook her head. "James told me he may have to delay having us visit until he finishes investigating the mayor's death."

Avrill made a face, then turned on her heel and headed to the kitchen. When Avrill could no longer hear, William faced Ellene and spoke to her in a whisper.

"I hope James doesn't suspect Marguerite. She appears to benefit more than anyone from his death."

"How so?" Ellene asked. She had not considered her to be a suspect.

"Eustace was a cruel man, and she is now free of him. She can find another husband who will treat her better. Also, she will inherit the estate and some money."

Ellene's expression shifted to one of alarm as her brows raised. "I know she wouldn't poison her husband. There must be others who would benefit from his death. She told James that Robert was their solicitor and

Eustace left a will. Would anyone else know what is in the will?"

"It's hard to say who Eustace might have told. James will find out the details in due time."

"According to Molly, Eustace is suspected of extorting various merchants and craftsmen in the county."

"I told James as much. He promised to look into it. I'll ask my friends if they know anyone who might bear a grudge." William rubbed his chin.

"We need to help Marguerite, don't you agree?" Ellene's tone was resolute.

William nodded before marching to his office, his footsteps echoing down the corridor.

Chapter Twelve

THE INVESTIGATION

A fter James made a brief stop at his office, he set off at a leisurely trot to visit the miller. Deep in thought, he pondered who could have poisoned Eustace and why. The mayor was corrupt and cruel, but so were many men. Driven by intense hatred or greed for Eustace's wealth, the poisoner risked burning or hanging to commit the murder.

James assessed each guest, imagining them as potential suspects in his mind. Anticipating questioning them filled him with embarrassment, causing his heart to race and his palms to sweat. They were his friends, all successful and respected in their occupations. He frowned and shook his head. With each passing day, his distaste for this job grew stronger and more unbearable.

Because estate owners suspected Michael was being pressured by Eustace to raise his mill fees, James called on him first. Situated a mile north of the village, the mill stood as a marker for Haver Hamlet. The rushing stream, which turned the wheel, flowed around the shunt. Weathered boards comprised the windowless walls.

The idle grinding wheel was visible on the ground floor. A stairway positioned against the far wall reached the upper floor, where Michael kept his office. He sat behind a crude desk, holding a ledger listing transactions in crude lettering. He was a stout, balding man, his white apron secured around his waist. Born in Haver Hamlet, he inherited the business from his father.

When James popped his head above the floor on his way up the stairway, Michael folded his stubby hands and placed them over his round belly.

"What can I do for you, Sheriff?" His face revealed his unease at James' visit.

"I came to talk to you about Eustace's death yesterday." James continued up the stairs and stood facing Michael with his feet planted, a determined look on his face. "Seems that he consumed poison." James had few encounters with Michael, so did not know him well. Thomas handled transactions for the estate involving grain and flour.

Michael's eyes widened in surprise as his bushy eyebrows rose. "Poison," he exclaimed. "How did he get poisoned?"

"That is what I'm trying to determine. What can you tell me about your dealings with him for the past two days?"

"Let's see." The miller pursed his fleshy lips and peered at the ceiling. "I've been here all week except for going to the banquet."

"And your wife? Has she been to Coeur de Lion recently other than the banquet?"

"No. Our business requires us to stay here and wait for customers. We never know when someone will show up and ask us to grind their grain." Shrugging, he showed his indifference.

"I heard people are angry with him about the increase in mill fees. Any truth to that?"

In surprise, Michael gasped. "Who told you that?"

"One of the estate owners. Don't forget, I own an estate and must pay the fees as well."

"He increased my fee for the privilege of running the mill. He claimed his costs went up, so he needed to collect more. Just business. He needed to make a living, too."

"How long has this been going on?"

"A year, maybe two. But it's not enough money for me to risk the hangman's noose. I pass the fees along to my customers. They grumble, but they pay. The nearest mill is Updyke Chase, and it would cost too much to transport the grain there and the flour back."

"Do you know anyone who might have a grudge against him? Or have a reason to harm him?"

"Why don't you ask Andrew about what Eustace tried to do to Molly? He may still have a grudge about that." He fidgeted in his chair under James' intense gaze.

"Thank you for that information. If you think of anything else, let me know." James determined the current evidence was inadequate to implicate Michael. "I'll be on my way. Just don't talk about the poisoning with anyone."

Michael reassured him he would not. James descended the stairs and rode toward the Smythe estate.

As James arrived at the Smythe estate just before the midday meal, he reflected on the warm relationship he had with Andrew and Molly. After entering the house, he could hear Molly and her cook chatting in the kitchen. The valet led him to Andrew's office.

Andrew looked up from the paperwork piled on his desk, then rose and greeted him. "To what do I owe this visit?"

James greeted his friend with a smile, but then his expression grew serious.

"This is an official visit. Zachary thinks Eustace died from consuming poison. I'm talking with all the guests at the banquet to find out what they know or saw."

Andrew's smile vanished, and he swallowed hard, feeling his throat constrict. "Poison you say. I can't believe it."

"Did you see anyone give Eustace anything unusual to eat or drink?"

"No. Yes. Marguerite brought him bread and honey during the dancing. I thought it strange after an enormous meal, but the man had his eccentricities."

"When was the last time you saw Eustace before the banquet?"

"Oh, at the council meeting. I guess that was over a week ago."

"What about Molly?"

"Not recently. Marguerite, Ellene, and the Throck-Mortons visited us the day before the banquet. The women chatted about Avrill's future marriage prospects and the fabrics Simon keeps in stock."

"Do you know anybody who has a grudge against him? Who might want to harm him?"

"The fee increase has people upset, but that won't cause a person to kill him."

"I heard Eustace attempted some mischief toward Molly. Can you tell me what happened?"

"Who told you about that?" Andrew appeared taken aback.

"It came up in my interviews. What was it about?"

"It happened so long ago. When we were newlyweds, Eustace backed her into a corner. He had his hands on her where he shouldn't. I stopped him. He never tried again. We never speak of it."

"Was he blackmailing you?"

Andrew's face froze with surprise, and his eyes widened in disbelief. "Why do you ask that? Was he blackmailing someone?"

"The accusation came up in my investigation. I won't divulge who made it. So, your answer would be?"

"No. I've heard rumors he was corrupt, but I can't confirm them." He thought for a moment. "Talk to Jonathon."

"Why is that?"

"Jonathon got in a fight with a smaller boy when he and Eustace were lads. The boy died. Eustace came to Jonathon's defense, asserting that the boy's death was an unfortunate accident. Therefore, Jonathon avoided being brought to trial. Rumor is Jonathon gave Eustace big discounts on his services. Jonathon always votes—voted—with the mayor."

"Might I speak with Molly?"

"Of course."

Andrew asked his valet to bring Molly to his office. When Molly appeared, James greeted her and explained his reason for his presence.

"Did you notice the bruising on Marguerite's neck when she came here recently?"

"No, her neck was clear."

"What time did she visit?"

"Early afternoon the day before the banquet. In addition, William, Ellene, and Avrill came by. William met with Andrew. We women chatted about fabrics and such. Marguerite disclosed she bought hers from Simon at a steep discount. I know I can't buy for the prices she quoted. Maybe

Eustace was forcing Simon to give them a better price. Eustace promised she could have a new gown in the fall made of some expensive imported fabric."

James thought for a minute. Perhaps he would visit Simon this afternoon. But first to the White Stag Inn and lunch.

"Would you stay for a meal, James? You must be hungry. I can tell the cook to set another place at the table."

"No, not while I'm investigating. I'll accept your offer once I figure out what exactly occurred."

"We understand. If you see Ellene and the Throck-Mortons, give them our love," Molly spoke with a cheerful lilt in her voice.

"I certainly shall. And please don't mention the poisoning to anyone for now." James nodded to the couple, and the valet ushered him out.

In the village, James made his way to his regular table at the White Stag Inn. The smell of ale, beer, and stew mingled with the odor of unwashed bodies of travelers and locals alike.

Bess appeared at his elbow. "Can I bring your usual, Sheriff?"

"Sure thing."

When she brought his food and drink, he held out his hand to stop her from leaving.

"Do you have time for me to ask you a few questions?"

Bess looked around to verify the few diners in the public area had been served. She nodded to the sheriff.

"A few days ago Eustace was in here talking to a stranger. Gray hair and beard, shabby clothes. Any idea who the stranger was?"

Bess looked blank for a minute, then snapped her fingers. "That was the wine merchant. They bargained for the mayor to buy some barrels of wine. Claimed he had it on his wagon outside and needed a new buyer because the original one couldn't take delivery. That's all I heard."

"Did you get the impression they knew each other or did business before?"

"No, they didn't know each other. The stranger introduced himself. Harry, I think his name was."

"Did the man have any distinguishing features? Could you identify him if he came in here again?"

"Let's see. He had a red scar from a burn on his hand and wrist."

"Bess, be a love and bring me more ale." A man across the room shouted and waved his empty tankard.

"Sorry, Sheriff, I need to serve him."

James gestured for her to go. So a stranger shows up with undeliverable wine. How did he single out Eustace? Why offer it to Eustace for a bargain? Marguerite recounted Eustace declared his intention to buy from Harry in the future.

James' stomach rumbled with anticipation as Bess brought his lunch and its enticing aroma filled the air.

A short distance from the White Stag was the village smithy's shop. James could smell the strong, distinct odor of burning coal and the sharp, metallic scent of hot iron as he neared the source. An intense fire burned in the hearth, heating the room. He found Jonathon, the village's blacksmith, working at the anvil. A muscular man, Jonathon had powerful arms and hands, black hair, dark eyes, and skin tanned from exposure to the sun. He wore a brown leather apron over his soiled linen shirt and threadbare breeches. Swinging the massive hammer in a steady rhythm, he beat the orange hot metal into the shape of a horseshoe.

"Jonathon, I need to talk to you a minute," James called out to him as he entered the building. Besides the smoke, it smelled of horses and human sweat. James made it his business to be friendly with Jonathon in case he needed weapons for his men or equipment for his horses. He wondered how the blacksmith secured a seat on the village council. After all, the man could neither read nor write. The trade paid well, or Eustace would have shunned the man. Assuming Michael spoke the truth, Eustace took advantage of him.

Jonathon looked up, ceasing his work. The sight of the sheriff at his door brought a smile to his face. He immersed the hot iron in a barrel of water. Steam rose until the orange glow turned dark gray.

"What can I do for you, Sheriff? Horseshoes, weapons?"

"This is an official visit. I recall you were at the mayor's banquet last night."

"I was. A shame about the old scoundrel."

"According to Zachary, it looks like he died from poison."

Jonathon's jaw dropped. "I thought he died from heart failure. How is Mrs. Ellingham holding up? Young woman like her needs to find another husband to look after her."

James ignored the comment. "Did you see Eustace before the banquet? Either the same day or the previous day?"

"Can't say as I did. He told me last week he would bring his carriage to me for repairs, but didn't show up. I saw his carriage outside the White

Stag, though."

"When was this?" James perked up.

"Must have been two or three days ago."

James saw Eustace with the stranger in the inn about that same time, and Bess verified the visit.

"Do you know of anyone who might have a grudge against the mayor?"

Jonathon rubbed his chin as he thought for a minute. "He was a cruel man. There won't be many tears shed at his burial. But to kill him?" He shook his head. "No. Everybody thought he was already dying, him being in such poor health. If I think of anyone, I'll let you know."

"I heard a tale about you and another boy fighting, and the boy died. The story is that Eustace testified in your favor."

"We were lads. While we were wrestling, he lost his balance and fell. Hit his head on a stone and never regained consciousness. I didn't kill him. I swear." Jonathon's cheeks flushed, and he spat out the words. "Eustace just told the justice of the peace what he saw. There wasn't even a trial."

James gazed at him a minute, but decided not to question him further. "If you think of anything else, let me know. Please don't discuss the poisoning with anyone else for now."

On his way to see Simon, James' thoughts turned to their rivalry over Ellene at the banquet. James was angry Simon tried to court Ellene, especially when he saw them dancing together. He could not imagine Ellene marrying anyone but him. Why did she keep turning him down?

Stepping into Simon's mercantile shop, James heard the soft chatter of two women as they discussed the various fabrics and trimmings available.

When he saw James, Simon's face registered shock, but he reverted to his obsequious manner with his customers. James felt out of place, so he stayed near the door, listening to the murmur of voices until the women completed their purchases and left.

James and Simon's eyes locked, and the tension in the room became palpable. Simon flushed as James closed the distance between them. James dwarfed Simon, his tall and muscular build contrasting with Simon's skinny body.

"Sheriff, how can I help you? Is this about Eustace? People say he died from poison."

James let out a heavy breath. So, word was spreading fast, despite his warnings. With a clenched jaw, James replied. "Yes, I came to ask about your dealings with Eustace. You were at the banquet, if I remember correctly."

Simon's lips drew into a tight line as he glared at him. "Yes. I so looked forward to the event. Most of the women wore garments made of fabric purchased in my store. I hoped it would entice others to visit me in the future."

"I don't remember seeing Pernilla there."

"My daughter just had a baby, so she could not attend."

"I'm checking in with all the banquet attendees to gather information on what they saw or heard. Do you know of anyone who might want to harm the mayor?"

"He had his detractors, but I know of nobody who would want to kill him."

"Can you give me any names?"

"No, just idle gossip." Simon glanced around, his eyes darting back and forth as though looking for an escape route. "Talk to Forest about his dealings with Eustace."

"Why is that?"

"I hear he avoids the mayor. Not sure of the reason."

"Is it true that you grant the Ellingham family exclusive discounts that are not available to your other customers? Is there some reason they receive preferential treatment?"

"Who told you that? Mrs. Ellingham buys more fabric than other ladies, so I provide a discount. Normal trade practice." Simon's voice held a firm tone as he stated his opinion.

James suspected he was lying. "When was the last time you saw Eustace before the banquet?"

"Well, let's see." Simon hugged one arm to his body, placed his elbow on it, and put his finger next to his lips. "Not since the last council meeting. But Mrs. Ellingham came by to pick up her new bodice and gown that afternoon."

"Did you notice anything unusual happen at the banquet before Eustace collapsed?"

"After I greeted him, I watched the ladies. They did nothing unexpected."

James was conscious of this because he noticed Simon was always looking at Ellene. "Well, if you think of anything that might be helpful, let me know. And please don't discuss the poisoning with others."

James started toward the door, then stopped and faced Simon. "Before I leave, I want to make one thing clear. I intend to make Lady Ellene my wife. Do not interfere. Understood?"

Color drained from Simon's face, and he nodded his head up and down.

Satisfied, James left the premises.

When he was back outside, James took a deep breath. He felt relief at having warned Simon about Ellene. Forest's goldsmith business was located across from the mercantile shop. The Babbages were last on his list of banquet guests. Forest was a stranger to James, as it was not his practice to purchase jewelry. He waited for two tinkers to pass by with their loaded wagons, then strode across the road.

Forest sat at his smelter when James entered his shop. James' massive presence filled the open space. They exchanged polite greetings.

"I assume you are here about the mayor's death last night?" Forest glanced at the sheriff but did not stand, continuing to work the molten metal.

"Yes. It seems Eustace consumed poison. I wondered if you saw anything suspicious before or during the banquet."

"Poison? That is distressing. My wife and I arrived just before you did. We do not socialize with the mayor except for his banquets. I noticed Marguerite served him bread and honey after everyone else had finished eating. Why her? Why not a servant?" He thought for a minute. "He rubbed his stomach all evening as though it pained him."

"When is the last time you or Harriet visited the Ellinghams prior to the banquet?"

"Not since the last one almost a year ago. Harriet and Marguerite are not friends. Eustace bought his jewelry from a goldsmith in London."

"Do you have any specific reason for disliking Eustace?"

A look of displeasure washed over Forest's face, his lips turning downward into a frown. "Eustace asked me to design a pendant for Marguerite when they first married. I spent hours on it. But when it came time for him to pay, he put me off. Each time I asked, he had an excuse. He even tried to remove me from the village council, but the other members blocked him. He is—was a bully, known for his cruel behavior towards others."

"Do you know of anyone who held a grudge against him or wanted him dead?"

Forest stopped what he was doing and stared at James. "Many in the village looked forward to his death. But to kill him? I know no one that brave. Everyone knew his health was declining. It would take a special reason to risk the hangman to kill him."

James sighed. What he learned from the guests was consistent. "If you remember anything or hear anything relevant, let me know. Do not discuss his poisoning with anyone else."

CHAPTER THIRTEEN

THEORIES ABOUT THE KILLER

Although it had already been a long day, James returned to Coeur de Lion to reveal his progress to Marguerite. He had uncovered nothing that would implicate the council members and their wives. The servants appeared not to have been involved, either. Perhaps if he found the plant itself, it might help him determine who introduced it into Eustace's food or drink.

Marguerite was in Eustace's office searching through his papers when the valet announced James. She hurried into the Great Hall to greet him. "James, I didn't expect you to return so soon. Do you have new information?" She searched his face for a clue regarding his visit.

The cloying scent of her perfume made it difficult for him to maintain a neutral expression.

"Zachery believes your husband consumed wolfsbane, a plant typically found near streams. I noticed a stream goes through your property. Have you found plants with purple flowers along the banks?"

"No, I have never seen the plant on our property. Regardless, I wouldn't pick them because they're poisonous."

"I would like to look in your kitchen, if I may."

"Of course." Marguerite's forehead furrowed.

James headed toward the kitchen, and she tried to keep up with his long strides. When James entered the kitchen, he ordered Prudence and her servant to stop what they were doing and step into the hallway. The cook protested as she left the room. Without speaking, the servant followed along.

Marguerite hovered while James inspected the baskets, pots, and other containers. He looked in the pantry and asked about the honey jar.

"I don't know where it is. We kept it in the pantry. The servants must have misplaced it when clearing the food after his death."

"Who had access to the jar?"

"I, like the servants, had access. He would regularly have bread and honey in the afternoon."

"Where was the jar between when he ate his snack and when he ate after the banquet?"

"When he asked for it during the dancing, I found it on a shelf in the pantry. That's where we kept it when not in use."

James frowned again, then went out the back door into the yard.

The back door was just a stone's throw away from a refuse pile filled with kitchen scraps and leftovers that produced a disagreeable smell. With a long stick in hand, he poked at the garbage heap. There, peeking through the roughage, was a purple flower attached to a green stem with leaves. It looked like wolfsbane. He grasped it, pulled it out, and inspected it. Someone had cut the stem of the plant with a knife.

"Marguerite, can you explain why this is in your rubbish pile?"

Her eyes opened wide with fear. "No, I can't. Is it wolfsbane?"

"Yes, it is."

"I don't know how it got there." She shook her head from side to side.

James stared at her. "I would also like to see Eustace's office."

Marguerite led James back into the house and down the hall to the office. James took a tour of the room, scanning the desk, tables, and shelves. The papers were in disarray, as though someone was searching for something. The honey jar was not there. Neither was the bottle of wine Harry provided for Eustace.

James stared at her, studying her response. She maintained her composure. Satisfied that he had discovered what he could, he addressed Marguerite.

"If you find the wine bottle or the honey jar, let me know so I can come get it. Do not empty it or clean it out. Thank you for your help. I'll take this plant back to my office as evidence."

Marguerite clenched her hands as she watched James mount his horse and ride towards Haver Hamlet.

James took the wolfsbane to his office for safekeeping, then left for the day. Riding at a leisurely pace towards Haver Hall, he couldn't help but notice the soft golden glow of the late afternoon sun. He rubbed his hand on his thigh in frustration, his mind a jumble of racing thoughts. Even after questioning the guests and the servants, he remained no closer to unraveling the mystery of who wanted Eustace dead. No one saw anything suspicious. Yet he found wolfsbane in the refuse pile behind the house. Anyone could have left it there. Because of the constant presence of servants in the kitchen, it would have been challenging to mix wolfsbane with honey and put it into the jar without being detected. Which meant someone may have witnessed the deed and lied to him.

No one remembered seeing any guests except Ellene and Edith in the kitchen, but neither woman had a motive to kill Eustace. Neither woman took the plant to the banquet. Marguerite was too young and naïve to plan such a murder. With her husband gone, she would be alone and unprotected in the world.

When James arrived at Haver Hall, Jeremy met him at the door.

"Please let Sir William and Lady Ellene know I need to confer with them." James' grim expression discouraged idle chatter.

Jeremy bobbed his head and went in search of his master. He found William in his office facing the door, enjoying the warmth of the sun on his back from the windows.

"Sir William, Sheriff Asher just arrived. He wishes to speak with you and Lady Ellene."

William's eyes opened wide with surprise. Maybe James found out who or what caused Eustace's death. "I believe Ellene is with Avrill in the sitting room. I don't want Avrill involved. We can talk to the sheriff here."

Jeremy nodded and left the office. A moment later, he reappeared, bringing James with him to the office. William greeted him and motioned for him to sit in a chair opposite him. Ellene arrived and sat next to James, who greeted her with a warm smile and grasped her hand before placing a kiss on it. He detected a hint of her lavender scent.

James furrowed his forehead, showing the weight of his thoughts.

"What is it, James? What news do you have?" Ellene posed the question quietly.

James looked at the siblings, but his gaze lingered on Ellene. He feared this would not go well.

"Zachary suspects Eustace died from consuming wolfsbane."

The siblings' eyes widened in surprise as they gasped.

"That plant is common around here. People learn from childhood not to pick it." Ellene shook her head in confusion. "Is he sure?"

"Let's say he has a strong suspicion. When I found out, I returned to Coeur de Lion. I looked for wolfsbane in the house and backyard. In the refuse pile in the backyard, I found a flower still attached to a stem cut by a knife."

"You think that was used to poison the mayor?" A worried expression crossed William's face. "But why would he eat it? I hear it tastes bitter."

"There are two things he had access to which no one else did. A bottle of wine and a jar of honey. Either might disguise the taste. The bottle and honey jar are now missing. I questioned the servants and the guests but could not discover any clues. I believe it had to be someone who had access to food preparation. Which leaves Marguerite, the cook, and the servants. I have ruled out Ellene and Edith, who also went into the kitchen."

A look of dismay covered Ellene's face. William closed his eyes as he weighed the implications. James waited for someone to speak.

"Is it possible someone else, like a tradesman or tenant, could have left the plant there? How long was it after the banquet that you found the wolfsbane?" Ellene's body grew rigid as her hands clenched, her shoulders rising with tension.

"I just found the plant this afternoon." James spoke in a low, deliberate voice. "It looked somewhat wilted, like it had been there for a while."

"Surely it was a servant. Marguerite would not do such a thing. I know her. She enjoys the luxury of being married to such a wealthy man." Ellene's cheeks grew hot.

"You know I respect what you think, Ellene. Still, how much do you know of her history before she reached Haver Hamlet?" James paused, his gaze drawn to Ellene's face as it reddened in annoyance.

"What about the other people I mentioned?" William interrupted. "Some men on the council had reasons to silence him."

"Today I talked to Jonathon, Michael, Andrew, Molly, Forest, and Simon. They did not meet with Eustace during the previous twenty-four hours. Neither did Edith or Harriet. They were not in the kitchen. The poison needed only minutes to act. Marguerite and her servants had the best access and opportunity. I just need to know who had a motive."

"But we are not sure how he consumed it." Ellene raised her voice in protest. "His health was poor. He may have died despite the wolfsbane."

"You are correct. We are not sure it was the honey. But the guests at the banquet had little or no opportunity to slip the poison into his food or drink. He and the guests received their servings from the same platters. Marguerite served the honey and bread to him alone. Still, I need to look for the stranger who met with Eustace in the afternoon to deliver wine."

"James, what can I do to help clear Marguerite?" Ellene's voice intensified.

James reached over to take Ellene's hand, but she snatched it out of the way.

"Don't interfere. Let me investigate to see if there is a reason to suspect her." James' voice was firm.

Ellene's lips pressed together in a tight line. James recognized that expression and knew Ellene didn't agree with him. Standing up, James faced William.

"I plan to wait until Monday morning to resume investigating. It would help Marguerite if you would talk with Robert White. He drew up Eustace's will."

"I'll visit him first thing on Monday morning."

Turning to Ellene, James tried to meet her eyes, but she gazed at her brother.

"Ellene, would you walk with me to the door? I would like to talk with you in private." James spoke more gently.

Ellene tilted her head upward to look him in the eye and gave a reluctant nod.

After they exited the office, James whispered. "Are you angry with me, Ellene? I don't want my investigation to interfere with our relationship. I still want your family to have dinner with Thomas and me soon."

"It is not just this investigation, James. It's that you never seem to trust me. I can help. Maybe I can find out information as a friend that they would not tell you in your official capacity."

"I don't want to put you in danger. If you discover something that threatens the person responsible, he may try to kill you as well." James paused and put his hands on her arms with a gentle touch. "You know how I feel about you, Ellene. I want us to have a long life together. I wish you would wear the brooch."

Ellene closed her eyes and took a deep breath. He was pleased she did not shake off his touch.

"James." Avrill cautiously poked her head out of the sitting room. "How are you? Are you staying for dinner?" She skipped down the hall as Ellene and James separated.

"No, I'm just leaving. I'll see you in a few days, after I finish investigating the mayor's death."

Avrill's face fell. "I'm looking forward to hearing about your journey to the north."

"It won't be long, Avrill."

Ellene took a moment to compose herself while Avrill distracted James.

"Walk with me to my horse." James held his hand out to Ellene.

After a moment of hesitation, she took hold of it, a cautious smile appearing on her face.

They were silent as they walked into the courtyard. He brushed his lips against the back of her hand. Saying goodbye, he mounted his horse and rode down the lane.

Chapter Fourteen

STOLEN WINE

The following morning, shirtless and armed, James and his men engaged in their daily training. James and Thomas practiced balance and coordination using their swords. The others sparred with daggers, swords, or staffs.

James enjoyed these workouts. He used the time to put aside concerns about crime and frustrations with courting Ellene to focus on his fighting techniques instead.

Four armed men rode up the lane at a gallop, stirring up a cloud of dust. James and his men stopped sparring, alert to danger, and the men formed a defensive line around James, facing the riders.

The leader signaled for the riders to halt. He bellowed, "Are you Sheriff Asher?"

"I am. What brings you to my estate?"

"We are looking for a thief."

"Did you expect to find him here?" James's face reddened with indignation.

"No, but he may be in the area. I came to alert you and advise you to be on guard." The leader's furrowed brow and clenched jaw betrayed his anger.

"Perhaps you would like to come inside and provide the details in a more private setting?" James gestured toward the house.

The man nodded and dismounted with a flourish. His doublet and breeches were stylish, and he wore a baldric carrying a sword and daggers. His companions also dismounted, but remained beside their horses. The leader handed his reins to a colleague. James sheathed his sword and led him into the house.

Together, they went to the sitting room. Wood chairs and a bench comprised the furniture. The walls were unadorned except for candle brackets. The warm sun's rays shone brightly through the windows. James motioned toward a chair.

"Now then. Give me whatever details you have." James sat across from his visitor, his face impassive.

"I import wine and sell it by the barrel to taverns and large estates. A man came to my warehouse claiming to represent an inn and loaded up his wagon with five barrels of wine. He presented the manager with a bill-of-sale marked paid in full. By the time we realized the document was a forgery, he had already driven away with the wine."

"Can you describe him and the wagon?"

"Short, thin, had gray hair and a bushy beard. Dressed in shabby clothes. Two draft horses pulling a flatbed wagon. The wagon held five barrels, marked with the name of my warehouse. He knew enough about wine not to steal the cheap stock."

James wrote the details in case he came across the thief. It sounded like the man who met with Eustace in the White Stag. "Do you have reason to believe he came this way?"

"No. We're going in all directions within a twenty-mile radius. The wagon could not go quickly with such a heavy load."

"He must have a buyer. That was a risk to steal it if he didn't." James reflected for a moment. "Anything else?"

"No, we'll be on our way. We have several more places to stop."

"Where can I contact you if we find him?"

"Contact the sheriff of County Norcross. He knows where to find me."

James walked with him to the courtyard. The merchant and his men mounted their horses and galloped away as James and his men watched.

James described the thief to his men, should they spot him. Despite it being Sunday, he needed to go to the village to check on any reports of illegal activity. Then a smile spread across his face as he remembered he would see Ellene soon. He hoped to find a way to win her affection. He could feel her attraction towards him, but she maintained a polite distance.

Chapter Fifteen

READING THE WILL

Ellene and William rode into the village early Monday morning. William stopped at Robert's office while Ellene continued her ride to visit Marguerite. The gentle wind usually had a calming effect on Ellene. She enjoyed listening to the birds singing and spotting wildflowers. But today, worry consumed her.

Although she defended Marguerite, she had to confess she knew little about her. Eustace brought her to Haver Hamlet and introduced her as his wife after he had been in London for an extended period. Ellene noticed Marguerite did not have the polished manners of the upper class. Still, wealthy men often married pretty women who were from a lower class. Marguerite made friends with Ellene, William, and the Smythes soon after she arrived.

When Ellene arrived at Coeur de Lion, a servant led Ellene to the sitting room, where Marguerite occupied herself with needlepoint. Her eyes were red and puffy, and she wore only a hint of perfume.

After chatting for a few minutes, Ellene broached the reason she visited. "James came by two days ago and told us about finding the wolfsbane in your backyard. Do you have any idea how it came to be there? It grows near the water. Have you noticed any plants growing nearby?"

"I've never seen it on our property, but I don't wander in the fields. I'm at a loss to explain why it was in the refuse pile."

"If there's anything we can do, William and I are happy to help. We believe an outsider poisoned the mayor."

Marguerite looked relieved. "I need all the support I can get. James' intense gaze frightens me. It's almost like—well—he suspects me." Suddenly, emotion overcame her, and tears flowed down her cheeks.

Ellene put her arm around her friend's shoulders until she stopped weeping.

"James takes his role seriously. I want to make sure he doesn't draw the wrong conclusions. Let's walk along the stream and keep an eye out for any signs of wolfsbane. If we don't see any, an outsider probably brought it here. Maybe a field worker cut it and threw it in the pile. We need to ask the outdoor workers if they saw anything suspicious."

Marguerite agreed, and Ellene stood and gestured for her to lead the way.

The women strolled out the back door and across the yard, taking the shortest route to the stream. The chickens squawked and flapped their wings as they scattered. After passing through a gate, the friends entered a field in which sheep were milling about nearby. Soon they approached the stream.

Water flowed between the banks, making a gurgling sound as it tumbled over the rocks in the stream bed. The bright pebbles on the bottom were visible through the transparent liquid. A thorough search along the banks revealed no trace of wolfsbane.

"Mrs. Ellingham," called a male voice. "Can I help ye?"

As they looked around, they saw the herdsman with the sheep, his crook in hand and his faithful dog sitting at his side.

"We're looking for wolfsbane. Have you seen any growing along the stream recently?" Marguerite shaded her eyes against the sun as she talked to him.

"That's poison, ma'am. Is that how the master died? I've meant to tell ye we're sorry to hear he died."

"Yes, thank you. I shall miss him terribly. Have you seen the plant?" She repeated, her impatience clear by the acid tone of voice.

"There was some last week, but I pulled them up by the roots. We don't want the livestock getting into it."

"Where did you put the plants?" Ellene's eyebrows furrowed in concentration.

"I burned 'em. Always do when I find it." He squinted and spat on the ground.

"Did you see any strangers around here the past few days?" Marguerite posed her question, her voice sharp and clear.

"Why, yes, I did. The day of your banquet, a man with a wagon loaded with wine barrels went into the barn. When he came out, no barrels. Just an empty wagon. They might still be there."

Marguerite's eyes widened and her jaw dropped as she heard the news. She glanced at Ellene. "We need to check. Eustace was furious that I accepted the delivery from our regular tradesman. He may have taken delivery from the other man without my knowledge."

Both women hurried to the barn. The dark and chilly interior had a pungent odor of horses and hay. They left the door open to let in the sunlight. In a corner, concealed in part by hay bales, were five wine barrels marked with the name of a warehouse.

The sound of horses in the courtyard interrupted their thoughts. They hastened to the barn door to discover the identity of the visitors. William and Robert rode into view and dismounted as they greeted the women.

"Marguerite," William called out. "I brought Robert to talk with you about Eustace's will."

"Well, come into the house. Ellene and I have some information, too."

Marguerite led them to the sitting room. Seated, the women waited for the men to speak.

"Marguerite, I went to Robert's office this morning to ask him about your husband's will. He brought it with him. It appears to be the original document."

"Are you aware of any other wills kept here?" Robert gazed at Marguerite.

"No, he never told me about his business or legal affairs. I searched his office but didn't find a will."

"Then we must assume this is the only one. I need to take this to the justice of the peace to be recorded." Robert gestured with a scroll in his hand.

"What does it say?" Marguerite sat on the edge of her seat. With wide eyes, she kept her attention fixed on Robert.

Robert unrolled the scroll with care and read the contents, interpreting the legal language so she could understand.

"The will leaves you a substantial amount of money to live on. And you may keep your clothing and jewels. But the house and real property are subject to entailment, known as a strict settlement."

"What does that mean?"

"If no male blood relative of Eustace can be located, the estate reverts to Queen Elizabeth. She can grant it as a political favor to another family or sell it."

"How would she know Eustace died?"

"I notified her majesty of the mayor's death. Since her brother Edward VI appointed Eustace as mayor, she should be aware he no longer occupies the office." Robert handed Marguerite the document. "You are required to move away from this estate."

Marguerite's eyes bulged with disbelief, and her hand shook. "But I thought the estate would be mine." She glanced at the paper. Ellene noticed Marguerite held it upside down and could not decipher the words. "Where shall I live? How long before I must leave?"

"It will take a while to determine if any heirs come forward. Callum Etchell, the justice of the peace, will interpret the legal restrictions. You need to have him appoint a guardian. I understand you have family in London?"

"No, not anymore." Marguerite's voice quivered, and she shook her head.

"Well, perhaps a friend can take you in. Or there may be a cottage you can rent with your inheritance. Surely, an attractive young woman like yourself will have many suitors in no time," Robert voiced his opinion.

Ellene observed Marguerite and William exchanging furtive glances.

"In the meantime, what about money to pay the servants? How am I to run the household? What shall I tell them about their employment? I know nothing about Eustace's business dealings." Her eyes brimmed with tears, and she twisted her hands. She turned to William. "Would you be my guardian?"

William looked surprised. "Y—yes, I agree to do that." He spoke in a calming, reassuring tone. "Robert and I can find out the servants' terms of employment, the estate's sources of income, and what bills are due."

"If you'll excuse me, I'll go to his office to gather his business records." Robert left the room and returned with several ledgers, which he placed in a pannier.

"Do you know where Eustace kept his signet ring? I didn't see it." Robert asked Marguerite.

"Yes, he keeps it on his desk. I'll go look for it." Marguerite left the room and was gone for several minutes. She returned with a puzzled look on her face.

"I couldn't find it. I'll have the servants search and send it to you when we find it," she said.

"Do you want me to stay here again tonight?" Ellene asked in a gentle voice.

Marguerite nodded in agreement, her eyes brightening. "Perhaps that would be best. Especially if James returns with more questions."

Ellene reached out and placed her hand on Marguerite's. "It will all work out. You'll see."

Marguerite's mouth curved in an attempted smile. Then she took a deep, shuddering breath and faced Robert. "Ellene and I found five barrels of wine in the barn. I didn't pay or sign for them. Perhaps Eustace did, without my knowledge. And the herdsman reported he saw a man deliver some wine the day of the banquet."

"Did the driver come into the house?" William asked.

Marguerite summoned the valet who attended Eustace that day.

"On the day of the banquet, did a tradesman call on my husband about delivering wine?"

"Yes, madame. He brought in a bottle of wine for the master. They met

102

in the office for a few minutes. The stranger left the bottle with the master, entered the barn with his wagon, and departed with an empty wagon."

"Could you recognize him if you saw him again?" William probed for more information.

"He was thin, had gray hair and a beard, and wore shabby clothes. I might recognize him if I saw him."

"What happened to the bottle he left?"

The valet shrugged. "I think the master drank the wine and threw away the bottle. I never saw it again."

"Thank you. That is all." Marguerite dismissed him with a wave of her hand.

After a few more minutes of discussion, the men went to the barn to inspect the barrels. Marguerite and Ellene waited in the courtyard. When the men returned, William grasped Marguerite's hands and gazed into her eyes.

"Don't worry. We'll let James know about the wine. It is not your fault."

"Thank you, William. I have complete faith in your ability to take care of me." Marguerite managed a wan smile.

When William nodded his head, Ellene's eyebrows shot up in surprise. Business advice was one thing, but taking care of her was quite another. She resolved to ask William what he intended.

The men bid farewell and headed to Robert's office.

Bewildered at the turn of events and her pending loss of status because of the will, Marguerite stared at her friend. "What shall I do, Ellene? I never expected to be homeless." A tear trickled down her cheek.

"You can stay with us at Haver Hall, and we will help you find a suitable cottage. William can help you find a husband." Ellene put her arm around the young woman's shoulders, and they went back into the house.

CHAPTER SIXTEEN

A STRANGER ATTACKS

L ater that day, Marguerite sought Prudence to plan their meals for the week. Looking through the back door into the garden for the cook, she noticed a hooded male figure slipping into the barn. The door stood ajar. She called out to Ellene, who was upstairs.

"Ellene, I think someone is lurking around the barn. I'm going out to see who it is."

"Wait for me. I'll be downstairs in a minute. We should go together," Ellene responded.

"I'll be fine. I suspect it is just a tenant." With a shrug, Marguerite went outdoors to discover the man's identity. To avoid startling him, Marguerite raised her voice while approaching the barn.

"Hello, is someone there? You in the barn. I suggest you come out now." She had no intention of confronting a thief armed with a knife or a staff. Her heart raced in her chest as she crept closer to the door. "Hello?"

She paused when she heard someone moving inside the barn. "If you leave immediately I won't have to involve the sheriff."

She waited a few minutes, but no one emerged. Upon seeing Ellene appear from the house, Marguerite strode to the barn and went through the door. She squinted in the dim light and caught her breath when she heard a noise behind her. A sudden and powerful blow filled her world with a thick and oppressive darkness.

Holding her hand above her eyes to shade them from the bright sun, Ellene hurried from the house to join Marguerite. She quickened her pace when Marguerite entered the barn. A moment later, a hooded male figure with a gray beard ran from the building and scrambled toward the woods. The figure carried a rolled-up piece of paper.

"Marguerite. Marguerite." Ellene shouted as she ran toward the barn. On the way, she picked up a large stick. When she reached the barn door, she moved with stealth into the building, fearful there may be someone else in there as well. She remembered how James' fighters held their staff, and she grasped the stick the same way. As her eyes grew accustomed to the darkness, she made out a body lying on the floor. A wave of horror washed over her when she realized it was her friend.

"Marguerite, where are you hurt?" She fell to her knees and felt for a pulse. Then she noticed blood pooling behind her friend's head. Satisfied she was still alive, Ellene ran out of the barn and called. "Help. Help. Someone attacked Mrs. Ellingham."

The stableman emerged from the field, and Prudence appeared from the garden.

"Where is she, Lady Ellene?" The stableman held his dagger, prepared to strike.

"She's in the barn, unconscious. A prowler hit your mistress on the head. Find Zachary and bring him here without delay."

The stableman saddled Marguerite's horse, then galloped down the lane and along the road to the village. Prudence hurried inside to collect water and towels. Ellene returned to Marguerite and attempted to stop the bleeding.

—ℓℓ—

After William finished his business with Robert, he headed back to Coeur de Lion to check on his sister and Marguerite. To his surprise, he witnessed the stableman galloping toward the village.

"Where are you going in such a hurry?" William stopped his horse and waved to the stableman to stop.

"It's the mistress." The stableman gasped for breath. "Someone attacked her in the barn. Lady Ellene sent me to fetch Zachary."

William's mouth gaped open in surprise, and fear sent his heart racing. The women had no man to defend them, other than a few servants. He spurred his horse into a gallop, the thunder of hooves echoing through the air. He felt his heart pounding as he arrived at the estate.

"Marguerite. Ellene." He shouted as he jumped from his horse and listened for a response.

He heard Ellene's voice reply. "William, we're in the barn."

William tied up his horse and ran into the barn to find Ellene holding Marguerite's blood splattered coif and partlet behind her head. In the dim light, Marguerite's limp body and pale skin made her look incredibly vulnerable.

"Marguerite is unconscious. I sent the stableman to get Zachary."

Marguerite moaned and her eyes fluttered as she regained consciousness.

"I'm here, Marguerite. I'll protect you." As he knelt beside her body, William's words were gentle. He put one arm behind her shoulders and

107

the other beneath her knees. He stood so as not to jolt her, then carried her toward the house. Ellene followed behind with the bloody coif and partlet. A sob caught in Ellene's throat.

In a rush, the stableman made his way to Zachary's house, seeking his help to tend to Marguerite's injury. Grabbing his medical supplies and mounting his horse, the physician took off at a gallop and arrived at the estate minutes later. He stopped his horse next to William, who was carrying the unconscious woman. He noticed the blood on William and Ellene's clothes.

"Is Marguerite the only one injured?"

"Yes, she has a wound on the back of her head." Ellene gestured to show the location.

"Can someone take my horse while I tend to her?"

Ellene stepped forward, her face pale with fear. "I'll take the reins until the stableman returns. Please help her." She remained in the courtyard waiting for the stableman.

William carried Marguerite into the house, followed by Zachary. He placed her on the table in the Great Hall and stepped aside so the physician could examine her. Prudence emerged from the kitchen with cold water and towels.

"Put those here." Zachary gestured to the table. "Get laudanum for her pain." He looked into Marguerite's eyes and unfastened her hair to see the wound better.

"Someone hit me. Oh, my head hurts. I'm so dizzy, I can't sit up." As she regained consciousness, Marguerite moaned. She winced as she felt the lump on her head.

William hovered next to her, his eyes fixed on the woman before him as he shifted from one foot to the other.

Prudence emerged from the kitchen with a flagon of herbal tea and a vial of medicine. Zachary cleaned the blood off the wound.

"It's a shallow wound, but you may have a headache for several days. Refrain from moving unless you must. Use cold towels to take down the swelling."

Zachary looked around the room. "Can someone help her up to her bedroom?"

"I will." William wrapped his arm around Marguerite and helped her off the table. "Shall I carry you up the stairs?"

"No, I can make it. Just don't walk fast." Marguerite mumbled, her words barely reaching their ears.

She put her arm around William's waist, and clung to him as they climbed the stairs to her bedroom. Zachary and her maid followed close behind. Her maid fluffed the pillows to prop her up as she reclined on the bed. Prudence appeared with the cold, wet towels, which she applied to Marguerite's head.

"I'll sit with her for a while if you want to go back to the kitchen," William said.

The cook hesitated, then nodded and left the room, followed by the maid.

"Have her take one sip of the laudanum for the pain about every four hours. She needs to rest for two or three days. I'll return tomorrow to check on her." Zachary gave William a pat on the back and then left the room.

Once Zachary and the servants had gone, Marguerite stretched out her hand to William. Her perfume drifted towards him.

"Oh, William. You're my hero. Comfort me." Marguerite's face was white, and there was a bloodstain where her wound oozed onto the towel.

Feeling the need to protect her, he sat on the side of the bed and pulled her close, feeling the silkiness of her skin. "Just stay calm. It may take some time for this nightmare to be over."

They gazed into each other's eyes, then William's face moved closer to Marguerite. She tilted her face up, and their lips met in a passionate kiss. They did not hear the footsteps on the stairs or in the hallway.

The stableman wasted no time heading to James' office after talking to Zachary. He did not bother to knock before he threw open the door. "Sheriff, somebody attacked Mrs. Ellingham. She's unconscious. Zachary and Sir William are on their way to Coeur de Lion."

James' eyes widened in amazement, and he grabbed his weapons before sprinting to his horse. He and the stableman galloped to Coeur de Lion. James saw Ellene standing with William and Zachary's horses as he entered the courtyard. He felt a thrill of fear when he saw Ellene, a dazed look on her face and blood on her clothes.

The men dismounted. The stableman took the horses while James rushed to Ellene.

"Ellene, are you hurt? Is that your blood?" James pulled her into a gentle embrace. "The stableman told me someone attacked Marguerite."

Ellene nodded. She pulled away and explained what had happened to Marguerite, gesturing as she talked. Together, they entered the house. Zachary appeared on the landing upstairs and descended into the Great Hall.

"How is she? Is she going to recover?" Ellene's hands were clammy as she nervously wrung them.

"She suffered a blow to her head, but she should be fine in a few days. If she gets worse, or falls asleep and won't wake up, send for me immediately." Zachary nodded his head, then left the house. They heard him ride away at a trot.

James looked back at Ellene. "Show me where you found her. And tell me anything you remember about the person who fled the barn."

James reached out and grasped Ellene's hand, guiding her towards the barn. Inside the structure, she pointed to where she found Marguerite. Flies congregated around the blood on the floor, their buzzing echoing in the room. James released her hand and searched the stable, peering in the corners and stalls. Gossamer strands of spider webs hung from the rafters. A small brown spider hung down from a web. James knocked it down and smashed it with his foot. He spotted five barrels of wine in one corner and noted the name of the warehouse on the barrels.

Ellene repeated the conversation with the herdsman earlier that day. "We talked to the herdsman. He saw someone snooping around the barn before the banquet. Maybe the wine seller came back? Maybe Eustace didn't pay him and now he wants to retrieve the wine and sell it to someone else?"

"I suspect that someone stole these barrels." Something glistened in the faint light. He bent over to pick it up. "Aha. Here is a ring. It's possible the prowler dropped it." James put it into a pouch. "Can you show me which way he ran?"

Standing in the courtyard in front of the barn, Ellene pointed in the direction the intruder fled. James followed the bent twigs and trampled underbrush into the woods but lost the trail when the underbrush grew thicker. He returned to Ellene's side, his brow furrowed with concern.

"He could have attacked you. I want you to go back to Haver Hall, where it's safer. I'll send some men to come here to guard Marguerite." His cheeks grew hot, and he balled his hands into tight fists.

"But Marguerite needs my help." Ellene knew he was concerned for her, but she resisted. "What if she had been here alone? She could have died."

"Ellene, you are just putting yourself in danger. She needs armed men to defend her."

"What if the attacker was the same person who poisoned Eustace? Maybe there is a plot to remove Marguerite as well?"

"All valid questions. Still, the attacker may have just been a passing vagabond who got caught. Or the thief who left the wine here." James took a deep breath, searching her face. "If he was a legitimate dealer, he would just approach her and not have to sneak in. For now, let's go in and see if we can talk to Marguerite. She may have seen or heard something that will help us. In the meantime, I'll alert the sheriff in County Norcross about where to find the wine."

As they walked to the house, James's grip on Ellene's hand was warm and reassuring. They ascended the stairs to Marguerite's bedroom together.

Upon entering the bedroom, James and Ellene were astonished to see William and Marguerite in a passionate embrace.

"What's this?" James broke the spell.

William separated from Marguerite and sprang to his feet. Marguerite fell back on the pillows.

"I—we—. It's not what you think," William protested, his hands raised.

"It's clear that your relationship is more intimate than you let on." James narrowed his eyes. "With Eustace gone, Marguerite is free to remarry. Is that why you are so attentive to her, William? Are you lovers?"

"No, no. We have done nothing wrong. It was just a thank you kiss." Marguerite raised her voice in objection.

"James, are you accusing William or Marguerite of being the poisoner because they are kissing each other?" Ellene's eyes widened in disbelief. She stomped her foot and shouted, "You have no right to accuse either of them."

James ran his hand through his hair before resettling his bonnet. It distressed him that the moment of closeness with Ellene had turned into confrontation with William.

"This case is becoming more complicated every day. Poison, an assailant, stolen wine, secret lovers." James rolled his eyes, then turned to look at Marguerite. "What can you tell me about the attack today?"

Marguerite described her experience while James listened.

"Are we dealing with one criminal or several? I need to get away and think." James pivoted and left the room.

William rushed after James and caught up with him in the courtyard.

"James, stop. I need to explain."

James came to a stop and directed his attention to William without uttering a word.

"Please believe me, James. I'm attracted to Marguerite, and I think she cares for me. But this was the first time we kissed. We have not discussed having a relationship because she was married. I kissed her in a moment of weakness."

James gave William a piercing stare. "I know you and Ellene well. Or at least I think I do. My knowledge about Marguerite is quite limited. I have encountered women who were driven to kill their husbands for many reasons. I need to discover all the facts. There is still a lot of information that is missing. But I want you to take Ellene away from here. It is not safe."

"You know she has a mind of her own. She wants to protect Marguerite."

"Yes, but she can't. Only armed men can do so. I plan to send two of my men to protect Marguerite until she moves. Tell Ellene she must go home to care for you and Avrill."

"Well, Avrill is trying her best to supervise the household, but she still has much to learn. I'll talk to Ellene." William shrugged his shoulders.

James mounted his horse and headed back to the village.

William returned to the house and ascended the stairs to stand outside Marguerite's bedroom. "Ellene, I need to talk to you."

Ellene had calmed Marguerite, who lay on the pillows with a cold cloth over her forehead.

"Marguerite, I'm going to talk to my brother now. Try to relax."

"Yes. Thank you. You are a dear friend." Her lips formed a faint smile.

William and Ellene descended the stairs to the Great Hall.

"Ellene, I changed my mind about you staying here tonight. I need you to come home with me. Avrill needs help. I rely on you to visit the tenants. James will send two of his men to protect Marguerite. Perhaps someone else can look in on her as well? Molly is only a few minutes away."

"But—Marguerite should stay in bed. After Robert read the will, news

114

traveled among the servants that the new owner might force her to move. Several servants left to seek employment elsewhere. She needs someone to supervise the servants who remain until she is well again."

"Surely a few days will not make much difference. Prudence can run the household. We need you at Haver Hall."

Ellene searched his face. She suspected James put him up to this, but he was right. Choosing Marguerite over Avrill and her brother was not an option for her. Ellene released a sigh. "Agreed. I'll ride over to see Molly and ask if she can check on Marguerite."

"It's strange she hasn't come to visit to comfort Marguerite." William stroked his chin. "I'll go with you to see Molly, then go home with you. I don't want you riding all that way by yourself."

Ellene returned to Marguerite's bedroom. "William insists I return to Haver Hall. Shall I ask Rev. Broun to visit you? I can stop by the church on my way home."

"Yes, I need to talk with him about the burial." Her weak voice faltered as it carried across the room.

"First, we are going to visit the Smythes and ask Molly to check on you, too. And James promised he will send two of his men to protect you."

Marguerite opened her eyes. "Of course, Ellene. I can't be selfish. Thank you for all you've done for me." She lifted her hand and extended it. Ellene's gentle touch enveloped hers in a reassuring squeeze.

"Goodbye, Marguerite. Don't fret. I will return." William called from the hallway.

The young widow listened as the siblings went back down the stairs. A tear trickled down her cheek.

When James arrived at Haver Manor, the men gathered around him, waiting for orders. He asked for two volunteers to protect Marguerite. The men hesitated, then Rusty stepped forward. His best friend, Twig, who was tall and thin, joined the redhead. As seasoned fighters, they knew what James expected. They wasted no time collecting a few belongings and their weapons, then trotted off towards Coeur de Lion.

CHAPTER SEVENTEEN

THE SMYTHES AND THE VICAR

Ellene and William found Molly overseeing a servant's knitting when they arrived at the Smythe estate.

"What a delight to see you both today. This is unexpected." Molly smiled at the siblings as she wiped her hands on her apron. Then she saw the bloodstains. "You both have blood on your clothes. Are you injured?"

"We're fine, but I'm sorry to say that we have distressing events to report regarding Marguerite." Ellene's forehead wrinkled in a frown.

"What's this? What has happened? Why do you have blood on your clothes?" Andrew emerged from his office when he heard their voices.

Ellene explained about the attack on Marguerite. "She needs someone to check on her. Would it be possible for you to go to see her tomorrow? Some of her servants have left already. James promised he will send two men to protect her, but she needs help with the remaining servants."

"The poor dear. I am fond of her. A young woman like her needs a husband to take care of her, don't you think?" Molly made a noise that sounded like a clucking hen.

"Molly and I will look in on her." Andrew and Molly exchanged glances.

Then he resumed in an offhand manner, "Do you know what will happen to the estate?"

William shook his head. "Robert produced Eustace's will. The original grant of Coeur de Lion from the Crown to the Ellingham family entails the estate, so only a male relative in the Ellingham bloodline can inherit. Eustace has no known relatives. Robert says if one does not appear, the estate will revert to the Crown. Marguerite will have to move."

"Ah, so someone may purchase it?" Andrew rubbed his hands together, eagerness radiating through him.

Ellene stared at him, stunned by his question. The idea of planning to buy the estate so soon after Eustace's death felt like preying on Marguerite's vulnerability.

William shook his head. "We'll have to see if a claimant emerges, and, if not, whether Her Majesty wishes to sell."

Andrew frowned when he heard the information. Then he changed the subject.

"As a member of the village council, I think we need to meet and select a new mayor."

"They have not laid Eustace to rest yet," William responded. "If I remember correctly, the Crown appointed the two previous mayors. The queen may expect to do so again."

Andrew made a dismissive gesture with his hand. "It could take months. If we select a mayor now, we could petition for Her Majesty's approval. Besides, there are issues to debate and vote on," Andrew insisted.

"I don't think there's any hurry." William sounded annoyed. "I suppose it won't hurt to at least meet. Since you live closer to the village than me, could you take care of contacting the other members? Just let me know what you decide."

"I'll do that," Andrew nodded.

"Will you stay a while? I would enjoy your company," Molly entreated.

"I wish we could, but we must go home. Ellene needs to rest from the traumatic experience. Perhaps some other time." William rested his hand on Ellene's shoulder. She looked at him for a moment before redirecting her attention to Molly.

"Yes, perhaps I'll be better company in a week or two. I'm exhausted. I can bring Avrill with me when I return, if that's agreeable?"

Molly nodded and smiled. "Having Avrill visit me is such a treat. I always cherish her company."

The siblings took their leave and returned to their horses. A few miles down the road, Ellene broke their silence.

"It seems to me Andrew is overly eager to name a new mayor. What do you think, William?"

"I agree. There is nothing pressing for the council to decide. I suspect he wants to take Eustace's place as mayor." He took a deep breath. "If the estate goes back to the queen, she may appoint an overseer and wait to award it as a political favor. She may want to appoint the next mayor for the same reason."

"In the meantime, Marguerite needs to find a different place to live. It is unfortunate they closed the convents. Widows used to rely on sheltering there. I told her you would help her find a husband." Ellene felt gratitude toward William that she could move back to Haver Hall after she lost her husband.

"She told Robert she cannot return to her family in London. Eustace never discussed her background. Perhaps we should invite her to move in with us." William's eyes took on a dreamy expression.

"Is there something going on between you and Marguerite that you haven't told me about? I noticed you danced with her almost every dance at the banquet. The kiss I witnessed suggests you are much more than friends. Avrill even asked me if you plan to marry her." Ellene looked at him from the corners of her eyes.

"I can't deny that there is a physical attraction between us. I did not plan to kiss her, it just happened."

"Well, take care. She's looking for a husband, and you might be a good candidate."

"Are you implying that she's trying to beguile me into marriage? I thought she was your friend?"

"She is my friend, but there are still so many secrets that shroud her. Taking her as your wife without knowing her better is a serious step indeed."

Ellene stopped at the church while William continued to Haver Hall. Constructed from stone in the previous century, the church stood near the Haver Hall estate. The thick walls kept it cool in the summer. Sunlight streamed through the stained-glass windows behind the pulpit, casting colorful patterns on the floor.

After tying her horse's reins to a nearby pole, she strolled into the dim sanctuary, the sound of her heels echoing in the silent room. Aromas of candles and incense lingered in the air. Ellene moved to the front pew and sat, then bowed her head. As the stress drained from her body, her shoulders loosened, and a sense of calm came over her. She caught sight of Broun as he moved around preparing for the burial service. When he looked her way, she spoke up.

"Vicar, I need to talk with you a minute, if you have the time."

A warm smile accompanied his response, and his eyes crinkled at the corners. "Of course, Lady Ellene. How can I help?"

Ellene explained the events at Coeur de Lion. "And we still don't know who poisoned the mayor. James suspects it was someone in the household. A sense of loneliness and dread surround Marguerite. She would appreciate it if you could sit and pray with her for a while."

As he heard the news, Broun's warm expression transformed into one of sorrow. "I will visit tomorrow. I need to talk with her about the funeral. Learning about the assault in her own barn distresses me." He shook his head. "And how are you feeling? Were you frightened?"

"Yes, I was. The prowler could have killed her. I took James to the barn to show him where the attack happened. When we returned, we walked in on William and Marguerite, sharing a passionate kiss. If people find out, it's possible they will conclude that one of them murdered Eustace so Marguerite could marry William. I worry about William being charged with murder. James is good at his job, but I know he sometimes can reach conclusions without all the facts. Pray for us, Vicar, that James will find the murderer soon."

"You know I will." When he spoke, his voice was gentle and filled with warmth.

"Thank you." With a pensive look on her face, Ellene remained in the pew, her mind deep in contemplation.

"You seem troubled. Is there something else you want to talk about?" Speaking gently, he paused, giving her the opportunity to gather her thoughts and respond.

"No. Yes. I suppose so," Ellene stammered. Her face twisted in sorrow, and a tear escaped from her eye. She wiped it away with her handkerchief.

Broun waited until she gathered the courage to talk. She took a deep breath and began.

"James wants to court me. My friends and family put pressure on me to marry him. But I'm content as a widow. Why can't they leave me alone?"

"I've heard their comments. Is it the thought of marriage that distresses you, or just marriage to James? Have you examined your feelings toward him?"

"I enjoy his company, and I feel more secure in his presence. But I'm afraid to marry again. My first marriage was stifling because my late husband controlled every aspect of my life."

"And you think James will do that?"

"Well, sometimes he gives me orders like I'm one of his soldiers."

"Do you obey?" Broun tried not to laugh.

"We usually end up quarreling, even though I know he means well."

"And he still wants to court you?"

She made a gesture of agreement.

"Is there something else?"

"I worry I won't meet his expectations as a wife."

"Why do you think that?"

Ellene hesitated. A heavy silence filled the room. "Well, he wants children."

"As would any husband. Is it an impediment?" He watched her with intensity.

"God has cursed me. I can't have children." Another tear rolled down her cheek.

"Why would God curse you in such a manner?"

"No matter how deeply I delve into my past, I can't find any clues or explanations." She drew a shuddering breath. "During my marriage to Lord Hunter, I had a miscarriage."

"I'm so sorry for your loss. You never told me."

"Hunter told me that God was punishing me for my sin. If I was a devout woman, the baby would have lived. I never conceived again. He wanted an heir, and he blamed me because I didn't give him one." Tears streamed down her face as she cried.

"I honestly don't know how I failed to be devout. I read my Prayer Book, attend church services, and help others in need. And if I can't fix what is sinful, will I be able to have children with James? How can I agree to marry him if I'm cursed?" She raised her head to meet the priest's gaze, her eyes swollen and her lips turned down at the corners.

"Lady Ellene, I understand your grief. Let me assure you, God does not punish a woman by causing the death of her child. We don't know why He allows it to happen. I have known many couples who had a miscarriage, followed by healthy babies. It seems like your husband blamed you to hide his own guilty conscience. No one can fix our sinful nature. Only through faith in God and true repentance are our sins forgiven."

Ellene paused, her eyes narrowing in thought. "How can I risk another marriage?"

"Life is a risk. Your late husband was old, and the fault may have been his. After all, you were not his first wife."

"That's right, I was his third wife. He had no children with his other wives." Ellene looked up in surprise. "But what if James blames me if it happens again?"

"You know James better than I do. Maybe you should discuss this with him."

Ellene gazed at the vicar. "I'm so thankful for your kind words. I will pray for guidance. Maybe Hunter was mistaken after all." Ellene sprang to her feet. "I must go home. Tomorrow, I need to visit Goody Pickwick."

Ellene's eyes glistened as she gave a sad smile and shuffled towards the door, while Broun's eyes narrowed in thought.

CHAPTER EIGHTEEN

AT HAVER HALL

That evening, James made his way to Haver Hall. Jeremy announced him to Ellene, who was in the sitting room with Avrill. Ellene stood and faced James with a look of annoyance as he entered.

"James, are you making sure I returned home? Did you tell William to insist that I come back?"

"Why? What did he say?" James' eyes widened in surprise. He shifted his weight from one foot to the other.

She glared at him. Avrill peeked around her aunt.

"Hello, James. How is the investigation going?" A sweet smile adorned Avrill's face.

James' expression softened as he shifted his attention to Avrill. "Many questions. No firm suspects yet. Rusty and Twig went to safeguard Marguerite. Thomas sends his regards."

Avrill's eyes widened with wonder, then her mouth curved into a delighted grin. "When can we visit Haver Manor, Aunt Ellene?"

Ellene gave James an annoyed look, then shifted her attention to Avrill.

"When James has time to entertain us. He's too busy right now."

"Can he eat with us tonight?" Avrill inquired with anticipation.

Ellene turned her head toward James. "I know you are on your way home. Don't feel obligated to stay."

James grinned at the women.

"I gratefully accept. Bridgette is a better cook than Agnes, but please don't tell Agnes I said that."

They all laughed, breaking the tension. Sorcha appeared at the door and announced dinner. Avrill went first, then James and Ellene followed. In a playful manner, she nudged him with her elbow, like a sister, and he smiled, seeing it as a positive gesture.

Tensions between Ellene and James eased during the meal. James and William discussed crops, livestock, and hunting. Avrill encouraged James to tell them the stories from his time spent with his family. Ellene tried to act disinterested, but she could not resist listening. She wanted to learn all she could about his family. They avoided talking about the attack and the murder.

After dinner, James invited Ellene to walk with him in the courtyard. As the sun moved toward the horizon, its rays colored the sky in a wash of orange and pink. Ellene felt the refreshing breeze on her face. While Clive fetched James' horse, Ellene questioned James.

"Do you have any suspects in the poisoning?"

James thought a minute before responding. "Not sure. What I don't understand is everyone knew the mayor was in poor health and probably would not live much longer. Somebody decided they couldn't wait for him to die naturally. That person expected it to look like a stroke or heart failure. He—or she—may have planned it to happen in the afternoon, so there would be no witnesses."

"I want you to be truthful with me. Do you think my brother and Marguerite are suspects based on them kissing?"

James expressed his frustration with a sigh. "Your brother confessed his attraction to Marguerite, and she to him. William stated that her marriage had previously prevented him from taking action. Now Marguerite is a widow, she and William can wait a respectable amount of time and then marry. That is all I'll say about them."

Ellene persisted. "Do you think that Marguerite or my brother poisoned the mayor so they could marry?"

James shook his head. "Not William. Marguerite had more opportunities, but she also had her status to lose. She's young and does not seem smart enough to concoct such a plan. Still, some people in the village suspect her. If they find out your brother and Marguerite love each other, they'll be even more suspicious."

"You must find out who did it and clear William and Marguerite." She paused briefly, then resumed speaking. "William and I called on the Smythes after you left. They agreed to check on Marguerite since they live next door. While we were there, Andrew was eager for the village council to select a new mayor and inquired about buying Coeur de Lion. It would be easy for Andrew to sneak over to the house. He could have met with Eustace and slipped him the poison in his office. Maybe you should look at him more closely."

"I talked to Andrew. He denies visiting Eustace before the banquet. Please don't get involved. Whoever did this is dangerous." James raised his hand and caressed her cheek with his fingertips.

"I can help, you know that." Ellene tried to ignore the warmth that flooded her body when his fingers brushed against her skin.

"No, it is too dangerous. I forbid it." This time, his voice was heavy with authority.

"You can't forbid me from helping my brother and my friend." Ellene folded her arms across her chest.

Rather than argue, James opened his arms and gestured for her to come to him, his inviting smile warming her heart. "Truce?"

Ellene moved forward slowly, letting him wrap his arms around her. He brushed her forehead with his lips, inhaling her lavender scent. He then held her away from him. When he spoke, his voice softened.

"I love you and I want you to be safe. I want us to have a long life together. Promise me you'll be careful. Someone wanted the mayor to die. Then someone attacked the mayor's widow. That person may try again. I don't want you to be a victim."

"I promise to be careful."

Clive led James' horse into the courtyard. James' lips brushed her hand, then he mounted his horse and rode off. She watched until he disappeared into the darkness. James had a captivating effect on her, and she felt secure around him. But when he started giving her orders, a wave of rebellion surged through her. She did not want to have him, or any man, control her again.

As the sun rose, Ellene prepared to deliver a basket of food to Goody Pickwick. The cook during Ellene's childhood, Goody filled their home with lively conversations and laughter, creating cherished memories. William provided her with a cottage and provisions, since she could no longer work because of her arthritis and hearing loss.

In the kitchen, Bridgette packed a basket with bread, cheese, meat, and fruit. Wisps of her auburn hair, streaked with silver, escaped from her coif as she bustled around the kitchen. Her hazel eyes lifted as Ellene entered the room.

"Basket's ready, Lady Ellene. Tell Goody hello for me."

"I shall. Has Avrill been downstairs yet?"

"No, I suspect she's still in her room. William rode out this morning to visit some tenants."

"Well, I'm off. I'll be back before lunch."

Ellene smiled as she picked up the basket and set off. Typically, she went by the church to talk with the vicar, but today she needed to hurry. The verdant field and delicate scent of the wildflowers evoked a sense of joy and peace. This early in the morning, most of the tenant families were in the fields making repairs or improvements before the heat of the day.

Her thoughts shifted to Marguerite and William. Was he interested in the young widow, after all? What did he know about her background? She hoped he would not be hasty in committing to marriage.

Despite the warm air, she couldn't help but shiver as her thoughts turned to James. She pondered if James would be cold and domineering if they were to be wed. What would happen if she took that risk? Although William would sympathize with her, he would not have any way of defending her. When she arrived at Goody's cottage, the sunshine of her mood had disappeared. Taking a deep breath, she forced herself to smile and knocked on the door.

"Goody. It's Lady Ellene." Ellene shouted so Goody could hear her.

"Is that you, Lady Ellene?" Goody popped her head around the corner of the cottage, white curls tumbling from her untidy braid.

Ellene's back was toward Goody. She let out a gasp as she jumped, her heart pounding in her chest. "You startled me, Goody. I thought you were inside. I brought you a few treats from our kitchen."

Goody hobbled around the corner, using a stick for balance. "It's such a fine day. I thought I'd sit in the sun for a while. The warmth helps my aching joints, don't you know? Do come through."

Ellene followed Goody into her cottage, then went to the table and settled the basket in the center. Goody handed her the empty one from her previous visit.

Goody, always having an ear open for gossip, asked Ellene about how Marguerite was coping with being a widow.

"A prowler attacked her yesterday in her barn. She has a lump on her head. Zachary told her to stay in bed for two or three days." Ellene's voice reverberated through the room as she shouted.

"I heard a rumor that she poisoned the mayor. I'm curious to hear if James agrees."

"No, that rumor is not true. He is looking at other suspects. I'll tell her you asked about her, shall I?"

"Yes, of course."

"I need to cut my visit short today. I'll be back in a few days. Send someone to the house to let us know if you need anything before then." Ellene hugged her and exited the cottage.

CHAPTER NINETEEN

VISIT WITH MARGUERITE

A fter eating a light breakfast, the vicar mounted his horse and set off for Coeur de Lion. Along the way, he encountered one of Marguerite's servants carrying supplies to the estate from the village. Broun slowed his horse to fall into step with him.

"How is Mrs. Ellingham?"

"She's not well, Vicar. Someone hit her on the head. Some sneak-thief in the barn."

"When did this happen?" Broun pretended he was just learning about the attack.

"Just yesterday. Lady Ellene was there and saw it happen."

"Oh, my. Did you see anything?"

"No, sir."

Broun steered the conversation to inquire about how everyone else was faring on the estate. Soon, they turned into the courtyard. A maid greeted the vicar as he entered the house.

"Vicar, we're so thankful you're here. Zachary told the mistress to rest for a few days. Besides suffering from a headache, she grieves for the master. The mistress is resting in her bedroom."

"Ah. Well, can you show me to her?"

They climbed the stairs to the bedroom, and the maid knocked on the door.

"Mistress, it's Rev. Broun. Can you meet with him now?"

"Show him in," came the muffled reply.

The maid opened the door to reveal Marguerite sitting in a chair holding a white linen handkerchief.

"Oh, Vicar, I'm so relieved to see you." She motioned him in and gestured toward a chair opposite her. She faced the maid and ordered, "Leave us alone and close the door." The maid frowned in disapproval before she closed the door.

Broun settled in the chair opposite Marguerite. Her perfume was so strong that it made his eyes water. "I heard about the prowler attacking you. How are you feeling?"

"My head hurts and my eyes are blurry. I need your prayers." Marguerite's voice quivered.

"Do you have anything to confess? Remember, this is confidential. I can't tell the sheriff what you say."

"You think I poisoned my husband?" Her mouth fell open with indignation as she jerked upright.

"I didn't say that. But did you?"

His stare made her so uncomfortable she fidgeted.

"No, I did not poison him." She stuck out her lower lip. "But I'm not sorry he's dead. He was a wicked man and whoever killed him did me a favor. We should bury him as soon as possible." Her voice was full of defiance.

Broun stayed composed despite her agitation. "The carpenter is working on his casket. When he finishes, do you want a funeral service in the church, including eulogies, a homily, flowers, and incense? Or just the burial at the grave site?"

"Since he was the mayor, the villagers expect the pomp associated with the service. I prefer you to hold the service at the church. Would you ask the village council members if they have any stories they care to share?"

"Of course."

"I'll have a wake here afterwards, but only for a few friends."

"I checked the church records and discovered his family owns several plots in the graveyard. A large stone monument marks the location. You can hire a stone mason to add his name and other personal information to the monument."

Marguerite sniffed, and her eyes brimmed with tears. "I never dreamed I would have to go through this. How do I live as a widow? I'm told I shan't inherit the estate but must move."

Broun gave her hand a gentle pat. "Things will work out. Your friends will be there to support you during the moving and resettlement process."

After talking for a while longer, he closed his eyes and offered a heartfelt prayer for her well-being before bidding farewell to her.

CHAPTER TWENTY

AN HEIR APPEARS

As the morning sun cast a warm glow on Haver Hamlet, a thin, angular man entered the village. Pulling his horse to a stop outside the White Stag Inn, he went inside to ask Bess for directions to Robert's office. When he arrived at his destination, he explained his mission to Robert's servant and demanded to be announced. The servant went to Robert's office, leaving him pacing at the entrance.

"Master. A man claiming to be Mayor Ellingham's son is here to see you."

Robert's jaw dropped. His son? Who could that be? Carlos Ellingham was dead. Impatiently, he gestured with a flick of his hand.

"Send him in."

Robert studied the stranger who sauntered into his office carrying a scroll. He wore a velvet doublet and breeches, with a white linen shirt. Lace adorned the collar and cuffs of his shirt, and feathers decorated his velvet bonnet.

"I understand you are the solicitor for my father, Eustace Ellingham." The man cast his eyes around the office.

Robert stared at him. "I am the administrator of his estate, Coeur de Lion. How do you claim Eustace as your father? He has no living son, sir.

No legitimate son, that is. His son's life ended when he was still a child."

With arrogance, the man snorted. "That is what my father was told. In fact, my father threatened my mother during a fit of rage. She assumed a false identity and moved to another town. A messenger told my father we both drowned in a shipwreck on the way to Spain, so he would stop looking for us. My mother died five years ago, and, as you can see, I'm quite alive." The man's lips curled into a sly smirk.

"I need proof. You could be anyone," Robert spluttered. "I've known Eustace for years. It was difficult to deceive him. What was your mother's name? What is your name?"

"My mother was Juanita. My name is Carlos. She claimed my father would deny me out of spite. That is why I waited until he died to return to Haver Hamlet to reveal myself. I have proof here." He brandished the scroll.

"What do you have in your hand?" Robert viewed the document with skepticism.

"It is my mother's marriage contract with Eustace." Carlos handed him the scroll.

Robert frowned as he untied the ribbon and unrolled the document. The faded ink and yellowed parchment looked like a document that was prepared many years ago. Robert was not Eustace's solicitor at the time of his first marriage. He was aware Eustace kept the contract for his first marriage in his office. Although Juanita would have had a copy, it was surprising she took it with her. Robert felt his mind racing. How would they validate his identity? If he was Carlos, he would inherit the estate. Would the queen also consider promoting him to mayor of the village?

"I must present this to our justice of the peace. He will decide the course of action. Where are you staying?"

"I expect to stay at Coeur de Lion." Carlos looked down his nose at Robert.

"The justice of the peace will make that determination. Besides, Mayor Ellingham's widow still lives there. I must inform her of your claim. Might I recommend the White Stag Inn in the meantime?"

"Where is that?"

"In the village. If you came from the north, you passed by there on your way here."

"Very well, I'll go to reserve a room." Carlos nodded his head and sauntered out.

Robert grabbed his doublet and bonnet, then rushed out the door with the scroll. His first destination was James' office.

James' desk displayed piles of papers in neat stacks. The papers rustled as he scanned each one before affixing his signature and putting it into one of several piles.

Robert barged in without knocking, prompting James to reach for his sword. He relaxed when he recognized the solicitor.

"James, the most astounding thing has happened." Robert was out of breath from sprinting to see the sheriff.

James stared at his friend. "What is it? Did someone confess to the murder?"

"No. A man just presented himself to me, claiming to be Eustace's son, Carlos. Eustace told us his son died as a child. This man claimed he was not dead, but merely in hiding with his mother. He presented this scroll of

MAYORAL MYSTERY: WEB OF LIES

the marriage contract between Eustace and his first wife, Juanita, as proof of his identity."

"Is it possible it's true? I didn't live here when their deaths were reported." His eyebrows lifted in a questioning gesture, betraying his curiosity.

"Possible but unlikely. Eustace saw them board the ship and saw it leave for Spain, but it never arrived. Weeks passed by before the owner declared the ship missing, leaving everyone to assume all passengers had drowned. We have no witnesses to their death, no bodies. The scroll looks authentic. It is old, somewhat soiled, and uses terms employed on legal documents from the time. I'm on my way to confer with Callum. If he can prove his parentage, he will inherit the estate."

"Where is he now?"

"I sent him to the White Stag. He wants to move to the estate immediately. I told him he must wait for Callum's decision, but Marguerite needs to know. She may want to move out before he moves in."

"You go find Callum. And take your time. I'll alert Marguerite about his claim. I notified the sheriff of County Norcross that the stolen wine is at Coeur de Lion, and he can collect it at his convenience."

James pulled a ring from his pocket and showed it to Robert. "By the way, I found this in the barn after the attack on Marguerite. If the attacker dropped it, it may help us identify him."

Robert's eyebrows lifted. "That looks like Eustace's signet ring. It wasn't in his office when I collected the ledgers. The stable is an odd place to lose it. I'll compare the ring to seals that were affixed to Eustace's documents. It looks like it will match."

"That poses the question of how did it get into the barn? There was no mention of Eustace notifying anyone about its disappearance."

Robert gave a negative shake of his head. "I guess that just adds to the mystery."

Robert left, closing the door behind him. James grabbed his doublet and bonnet, retrieved his horse, and set off at a trot to see Marguerite.

A messenger from the undertaker told Marguerite the carpenter finished Eustace's casket, and Broun scheduled the burial on Wednesday. After the messenger left, she laid out her mourning clothes to wear to the funeral. She heard hoofbeats in the courtyard and headed toward the front door, hoping to see William.

When James arrived at Coeur de Lion, he looked for Rusty and Twig, but they were not there. Their horses were also missing. Leaving their posts was out of character for them. James dismounted and hurried up the stairs.

Marguerite threw open the door. Her expression changed to surprise when she recognized him. "Sheriff, I didn't expect you. Do you have news about the killer? Or the prowler?"

"No, neither. But there is a recent development which will affect you. I think you need to sit down to hear this." He paused. "By the way, where are Rusty and Twig? They are supposed to be protecting you."

"Oh, I sent them away. They're probably back at Haver Manor by now."

"Why did you do that? You are not safe." James stood there, his jaw dropping in astonishment.

"I don't want strangers here, always watching me." She shuddered, then led him into the sitting room and sat down in the plush velvet chair. James remained standing.

"Tell me your news, Sheriff."

"A man appeared at Robert's office this morning. He revealed he was Carlos, Eustace's deceased son, and insisted on his entitlement to inherit the estate."

Marguerite's breath caught in her throat. "NO. It can't be. Carlos is dead. Eustace assured me of that. What proof does he have that he's Carlos?"

"It looks like he has the marriage contract on a scroll from the mayor's first marriage. He claims Eustace drove his mother out in a fit of rage and they adopted a false identity. Then his mother sent a man to Eustace to tell him they both died at sea."

Marguerite let out a long breath and shook her head with deliberate slowness. "No, no. It cannot be true. Eustace was so sure. The man is an impostor, I know it."

"Robert took the scroll to Callum to alert him about the claim. I came to warn you. If given approval, Carlos will move into this house, and there will be nothing you can do to stop him. Unless you want to share the house for a few weeks, I suggest you arrange to move somewhere else. Have you contacted your family yet?"

Marguerite scrutinized James, but his stoic expression revealed nothing.

"No, I prefer to remain in County Havershire. Thank you for the warning. I'll start packing my things. William and Ellene offered me a room at Haver Hall." She spoke in a slow, deliberate way, her forehead creased in a frown.

"As you wish. I must return to the village. Best of luck to you." James left the house and headed to his office. It puzzled him why she sent away the bodyguards and seemed so reluctant to return to her family. Did it have anything to do with her relationship with William?

After leaving James' office, Robert rode to Callum's house with the scroll. A hearing was in progress, so the valet told him to wait at the entrance. After the hearing ended, the clerk summoned him to the office. Callum's eyebrows made a thick gray line on his forehead as he examined Robert.

"What can I do for you today, Robert? Any break in finding out who poisoned the mayor?"

"No, Your Honor. Although I come on a related matter."

"Proceed." The justice rested his hands on the desk.

Robert described his meeting with Carlos that morning, then handed the scroll to the justice.

"His story is unlikely. I expect Eustace contacted the ship's owner to confirm its loss at sea. It would be unusual for an upper-class Spanish woman to live in hiding for that many years. Still, he asserted his right to take possession of the estate in a timely fashion."

Callum unrolled the paper and gazed at it for a few minutes. "Har-rumph. Persuasive, but not conclusive. There must be other evidence. I mean, we have presumed the child—er—man to be dead all these years. Why wait until now to reveal himself?"

"He maintained he had to bide his time until Eustace passed away, because he was certain Eustace would deny being his father. He brought the marriage contract to me since I represent the estate. How do you want to proceed?"

"We need to hold a hearing. If anyone has evidence he is not the son, that is the time to present it. We need Mrs. Ellingham's opinion, since she was married to Eustace. What about any other witnesses who knew the wife and child?"

"It's been about thirty years, so few remain. I need to find out where Carlos lived before he arrived here, and what those people know about his parents. One can assume he's prosperous from his expensive clothes and impeccable grooming."

"Harrumph. Work with the sheriff to find evidence either way. If he is Carlos, so be it. If not, we don't want to hand him the estate. I will schedule a preliminary hearing in two days, and we will proceed based on the outcome."

Robert left the scroll with the justice to review. He headed to James' office to tell him the outcome of his meeting.

James was in his office and welcomed Robert when he arrived. Robert related his conversation with the justice. They agreed it was essential to uncover Carlos' past.

CHAPTER TWENTY-ONE

WILLIAM VISITS MARGUERITE

In his capacity as administrator, Robert ensured Marguerite had adequate funds to cover the estate expenses until the justice of the peace rendered a verdict on ownership. Meanwhile, he collected, recorded, and held for safekeeping all funds to be paid to the estate.

While examining the ledgers, Robert noticed discrepancies in what Eustace listed as due and what the crofters claimed they were charged. According to their claims, Eustace compelled them to pay more than the agreed amount. The mysterious wine dealer did not return to receive payment or claim his merchandise. The warehouse had collected the wine barrels from Coeur de Lion. Simon's bill for Marguerite's clothes for the banquet was less than Robert expected. He believed he uncovered corrupt practices by the mayor.

As William set off to visit Marguerite, the intoxicating sensation of her kiss filled his mind. Seeing her struggling with her problems, a strong urge to protect her washed over him. He could tell that Ellene did not approve of his affection for the widow, as she advised him to take his time before getting married. Still, a longing for a life partner and a son and heir filled his heart. Marguerite reacted positively to his romantic gestures.

He stopped at Robert's office to discuss his progress with the Coeur de Lion ledgers. Robert revealed Carlos' claim and its potential impact on Marguerite's living arrangements.

When William arrived at Coeur de Lion, a servant answered his knock at the door. "Mrs. Ellingham is in the sitting room. I'll announce your visit."

Marguerite heard their voices and emerged from the sitting room, perfume trailing behind her.

"William, I hoped you would come. Please join me." She gazed at him with a half-smile and held out both hands.

Her stunning beauty and vulnerability struck William. The aroma of her Italian perfume overwhelmed him. He wanted to wrap his arms around her and make her feel safe. Instead, he kissed one hand and returned his arms to his sides.

"I stopped to see Robert on the way. He told me about the man who claims to be Eustace's son. Do you think there is any truth to it?"

"No, Eustace always told me his son died. You knew Eustace for many years. What do you think?"

"I was a child when his wife and son died. I don't remember Carlos at all. Eustace never talked about his first family. I can't confirm his identity." William shook his head. "If you decide you must move soon, remember, Ellene and I offer you the use of our house until you can find something more permanent."

"That decision can wait, can't it?" Marguerite fluttered her eyelashes.

She moved close to him and rested her hand on his chest.

William breathed in her heady, alluring fragrance, and his pulse quickened. "Yes, of course," he gulped. Standing face to face, he recognized the depth of his longing for intimacy with a woman.

Marguerite noticed a servant standing in the Great Hall, waiting for further instructions. "That will be all. You may return to your duties." When she spoke, her voice cut through the silence like a knife.

When the servant disappeared, Marguerite slipped her slender hand into William's. She rested a finger on his lips, then led him to the sitting room. She shut the door and faced him as soon as they entered. William gazed at her beautiful eyes and her alabaster skin.

Tears welled up in her eyes as she whispered. "Oh, William, how I long for you to kiss me." She tilted her head and pursed her lips. William accepted the invitation by taking her into his arms and pressing his lips against her mouth.

"Someday soon we will reveal our love to the world. Perhaps we can have a double wedding with Ellene and James," she teased.

"Has Ellene accepted James' proposal?" At the mention of marriage, William's eyebrows shot up in astonishment. This relationship with Marguerite was progressing faster than he expected, and he tried to clear his head.

"Not that she told me. But she will. She may soon have no choice." The corners of her mouth twitched downward before curving back up into a smile. With a second kiss, she allowed herself to linger, relishing the sensation of their lips pressed together.

"Why do you say that?" His voice choked with emotion.

"Oh, let's not talk about her. Let's talk about us. Do you want to marry me, William?"

"You're a beautiful woman. Any man would consider himself lucky to have you as his wife." The aroma of the perfume made him lightheaded.

"When I'm your wife, I'll be mistress of Haver Hall. And soon you will find a husband for Avrill. It will be just us and our children. Our sons."

As William leaned forward, his lips met hers once more in a passionate and lingering kiss. "That is something to look forward to."

After William returned to Haver Hall, he went straight to his office, where he sat staring out the window. The encounter with Marguerite had him feeling out of sorts. His cheeks were flushed, and a sheen of sweat covered his forehead when Ellene joined him, interrupting his reverie.

"Is Marguerite recovering from her injury?"

"She's doing well physically. Still, most of her servants quit. She was in the sitting room this afternoon. There is a surprising development." William described what he knew about Carlos and his claim.

"Do you think it is possible Carlos is still alive?"

"I suppose it's possible. That is not my problem to solve, thankfully."

"Could he make Marguerite move out before she is ready?"

"I doubt he can force her to leave before the will specifies, but she probably would not want to stay if he moved in. I repeated our invitation, making sure she knew she was always welcome here." William frowned. "Robert and I discussed Eustace's business dealings. Robert analyzed the ledgers, but Eustace did not keep accurate records. We are unsure of the assets and liabilities." He paused. "How is your relationship with James progressing?" William spoke casually. "Are you going to marry him? Marguerite thinks you two are serious."

"Despite him giving me the brooch, a family heirloom, we are not serious." She gave a slight shrug. "I told him I did not want to commit to a more formal relationship. We are friends, but I'm not ready to give up my independence and submit to a husband." She searched her brother's face. Why would he discuss her status with Marguerite? Had he told her about James' gift?

"You need a household and family of your own. I have letters from families interested in a match with Avrill. When she is married, you will have no children to nurture. James possesses qualities that make him an ideal husband and father."

Ellene's face flushed, and she clenched her jaw before she answered, her voice tight. William's words caught her off guard. She wondered why he said that.

"Did James put you up to this? I refuse to be forced into a marriage that I don't want. If you don't want me to live here, just say so. I shall use my inheritance from Lord Hunter to rent a cottage," Ellene snapped back.

William endeavored to pacify her with a sincere apology. "No, I don't want you to leave. I enjoy having you here. I just want you to consider your own needs. Speaking of James, how is his investigation going?"

"He won't tell me much. I wonder if the poisoning could have been an accident. Maybe someone cut the stem because of the beautiful flower, took it to the kitchen, and it made its way into the honey."

"Well, that's not likely, is it? Does James think it was an accident?" William's eyebrows shot up in surprise.

"No, he thinks it was intentional, that poisoning Eustace must have been deliberate. There are few suspects." A heavy sigh escaped Ellene's lips, a tangible manifestation of her mounting frustration.

"It's possible Eustace was threatening someone. Maybe the poisoner thought they had to kill him before he could follow through with the threat." William shrugged again. "What about a servant who disliked Eustace? Or one who thought to protect Marguerite after Eustace attacked her?" William contemplated, rubbing his chin as he spoke.

"The herdsman saw a prowler a day or two before the attack on Marguerite. And the wine merchant never returned for payment or to retrieve his wine. No one has found the bottle of wine that he left with Eustace. The mayor did not share the wine with Marguerite or the servants. No one else dropped by after Eustace received it, and it was missing after the banquet." Ellene chewed her lower lip.

William rubbed his chin. "What do we know about the prowler? Why did he go into the barn? Was he also the tradesman who sold Eustace the stolen wine? Was he after the barrels he left there? If so, where was his wagon to carry them away? If it was a legitimate sale, he could have confronted her in the house instead."

"Maybe the tradesman stole it, and Eustace threatened to report him to James after he received the wine."

"In my discussion with James, I pointed out the council members who may have a motive and highlighted specific occurrences that seemed suspicious. Simon gave Eustace a huge discount on fabric. Eustace put Jonathon, who is lower class and illiterate, on the village council and he always voted the way Eustace did. He charged Michael high fees to maintain the mill. Andrew is eager to buy the estate and become the next mayor. Despite spending hours on it, Forest never received compensation for his work on the exquisite piece of jewelry he created for Eustace. According to

James, everyone has an alibi. Marguerite and her servants have the weakest defense."

The siblings were still, their minds elsewhere as they reflected on the possibilities.

Ellene's eyes grew heavy as she let out a yawn. "I'm feeling tired, so I'm off to bed. Tomorrow is the burial. We can sleep on the questions and maybe have a better answer in the morning."

CHAPTER TWENTY-TWO

THE BURIAL

O n the day of Eustace's burial, a blanket of gray clouds hid the sun, creating a dreary and solemn atmosphere. A gray stone monument engraved with the name 'Ellingham' towered over the graveyard beside the church. Next to it rose a mound of soil, just dug that morning. In the background, two men holding shovels observed the events.

The undertaker inspected the church and grounds, making sure everything was in order for the burial. Inside the church, soft light from the flickering candles illuminated the walls, and the air was heavy with incense. A large coffin rested on wooden supports near the pulpit. Someone placed fresh flowers on the lid.

Rev. Broun greeted the mourners as they arrived. Ellene, William, and Avrill rode to the church in their carriage, arriving first. They planned to ride to Coeur de Lion for the wake after the service finished. Ellene and Avrill glided to their pew while William waited at the entrance for Marguerite to arrive.

Soon, the Ellingham carriage pulled up to the front of the church. Marguerite emerged, dressed in a black bodice and gown with a white partlet, skirt, and French hood. Her veil covered her face, and she held a white handkerchief in her right hand. The aroma of her perfume lingered in the air. William helped her down from the carriage and escorted her to her pew, the ornate wood polished to a shine. He then went to sit with his family.

The Smythes, Jonathon, Simon, the Babbages, and the Milners arrived soon after. Robert, Zachary, and Callum, accompanied by their wives, filed in. A dozen others from the village came to pay their respects.

When James arrived, he stopped at the entrance and surveyed those seated to see who was there, then strolled up the aisle and sat beside Ellene instead of in his own pew. She gave him a brief smile before resuming her solemn expression. She ignored the buzz of chatter coming from the congregation. Gossip about their relationship had already started.

Carlos hid in the woods nearby, waiting for everyone to enter the church. When the last person disappeared inside, he strode up to the entrance and threw open the door. He wore his velvet doublet, breeches, and bonnet. Aware that all eyes were now on him, he sauntered down the aisle to sit beside Marguerite in the Ellingham pew. This was the first time most of the congregation saw him, although rumors already circulated about his identity. The buzz from the mourners grew louder. No one could see Marguerite's expression behind her veil. James tensed, worried there might be a confrontation.

Ellene glanced around at the mourners. When she attended funeral services in the past, she would hear the mournful sound of women crying into their handkerchiefs and see men bowing their heads. However, on that day, those waiting murmured to each other, filling the air with a sense of anticipation. While she mourned any loss of life, her limited interaction with and low regard for Eustace tempered her sadness.

Rev. Broun processed to the pulpit and began the service. He read from the Bible and the Book of Common Prayer, then delivered a brief homily about death and the afterlife. Ellene felt the service lacked warmth because none of his colleagues gave heartfelt testimonials or personal anecdotes about Eustace. Just as the vicar prepared to give the benediction, Carlos stood and faced the congregation.

"For those who have not met me, my name is Carlos. I'm Eustace Ellingham's son. Years ago, he thought I had died when my mother and I went to another town and assumed a false identity. But now I have returned and intend to take my rightful place at Coeur de Lion. I shall petition Her Majesty the Queen to appoint me to fill my father's role as the next mayor of Haver Hamlet."

Loud gasps filled the church as the shocking news spread among the mourners. James stood, preparing to remove him from the building. Broun signaled for silence by raising his hand.

"Now is not the time or place, sir. Please return to your seat," the vicar stated in a firm voice.

Carlos smirked, but he sat as directed. Broun shot a piercing glare at James, who resumed his seat beside Ellene. The vicar's voice filled the church as he delivered the benediction.

Six vigorous men lifted the coffin and carried it down the aisle and out the doors. Broun followed, and Marguerite took her place behind him. Then came Carlos, strutting and wearing a smirk, pleased with the commotion he caused. The Throck-Mortons, Ellene, and James were next. In a solemn procession, the mourners emptied the church and assembled around the open grave.

During the burial rite, Ellene noticed Carlos peeking out of the corners of his eyes to watch people's responses. Marguerite lifted her veil part way and dabbed her eyes with her handkerchief. The pallbearers lowered the coffin into the hole and Marguerite dropped soil and flowers on top of the coffin. Carlos mirrored her movements, following her lead step by step. James noticed a burn scar on Carlos' hand and wrist when he extended his arm to drop the soil on the coffin.

After the service ended, some mourners formed groups to chat, while others went to retrieve their horses and carriages.

Carlos stood tall, facing Marguerite with determination in his eyes. "Allow me to introduce myself. I'm your stepson, Carlos Ellingham."

"I'm aware of your claim. My solicitor advised me to communicate with you through him until we hear from the justice of the peace." Turning her back on him, Marguerite marched over to where William stood with Ellene, Avrill, and James.

"Please come to my house. Prudence is preparing some refreshments. I dread the the thought of spending the afternoon alone."

"We'll be there." William assured her with a sympathetic smile on his face. Taking her arm, he escorted her to her carriage.

"I'll ride with her. I should be nearby if Carlos causes trouble." James squeezed Ellene's hand, then mounted his horse and set off after Marguerite's carriage.

William made his way to where Carlos stood, watching the carriage disappear.

"Mr. Ellingham, I'm Sir William Throck-Morton. I'm told we played together as children."

Carlos greeted him with a half-smile. "Forgive me if I don't remember. I was quite young when I left the area. My mother seldom spoke of her life here."

Ellene and Avrill joined William as he and Carlos talked.

"This is my sister, Lady Ellene Hunter, who wasn't born yet when you left, and my daughter, Lady Avrill." William searched Carlos' face, trying to jog his memory.

"Carlos, it's sad you were away so long. Where did you and your mother live?" Ellene inquired.

"In Cheapside, near London. My mother had wealthy friends there who took us in."

"What a coincidence. I lived there when I married Lord Hunter. Surely you heard of him?"

Carlos blanched, his body tensing up in response to her statement. "Lord Hunter? Oh, yes. And you are his pretty bride. I remember seeing you out riding together."

The Babbages and Smythes interrupted them as they walked up and introduced themselves to Carlos.

"And what is it you do for a living, may I ask?" Forest inquired.

"I'm a goldsmith. My mother apprenticed me to Mr. Silverstein, one of the finest jewelers in Cheapside."

Ellene's eyebrows drew together in a frown. "How long ago did you become his apprentice?"

"About fifteen years. Last year, I set up my business." Carlos glanced around and saw the vicar headed in their direction.

"When did you say you left Cheapside?" Ellene looked puzzled.

"Why, just a week ago, when I heard the news of my father's death. If you will excuse me, I need to meet some others before they leave." Carlos backed away, then sprinted off to the group furthest from where the friends stood.

"Is something wrong, Ellene? You look unsettled." William had watched her as she talked with Carlos.

Broun joined the group. "I see you are getting acquainted with Carlos. I plan to get to know him better in the future."

"Are you coming to the wake at Coeur de Lion?" Ellene raised her eyebrows.

"Yes, but I must stay here until everyone leaves. Will I see you there?"

The family confirmed that they were going to the wake. The Babbages and Smythes confirmed their intention to head there as well. Ellene, William, and Avrill climbed into their carriage to make the journey to Coeur de Lion. The last of the mourners drifted away after a few minutes of conversation. Grave diggers stood nearby to shovel the dirt onto the coffin after the mourners left.

Carlos' face twisted into a scowl. His fists clenched as he strode towards his horse. He would show the villagers not to ignore him. They could do nothing to stop him from taking over the estate. If Marguerite was nice to him, he might let her stay. He mounted his horse and set off at a trot back to the village. His thoughts turned to what he would do as mayor. The first thing would be to replace the sheriff and the current members of the village council with men who would be loyal to him.

James caught up with Marguerite and rode beside her carriage to the estate. When they arrived, he helped her climb down and she went inside.

Marguerite went to her bedroom and returned without the veil covering her face. James could see her eyes were red and swollen from crying.

As the guests trickled in, they sat or stood in small groups, talking in hushed voices. Aromas of the cook's creations wafted through the air, tantalizing Marguerite's guests. Servants brought refreshments and placed them on the tables set up in the Great Hall. This time, there were no musicians and colorful clothes, unlike the spirited banquet a few days ago.

James circulated among the guests, hoping to overhear a careless conversation that might give him some clues regarding Eustace's death. Ellene helped with the servants while Marguerite greeted the guests as they arrived. Avrill joined Molly, Harriet, and Edith, feeling a sense of relief at being in the company of friendly faces. The Whites, the Etchells, the Morgans, Jonathon, and Simon were among the other guests. Broun was the last to arrive. William made his way to the group of councilmen.

"Isn't it amazing that the mayor's son is still alive? Still, I thought his speech during the service was rude," Molly said with a frown.

"Were you living in this county when he was a little boy?" Avrill wanted to know.

"Andrew and I had just inherited his uncle's estate when Eustace told us his wife and son died. I was new to Haver Hamlet. Andrew knew the mayor and his family, of course, but I did not meet him until months later."

Harriet drew her lips into a thin line. "His first wife and son were strangers to me. I came to Haver Hamlet some years after they died."

Edith stated she had never met the mayor's first wife and child.

"Papa was told he played with Carlos, but he was too young to remember. Aunt Ellene wasn't born yet." Avrill recounted what her father told her.

Everyone savored their food and drinks. With full stomachs, they gathered around Marguerite, offering their heartfelt sympathy and promises of help in the weeks to come. Soon, they returned to their own businesses and homes.

After the guests departed, and only Ellene and the Throck-Mortons remained, James approached Marguerite. Her perfume was so strong that it made his eyes water.

"Do you intend to stay in this house tonight? I can still send my men to protect you."

"Despite my change in status, it remains my home, at least for now."

"Then I advise you to lock your doors and stay out of the barn. We're still looking for the man who assaulted you."

"Thank you, Sheriff. I appreciate your concern." Marguerite gave a sweet smile.

James' gaze caught Ellene's, and he motioned for her to come outside with him. They met at the door and went a few steps away from the entrance.

"Ellene, I need to go tend to some other matters." He clasped her hand and raised it to his lips. "I hoped you would wear my brooch today. Soon, yes?"

"James, I'd rather not discuss that now." Ellene's heart raced as she blushed, stammered, and tried to pull her hand away.

James chuckled and released her hand. Ellene found it maddening that he was so sure he would win her affections.

"Um, James." Ellene placed her hand on his arm.

"Yes?" He lifted his eyebrows as a sign that he was actively listening.

"I spoke with Carlos after you left. He claims he and his mother took refuge in Cheapside, the neighborhood where I lived during my married life. According to him, he saw me riding with Lord Hunter, which we never did. When Forest asked about his occupation, he declared he had served as an apprentice to Silverstein, the esteemed goldsmith at Cheapside. Silverstein took only family as apprentices. That was one of the few shops I visited with my husband, and I never saw Carlos."

"Maybe he has been gone from there for a while?"

"He claimed he lived there until just last week. What he says just seems wrong."

James studied her expression. "You and William stay alert. I have no proof Carlos is not who he claims to be. Let me know if you hear anything else amiss. I hope to see you again soon." He nodded and headed to his horse.

Then only Ellene, William, and Avrill remained at the estate with Marguerite.

"Marguerite, what will you do about Carlos? What if Callum rules in his favor?" Ellene had a worried look as she rested her hand on Marguerite's arm.

"I shall leave, of course. I can't stay in this house with a strange man, even if he would allow it."

Ellene exchanged glances with William. "Stay with us. We have extra rooms. And it will keep you away from the turmoil of the village. It will be safer than staying here if the prowler returns." Ellene reached out and clasped Marguerite's hand.

"I fear the villagers would gossip. It would be unseemly to live with an unmarried man." Marguerite glanced at William out of the corner of her eyes.

"Silly, you would live with Avrill and me, too. Please consider it. At least until you have time to make other plans. In the meantime, James is working on who killed Eustace and who attacked you." Ellene sought to ease the young woman's worries.

In the end, Marguerite agreed that if Callum granted Carlos the estate, she would move to Haver Hall.

Chapter Twenty-Three

GOODY REMEMBERS

During breakfast the morning after the burial, Ellene shared her plans for the day with William and Avrill.

"It is time I visit Goody Pickwick. I have neglected the poor dear and she must need food. Besides, she knows so much about the history of this area, she might shed light on Eustace's first family. Avrill, would you like to come with me?"

"Oh, do I have to? I'm busy." Avrill expressed her complaint in a whine.

Ellene's eyebrows flew up. "Doing what? Goody enjoys your visits, you know."

"She can't hear, and I must shout. Besides, she won't remember if I visited because she forgets things. Anyway, I promised to help Bridgette in the kitchen."

Ellene realized Avrill would make excuses, so she relented. "Well, I'll stop by the church and see Rev. Broun, then visit Goody. Avrill, since you are going to the kitchen, help Bridgette prepare a basket of food. I'm going to change my shoes and get a shawl." Ellene rose from the table.

William listened to the exchange between Ellene and Avrill, but did not comment on it. Instead, he said, "Give Goody my best, will you?"

"Of course." Ellene nodded and left the room.

A smirk crossed Avrill's face when Ellene was no longer in sight. Aware of her father's watchful eyes, she scurried into the kitchen to confide in Bridgette about the urgent need for the basket of food.

When Ellene entered the kitchen, the basket, full of food and covered with a clean linen cloth, was ready for her. Avrill fiddled at one end of the table, trying to look busy. Ellene thought Avrill's actions were odd. Could she be up to something? Ellene resolved to question her more closely when she had the time. She was already dealing with too many mysteries.

Outside, Ellene felt the warmth of the sun and the soothing touch of the breeze on her cheeks. Oh, how lovely it would be to spend the day relaxing, maybe riding her horse to the woods by the stream. She could feel her stress melt away as she strolled through the meadow surrounded by the sweet scent of flowers. But her mission that day meant she would have to wait for another opportunity.

She noticed as she passed by the fresh grave someone placed flowers near the Ellingham monument. The only sound she heard was the chirping of birds in the distance. Broun kept the church unlocked during the day in case a parishioner wanted to pray or seek his counsel. Soon she arrived at the wood front doors of the church and entered the cool stone structure. After her eyes adjusted to the dim light, she strolled to their family pew and sat.

A bang followed by a crash startled her out of her reverie. Alarmed, her heart thudded in her chest. Ellene jumped up and looked for the source of the noise. She saw the vicar picking up an object from the floor.

"Vicar, are you hurt? What happened?"

"Oh, Lady Ellene. I didn't see you there. I tripped in the dim light and knocked over a candlestick. No harm done." He ambled to the pew opposite her. It made a slight creak as he sank into it and faced her. "Is there a special reason you stopped by?"

"There is." She paused. "I know you haven't lived in this county long. And I know you keep confessions confidential. But I wondered if Eustace ever talked about his first wife and child?"

"Only to say they died while away on a journey. There did not seem to be anything remarkable about the story. He expressed sorrow about their deaths. I suppose you are curious about Carlos?"

"We spoke after the funeral about his time at Cheapside. His description was not accurate. I wonder if he is telling the truth."

Broun shrugged his shoulders. "I have witnessed people returning from the dead before."

"Well, his story was that Eustace drove his mother away. Was there gossip about conflicts between him and Juanita?"

"Not since I arrived here." He shook his head.

"Did you know any clergy who knew them?"

Broun studied Ellene's face and shook his head. "You are going to put yourself in danger, Lady Hunter. Tell James what you know and let him follow up."

"I did. He promised to look into it. But my inquiries are harmless enough. If I find out anything more, I'll tell him."

Broun drew a deep breath. "The vicar who was here when Carlos was small died five years ago. Goody may remember something, however. She has a wealth of knowledge about the villagers."

"Thank you, Vicar. Any information right now may help. Oh, if Callum rules the stranger is indeed Carlos, Marguerite will come to live with us until she can make other arrangements."

"Good to know. I shall remember to drop by to minister to her spiritual needs." His face crinkled into a comforting smile.

Ellene rose and picked up the basket, then bid him farewell. She stepped back into the sunlight and continued her journey to Goody's cottage. When she arrived, she found Goody outside, enjoying the sunshine.

"I have a basket of food for you," Ellene shouted. "Shall I take it inside?"

"Thank you, dear. I'll go with you. All this sunshine makes me quite thirsty," Goody shouted back.

Ellene held the door open, and the elderly woman, with a hobbled gait, made her way into her small cottage. Ellene followed her inside and put the basket on the table, then ladled some water into a cup for her. After a few minutes of casual conversation, Ellene posed her questions.

"Do you remember Mayor Ellingham's first wife and their son?"

Goody's forehead wrinkled as she pondered the question, then her face lit up. "Yes, I do. Her name was Juanita, and he married her in Spain. She had tawny skin, dark eyes, and coal-black hair. She was beautiful. He didn't know Spanish, and she was learning English. They visited your father and mother at Haver Hall a few times. You weren't born yet, and William was about five years old. People assumed that William and Carlos would become friends since they were close to the same age."

"William doesn't remember Carlos, and he appears to not remember my brother. Carlos is an odd name for a boy, don't you think?"

"I believe it was her father's name. He had an estate in Spain, you know."

"What happened to them? Some say they died at sea."

"That is what we heard. Eustace told your father that Juanita went to visit her family and took Carlos so he could meet her relatives. He was informed by the ship's owner that their ship sank during a storm in the

Channel, and all who were on board drowned."

"How sad for them. Might someone have saved Juanita and Carlos, but they never returned to Haver Hamlet?"

"Why would you ask that? What has happened?" Goody's eyebrows lifted in surprise.

Ellene described Carlos' arrival, his claim that Eustace drove his mother away in a fit of anger, and she assumed a false identity. "Were there any reports of Eustace abusing his wife, or her being afraid of him?"

"Eustace was always ill tempered. But you could see he adored her and the boy."

"Carlos told me they lived in Cheapside, where I lived with Lord Hunter, but his description was inaccurate. I told James, but he is currently busy investigating the murder."

"Tsk," Goody exclaimed in disapproval. "James has his hands full. First someone poisons the mayor, then someone attacks the widow, and a man who is supposed to be dead arrives, claiming to be the mayor's son." She reached over and patted Ellene's hand. "How is James, by the way?"

"I've spent little time with him since he returned from visiting his father. He seems well, however."

"Never fear, dear. I'm sure he's still interested in you."

Ellene gaped and blushed. "What makes you say that?"

"Everyone knows he is courting you. You would make a lovely couple."

"But you don't even know him," Ellene protested.

"People tell me things." Goody gave a wink. "I hear he danced almost every dance with you at the banquet."

"Yes, he and Simon were vying for my attention." Ellene giggled, then grew serious. "I'm not ready to remarry yet. The Earl de Beauvoir invited

Avrill to her cousin's wedding, at which she will meet many eligible young men. It is my mission to help her prepare."

"Avrill will make a lovely bride," Goody said. She sounded like a cooing bird.

Ellene nodded in agreement. "I wish I could talk longer, but I must go now. Seeing you again made my day much brighter. Take care of yourself." Ellene stood and hugged her friend, picked up the empty basket from the previous visit, and hurried from the cottage.

It annoyed her that people were talking about James and her. She felt a surge of rebellion against their relentless pressure to accept his proposal.

CHAPTER TWENTY-FOUR

AVRILL'S SECRET

Having received confirmation from Goody of the mayor's history, Ellene started back to her house. Something bothered her about Goody's description of Juanita and Carlos. If Juanita had tawny skin and dark hair, would Carlos' complexion be so fair? Can his physical appearance suggest something different from his claims?

Laughter floated across the field, interrupting her thoughts. Looking around, she spotted a girl and man sitting beneath a shade tree in deep conversation. A horse grazed nearby. What were they doing? From a distance, she guessed the girl was a tenant's daughter. She adjusted her route to uncover the couple's identity. As she drew closer, she recognized Avrill and Thomas.

"Avrill," she shouted. "Why are you in the field? You told me this morning that you were planning to work with Bridgette." She strode towards the couple.

Hunching her shoulders, Avrill turned toward Thomas. "Oh, no. I told Aunt Ellene I would work in the kitchen this morning. She'll be angry with me."

Thomas stood, faced Ellene, and bowed. He was as tall as James, but not as muscular. He flicked his blond hair from his eyes. "Lady Hunter, it's delightful to see you. I was riding by when I spotted Avrill and stopped to talk. My apologies if I kept her from her duties." He clasped his hands in supplication.

Ellene ignored him and focused on her conversation with her niece. "You told me you were planning to work with Bridgette. Why are you in the field with Thomas? I thought you knew better than to meet a man without a chaperone."

Then she confronted Thomas. "As for you, Thomas, does James know you are here?" Ellene noticed the tension in his body and his furrowed brow. Was Thomas' interest in her niece greater than she suspected?

"He sent me out to check on his estate. Avrill and I didn't plan to meet. We started talking and lost track of time."

Ellene fixed her gaze on Avrill, who hung her head. "Come to the house, Avrill. You need to explain to your father what happened."

"But, Aunt Ellene, nothing happened. We were just talking." Avrill's eyes glistened with tears.

"That is beside the point. Our goal is to protect your reputation for a suitable match. Or perhaps you don't want that?" She pointed toward the house. "Go. No argument." She pointed toward Thomas. "You come with us."

Thomas and Avrill went side by side, Thomas leading his horse. Ellene strode ahead, her expression downcast.

"Clive," she called out as they approached the courtyard.

"Yes, Lady Ellene." Clive came out of the stable.

"Do you know if William is here?"

"Ma'am, he just left for the village and won't be back until this afternoon."

Ellene thought for a minute, then decided. "Would you saddle horses for Avrill and me? We're going to Haver Manor to talk to James. Let Thomas water his horse while he's waiting. Avrill, put on your riding clothes. We will leave as soon as we both change, and the horses are ready."

When the women disappeared into the house, Clive peered at Thomas and smirked. "Things not going so well with Lady Avrill?"

Thomas sighed and scuffed the toe of his boot in the dirt.

Turning on his heel, Clive flashed a grin before striding towards the stable. Thomas followed, leading his horse to the water trough.

Ellene and Avrill dressed in their riding clothes, then joined Thomas and set off toward Haver Manor. Ellene realized she did not know what she would do if James was not home. Avrill and Thomas rode side by side, the only sound being the clip-clop of their horses' hooves on the dirt road. The trio turned into the lane leading to James' estate. As they approached the house, Ellene saw the men sparring in the yard. When she saw a tall, auburn-haired man, her heart skipped a beat. He wrestled with another man while a group watched. He had removed his shirt, and she caught herself admiring his muscular arms and torso.

One man shouted that riders were approaching, and all the men stopped to watch them draw near.

"Lady Ellene and Lady Avrill, what a pleasant surprise." James' face lit up with a delighted smile.

"I must speak with you in private. It concerns these two." Ellene's lips tightened into a frown as she gestured toward Avrill and Thomas.

A soft chortle from someone made Ellene look around to find the source. The men all looked toward the ground or the field, anywhere but the guests.

"Is something amiss?" James' expression changed. He searched Thomas' face, but the man was stoic.

James put on his shirt while the men resumed their practice. He reached up to help Ellene off her horse, his hands holding her at the waist, her hair brushing against his face as he leaned in close. James wore a puzzled expression as Ellene pulled away from his embrace.

"Come inside. Do you want something to drink?"

"No, thank you. We won't stay long." Ellene shook her head.

Thomas helped Avrill dismount. Tears glistened in her eyes, and her cheeks were red with embarrassment.

They gathered in the Great Hall, and James gazed at Ellene, waiting for her to speak.

Ellene drew a deep breath. "I found Avrill and Thomas meeting in our pasture. Avrill told me she would stay in the house this morning, but she was in the field talking to Thomas. They did not have a chaperone present. Thomas told me you sent him to check your estate. I'm concerned about Avrill's reputation. William is not home at present, and I believe this is serious enough that I need to address it without waiting for him to return."

"Sir, I meant no harm. I stopped to greet her during my ride. Avrill and I have similar interests, and we enjoy talking." Nervous, Thomas stumbled as he tried to explain.

James shifted his gaze to Thomas. "We will discuss this later."

"James, please don't blame him. It's my fault. He rode by when I was walking in the pasture, and we started talking, and we lost track of time." As her words tumbled out, tears rolled down Avrill's cheeks.

James put his arm around her shoulders. "Now, Avrill, calm yourself. Thomas is my steward and an honorable man. I don't believe he would try to take advantage of you."

Ellene looked on astonished. Crying was a trick Avrill used to get her way, and James fell for it. Good to know.

Avrill stopped sniffling. "Then it is all right? You aren't angry?"

"No, I didn't say that. You should not meet with a boy or man without a chaperone. Aunt Ellene and your papa will impose your punishment. I'll talk to Thomas about his consequences."

Thomas set his mouth in a grim line, his worry unmistakable.

"Ellene, I think we should arrange regular visits so Avrill and Thomas can spend time together. You can plan to have a chaperone present." James' eyes crinkled when he smiled.

Ellene responded with a nod. "I'll propose that to William."

Ellene and James stared into each other's eyes, the air between them charged with electricity. Avrill and Thomas shared a knowing look. Ellene could feel the heat rising to her neck and broke the silence.

"Well, Avrill and I must return. Thank you for being so understanding."

Although James smiled at Ellene, she did not return it. She was still angry with Avrill.

"I'll ride back with you. Even though it's a short distance, the roads are dangerous. Give me a minute to find a clean shirt, my baldric, and a bonnet." He looked at the steward. "Follow me."

James and Thomas went up the staircase and conferred after moving far enough away so the women could not hear.

"You know how protective William is of Avrill. I know you to be an honorable man, but I don't want to rile William." James shook his head. "It seems the Throck-Morton women are difficult to win. But don't damage Avrill's reputation because I don't want to fight William. I would win that battle, but it would help neither of us win our ladies." He made a face before pivoting to proceed to his room.

A short time later, James and Thomas helped Ellene and Avrill mount their horses. On their way to Haver Hall, James chatted with Ellene. When they arrived, he helped Ellene and Avrill dismount.

Avrill whispered, "Thank you, James."

He winked at her, and she stifled a giggle. Ellene glared at them, but they betrayed nothing. Avrill ran to the house while Ellene and James stood in the courtyard waiting for Clive to collect the horses.

"You realize Avrill cried to gain your sympathy, don't you?" Ellene spoke up.

"Yes, I'm familiar with that tactic. Many women use tears to melt a man's heart. I haven't noticed you using it." James grinned, a mischievous twinkle in his eyes.

Ellene made a face. "No, I don't. Is Thomas serious about Avrill? I can't believe William would allow him to court her."

"Thomas is from a prosperous family, but his older brother will inherit the family estate. Since William's only heir is Avrill, he would do well to select Thomas as her husband. He could effectively manage Haver Hall should William become disabled or die."

"Lately, my brother speaks of getting married and having more children.

He may have a son who could inherit the estate."

"Did this talk of marriage start after Marguerite became available?" James gazed at Ellene until she fidgeted.

"I see. Ellene, I enjoyed seeing you today. I miss you when we're apart." James reached out and caressed Ellene's cheek.

"I enjoy seeing you, too. I hope you are making progress with your investigation."

"Of course." He leaned over and kissed her hand. "You and I must have a serious conversation about our future. Soon." He kissed her hand again as Clive arrived to take the horses. "Goodbye, Ellene."

"Goodbye, James. Be careful."

Ellene watched as he climbed onto his horse, the leather of the saddle creaking beneath him, and rode away. Ellene's gaze followed him until he rode out of sight. With each passing day, he revealed new layers of complexity that she hadn't seen before. Their conversations always ended with pressure to make their relationship official. She wanted it to be her own decision, not something forced upon her.

Chapter Twenty-Five

ENTAILMENTS

Marguerite began packing for her imminent departure from Coeur de Lion. Tomorrow the justice of the peace would hear Carlos' claim that he should inherit the estate. She feared Callum would decide in his favor. Thankful for William and Ellene's offer to take her in, she couldn't help but smile at how much William cared for her.

She placed her belongings in the various trunks that were scattered around her bedroom. When she was certain none of the servants were nearby, she used the private passage leading from her bedroom to enter Eustace's bedroom to search for money and jewelry. She selected the biggest jewels from his jewelry box and filled a purse. After tiptoeing back, she stored the purse in a secret compartment in one trunk, along with her own jewels.

She heard William arrive in the courtyard. He rushed up the front stairs and knocked on the door.

Prudence shuffled from the kitchen to greet him. "The mistress is upstairs in her bedroom. Wait here and I'll go tell her you've arrived."

"No, don't trouble yourself. I know where to find her."

Prudence frowned as she raised her voice, her indignation palpable in the room. "It's not fitting for a young widow to meet a gentleman in her bedroom."

When she heard the cook call out, Marguerite appeared at the top of the stairs, with a smile on her face. "I'm glad you're here, William. I'm seeking a muscular man to assist me in moving a trunk."

William slipped past Prudence and ran up the stairs two at a time. Prudence shook her head in a disapproving manner and returned to the kitchen, muttering. William and Marguerite clasped hands and strolled toward her bedroom together. Her perfume was everywhere, filling the air.

"Has the prowler returned?"

"No. Perhaps he was frightened away." Marguerite shook her head and smoothed her satin skirt. She had dark circles under her eyes, a sign of her sleepless nights.

"Or what he wanted is no longer here." William lifted her hand and brushed it with his lips. "Are you packing to move to Haver Hall?"

"Yes, I'm packing my clothes and other items Eustace left for my inheritance." She set her lips in a thin line. Her jaw clenched in defiance.

"Do I need to send a wagon for your things?"

"Yes, I only have a carriage, which won't hold all my trunks. I can't express how grateful I am to have someone like you to take care of me. Are you sure Ellene and Avrill agree for me to move there?"

"Of course. You are Ellene's best friend. Avrill likes you as well."

Marguerite sidled close to William and put her arms around his neck. Their bodies pressed together in a tight, comforting embrace. As she looked up, he planted a soft kiss on her lips.

"Oh, William. I long for the time when we can be together every day. Just you and me at Haver Hall." She gazed into his eyes.

"My darling, I adore you. But surely it is too soon to speak of marriage."

William kissed her again. Reluctantly, they separated when they heard footsteps on the stairs.

William moved to the door by the time Prudence reached the bedroom.

"Mistress, I need to talk to you about supplies for the kitchen. Is it convenient now?" Prudence peered at William out of the corner of her eye.

"I'm just leaving."

"Goodbye. I'll see you soon." Marguerite watched his back until he disappeared. His footsteps echoed down the hall before he descended the stairs.

The same day, Robert met with Callum at his home to discuss Carlos' claim of heirship. With his hands clasped together, the justice fixed his eyes on Robert.

"I find no fault with the document produced by the claimant. Unless you can produce some evidence he is not the son, I must make a preliminary determination to grant possession to him. Mrs. Ellingham has thirty days from the mayor's death to vacate according to her marriage contract."

"I will let her know, Your Honor. James has not had time to investigate the man's background. We have no proof he's lying about his identity."

"Harrumph. If you find the man is an impostor in the future, the Crown can bring charges against him and remove him."

"Yes, Your Honor." Robert gave a slight bow and retreated from the justice's office.

Carlos sauntered into Robert's office and draped himself in the chair facing the solicitor.

"Mr. White, do you have any news for me about my claim to Coeur de Lion?" Carlos' voice revealed his annoyance, even though his words sounded polite.

"The justice of the peace scheduled a hearing tomorrow at one o'clock at his home. I suggest you arrive early. Remember, I represent the estate in this matter, so I cannot represent your interests." Robert's gaze locked on his unwelcome visitor. He had a strong dislike for the man but thought it wise to keep the relationship positive in case the justice awarded the estate to him.

"I want to petition the queen to appoint me as mayor in my father's place."

"I can handle that after the hearing."

"This is taking too long. I must pay for a room and meals while I wait. I demand an advance on the estate to cover my expenses." Carlos clenched his fists.

"You could go home and return tomorrow for the hearing."

"But the journey there would consume half a day, and it would require another half a day to make the return trip."

"Surely you have the means to stay in the inn another day or two. What did you say was your business before coming here?"

"I'm a goldsmith. I design jewelry and other items for wealthy clients." Carlos threw up his hands, his eyes darting from side to side. "It's important we resolve this issue. I'm eager to go back home to close my business. Then I can focus on managing the estate."

"Of course. Where is your shop located? Perhaps I could send a letter to your business associates for you?" Studying Carlos' face, Robert noticed a brief flash of alarm on his features before it vanished.

"I'll send the message myself."

"But surely you can tell me where you live."

"It's not your concern. I shall close my business and move here once the justice grants me my father's estate." Carlos sprang up, his chair scraping against the floor. "I see there is no further need for conversation. I'll see you tomorrow." He pivoted and rushed out of the office.

Later that morning, James stopped at Robert's office to find out the time of the hearing.

"It's tomorrow at one o'clock. Callum indicated he will grant possession of the estate to Carlos." Robert paused. "Carlos and I talked this morning. He wants to move in immediately. He also wants me to petition the queen to appoint him as the mayor."

"So, what can we do about it?" He recounted Ellene's suspicions.

"We would have to inquire among his acquaintances. I asked where he lives and what he does to earn a living. He claimed he is a goldsmith but would not tell me where he lives. He mentioned it was about a half day's ride from here." Robert gazed at James.

"Half a day? He told Ellene he lives in Cheapside. That is more than a day's ride from here."

The men stared at each other for a moment, then James broke the silence.

"Do you have a map? We can see which villages are half a day's ride from here."

Robert located a map of the surrounding area. The men determined Updyke Chase was within a half day's ride.

"I can visit the village and find out if he lives there. In that case, I'll uncover whatever I can about Carlos. But I can't be back in time for tomorrow's hearing."

"If you find out he is a fraud, we can arrest him when you return. Still, Marguerite will have to move from the estate regardless of his identity. It is just a matter of when."

"I'll set out tomorrow morning. Before I leave, I need to take care of some business at the manor."

A local vagrant, known for trading information for a pint of ale, crouched in the bushes below the window in Robert's office. His clothes were dirty and patched, his hair tangled and greasy.

After James left Robert's office, the vagrant crept away to the White Stag Inn. When Bess' back was toward the entrance, he slipped inside and climbed the stairs to the upper floor where guests rented rooms. He tapped on a bedroom door.

Carlos cracked open the door. Seeing the vagrant, he opened it all the way to let him into the room, then quickly shut the door.

"I've news for ye. I followed the sheriff like ye asked."

"Good. What did you find out?"

"Well, keeping up with him is thirsty work. Maybe a copper or two for a drink would help me remember."

Carlos pulled out two coppers and waved them under his nose. The vagrant tried to take them, but Carlos snatched them away.

"These are yours if you tell me something useful."

"Seems the sheriff thinks ye aren't really the mayor's son. Plans to go to Updyke Chase to ask some questions."

"When?" A chill ran down Carlos' spine, causing him to shiver.

"Tomorrow morning."

"Well, it seems you earned your coins. Enjoy your drink."

The man grabbed the coins and fled.

Carlos put on his bonnet and doublet and headed out of the inn. In a nearby stable, he found two men and a youth who made their living by robbing travelers. The two men were in their twenties and had been criminals for many years. The most recent addition to the gang was a youth in his late teens.

With a forced nonchalance, Carlos leaned against the wall, concealing the anxiety bubbling within. "I have a job for you. Seems the county sheriff plans to go to Updyke Chase and ask awkward questions about me. I'll be in trouble if he comes back."

"What's this caper worth to ye?" The head of the gang chewed on a straw.

"He's taking a purse of gold coins. It'll pay for any—um—expenses you encounter."

The man narrowed his eyes. "I know him. He has a big estate. Trains men how to fight."

"Should not be a problem for the three of you to take out one man, especially if you take him by surprise."

"Understood. Although it might be better to be waiting for him than to follow him."

"Suit yourself. Just make sure he doesn't return."

CHAPTER TWENTY-SIX

CHANGE OF OWNERSHIP

C allum held hearings in the Great Hall of his residence. His table was at one end of the room, and the servants arranged chairs and benches for the parties, their advocates, and witnesses. Marguerite arrived at Callum's house for the hearing regarding the will and Carlos' claim to the estate. She wore mourning clothes and a veil over her face. Her perfume's scent drifted through the room.

William sat next to Marguerite, expecting to be formally appointed as Marguerite's guardian. Robert was nearby since he represented the estate.

Carlos smirked as he strutted to a bench near the justice of the peace. When the clerk announced his case, Callum called Robert to address the issues of the case. Callum quickly agreed to William being Marguerite's guardian.

Next they took up Carlos' claim on the estate. He stood in front of the justice to tell his story. Carlos told how his mother took refuge with wealthy friends at Cheapside and hid him as a child from a dangerous father. He recognized his opportunity to emerge from hiding and claim the estate when he heard Eustace died. Callum questioned him about his possession of the marriage contract as evidence his mother was Juanita, Eustace's first wife.

Callum then directed questions about the document to Robert. The solicitor described his search for Eustace's copy of the marriage contract in the house but failed to find it. He admitted there was no evidence the one presented by Carlos lacked validity.

With no person present able to refute Carlos' claim, Callum ruled Carlos was Eustace's son and could forthwith take possession of Coeur de Lion. However, he had to permit Marguerite to stay until thirty days after Eustace died. Carlos expressed his gratitude to the justice. He gazed at Marguerite, and a delighted smirk spread across his face.

When Callum adjourned the hearing, Marguerite stormed out of the house and climbed into her carriage to return home. William pursued her to the carriage. A few people passing by stood in a half circle around the vehicle, eyes wide with curiosity, as they whispered to each other and gawked.

"What do you intend to do, Marguerite?" William rested his hand on the side of the carriage.

Marguerite's face remained hidden behind her veil. Even with no outward signs, he could sense her anger through the bitterness in her voice. "It seems I must make haste to move out of the house. I accept your offer to join you at Haver Hall."

"Come with me now. We can retrieve your possessions later. I have concerns about your safety."

"He'll not harm me. I'll keep my bedroom door locked. Besides, I need to finish packing. Tomorrow, my love, I will join you." Marguerite whispered so the onlookers would not hear.

"Let me know when you're ready and I'll bring my wagon." William grasped her hand but refrained from kissing it. The widow and the carriage drew too much attention from the onlookers.

After the hearing, Carlos went to the inn for a drink, then retrieved his belongings and rode to Coeur de Lion. Riding into the courtyard with pride, he surveyed the house and grounds with satisfaction. He spotted chickens, ducks, and geese in a side yard which contained a small pond. He could see fruit trees and grain in the fields, sheep in the pasture, and the stream beyond.

"This is a fine place to live," he murmured. He dismounted, tied his horse, and went to the front entrance. Instead of waiting for a servant to greet him, he threw open the door, sauntered into the house, and stood in the Great Hall. Aromas of food cooking emanated from the kitchen.

"I'm here at last, Mrs. Ellingham. I desire to see my new home." A smug look on his face, he yelled into the vacant room. He peered up the stairs, wondering if Marguerite was there. When she and the valet approached from behind, he jumped.

"Mr. Ellingham, this is your valet. He will show you the master's bedroom and the other rooms. My bedroom is private. I warn you to respect that." Marguerite's voice was icy, her face without expression.

"Of course, Mother. May I call you Mother?" He smirked, as he was several years older than she was.

"No. Mrs. Ellingham will do." Marguerite glared at him.

Carlos smirked again before turning to the valet. "I'm eager to see my new home. You may show me around."

Walking ahead of Carlos, the valet ascended the stairs and led him to Eustace's room.

"This is the master's bedroom, sir."

The wall of windows caught Carlos' attention. He crossed the room to look out on the estate but found a tall tree blocking his view. He resolved to have the tree removed so he could see his property unobstructed.

Taking up the center of another wall was an immense fireplace. A door led to Marguerite's room, but he found it locked from the other side. The headboard of an enormous bed backed up against a wall. Scattered around were several upholstered chairs. A night table with a silver candlestick stood beside the bed. A pile of goose down pillows rested at one end of the bed. Tapestries adorned the walls. A washstand held a basin and pitcher.

Eustace's clothes hung in the wardrobe, and his fine leather boots lined up on the floor. Many of the doublets and breeches had food stains and other signs of wear. His bonnets, decorated with gold trim, feathers, and jewels, rested on a shelf. The clothes and boots were too large for Carlos, but he speculated that a skilled tailor could alter the clothes to his size. He was not as confident about the boots.

"I shall need a tailor. I require him to alter the finer garments to fit me." He signaled the valet with a wave. "My panniers are with my horse. Have them brought to my room."

Carlos was eager to explore the rest of the house, so the valet showed him the other rooms on that floor. At Marguerite's bedroom, he turned the handle and shoved at the door, but it was locked. The valet pressed on a section of wall in the hallway, which opened to reveal a priest's hide. Eustace converted it to a closet, where he stored old weapons and armor, trunks, and various other items. Carlos noticed a portrait of a tawny woman with black hair and a toddler playing at her feet. The toddler had dark hair like the woman.

"Who is the woman in the portrait? Is she family?"

"I don't know, sir. Perhaps Mrs. Ellingham can tell you."

"Well, I shall dispose of it later."

Having explored the upper floor, the valet took him downstairs to look in the sitting room and the office. When they entered the kitchen, Prudence stopped her meal preparations and bowed.

"Welcome to your home, Mr. Ellingham. I have started the evening meal." She described the food she planned to serve.

"I'll let you know what I like for my meals. Starting tomorrow morning, I want eggs, bread, and ham," he proclaimed in an arrogant tone.

"I'm sorry, sir. We don't have ham," the cook replied confidently.

"I said I want ham." He rather enjoyed ordering people around.

"But we don't have pigs on the farm. I would have to find someone who recently butchered a pig and buy it from them."

"Then do so." The room reverberated with the sound of his loud cursing. "Woman, do as I tell you, or you shall have to look for other employment."

Her face darkened with a scowl.

Paying no attention to her, Carlos redirected his focus to the valet. "Now to the barn."

Carlos sauntered into the barn, but once inside, he began poking the straw with his foot. When he looked at the corner where the man had left the stolen wine, all he saw was straw.

In the field, the herdsman joined Carlos and the valet and pointed out the sheep Eustace allowed the tenants to keep in the pastures.

"Get rid of the sheep. I hate mutton. Sheep are a nuisance and a bother. I want pigs to provide me with bacon and ham." Carlos waved his arm in a dismissive gesture. He glared at the valet.

"Take me to the office and bring me wine. I intend to go over the estate's ledgers."

Behind his back, the valet and herdsman made a disrespectful hand sign toward Carlos before the valet followed him into the house.

In the office, Carlos settled in the large chair behind the ornate desk. He grabbed the flagon of wine from the valet and gulped it down, releasing a satisfied burp when he was done. Then he asked the valet, "Where are the estate's ledgers?"

"I don't know, sir. Mrs. Ellingham can tell you."

"How would she know?" He frowned at the valet. "Alright, go fetch her. And bring more wine."

While he waited, Carlos studied the room. Silver candlesticks, upholstered chairs, and tapestries decorated the office. They should fetch an acceptable price should he decide to sell them.

The valet found Marguerite in her bedroom and told her Carlos summoned her. She took her time in making her way to the office. The valet arrived behind her with more wine.

"I understand you want to see me?" Her face was like a mask, hiding any hint of feeling.

"Where are the estate's ledgers? I need to scrutinize them carefully." Carlos scowled, his fingers forming a tight fist.

She looked down her nose at the interloper. "Mr. White has them. He must account for money to the justice of the peace as part of the probate process. He left me only enough money to buy food and drink and pay the servants for the next week. I understand you want Prudence to buy ham for breakfast?"

"Yes. Why are people here so stupid? I want some ham for breakfast. Every morning." He spat out the words. His slender face, pointy nose, and beady eyes reminded her of a weasel.

"There is not enough money to buy it. If she does, there will not be enough to pay the servants and buy other food." Marguerite tried to make her argument sound reasonable.

Carlos pounded the desk, causing the papers and jar of ink to jump. "I'll see what Robert has to say about this. Eustace—my father—was rich. I should be rich too. Where is the money?"

"My late husband did not involve me in those matters. He gave me an allowance to manage the kitchen and pay the servants. Nothing more."

"Bah. Leave me. I've nothing more to say to you." He looked at the valet, who stood behind Marguerite, holding a bottle of wine. "What are you waiting for? Put the bottle here on the table."

When Carlos stumbled into the dining hall for dinner, he slurred his words and his steps were sluggish. He stumbled to the table and sat at the head. Marguerite sat at the foot, as far away from him as possible. Prudence brought out the food, serving him first. Marguerite stared at her plate, pushed the food around, and spoke as little as possible. He gobbled down his food without acknowledging her and stumbled out of the dining room.

Marguerite went to the kitchen to confer with the cook.

"I can't stay here. William will bring his wagon tomorrow so that I can leave. The valet told me Carlos had already tried to force his way into my bedroom. He'll ruin the estate in weeks. You and the others must decide your own futures."

"I'm not afraid of the likes of him. He has a nasty temper like the master. If I were you, I'd wait to move my things until he goes to the village to talk to the solicitor."

As William came back to Haver Hall from the hearing, his face betrayed his displeasure. Marguerite's decision to stay at the estate for an additional night appeared unwise given Carlos' immediate relocation there. William flung his reins at Clive and stomped into the house. He encountered Ellene in the hallway after she emerged from the sitting room. As soon as she caught sight of him, her expression shifted to one of concern.

"How did the hearing go? Did Callum grant Carlos the estate?"

"Yes, he did. Carlos plans to move in today. Marguerite wants to move here tomorrow. I told her we'll provide a wagon and driver for her things. She'll send a messenger to let us know when she's ready."

"I had better have Sorcha prepare a guest bedroom. Which one do you think she would like? The one closest to Avrill and me?"

"I want her in Desiree's room." He spoke with authority, but did not meet her eyes.

Ellene's mouth hung open as she gazed at him. "Why her room? I thought you did not want anyone to use it."

"Why not?" William's tone was sharp and defensive. "Marguerite is a close friend and the former mayor's widow. We don't know how long she may stay. She'll no doubt come with all her possessions, so she needs the larger room." He refused to make eye contact.

"I understand, but it's unexpected because you were so strict about not allowing anyone, including your daughter, into Desiree's room." Ellene's expression showed her confusion at his change in attitude.

"Maybe it's time." He glared at Ellene, as though daring her to contradict him. "I'm going to my office. Have Jeremy bring me some wine." He spun around and his boots clacked against the hard floor as he stalked down the hallway. Ellene watched him until he disappeared into his office and slammed the door.

On Friday morning, James packed a pannier and donned his leather jerkin and baldric. Apprehensive that he might encounter bandits, he picked up his sword, a firearm, and several daggers. The sooner he discovered Carlos' true lineage and could return, the better. Only Robert and Thomas knew about his destination. He debated whether he should let Ellene know what he had in mind, but chose not to, so she wouldn't worry. As he left, he gave parting instructions to Thomas.

"I have a half day's ride to Updyke Chase. I should return tomorrow evening or the following day. If anyone inquires, they are not to know the specifics. Just say that I'm away on business. If Ellene asks, tell her the truth but warn her to keep it confidential. If I'm not back the day after tomorrow, send someone to look for me."

"Are you sure you want to travel there alone? There are bandits on the roads."

"I can travel quickly and be less obvious if I'm alone."

"Safe journey, sir. I'll watch over the estate." Thomas swept his blond hair away from his eyes with a flick of his head.

James mounted his horse and set out on his journey. Along the way, he encountered tinkers and traders traveling the road in both directions.

Their wagons rattled with clanging goods and creaking wheels. He was relieved that he had someone to share the long journey with. As the wagons rolled by, a thick cloud of dust enveloped the air, making him cough and cover his nose.

Arriving at Updyke Chase late in the afternoon, James found the local inn. He stopped at the stable and paid for a stall and provisions for his horse. Then he arranged for a room and supper for himself. He strolled around the village to get a sense of the inhabitants and shops, most of which were already closed for the day. Then he ate a hearty meal and went to bed.

James' time in the military turned him into a light sleeper, and he kept his dagger nearby. During the night, he awakened to the sound of footsteps coming from the hallway. Then he heard a knife scraping against the door.

Someone was trying to force his door open.

On that cloudless night, the silver light of the moon illuminated the room. He sprang out of bed, tiptoed to the door, and held his dagger ready. Without a sound, he unlocked the door and threw it open. Two men tumbled onto the floor.

He picked up one by his hair and held his dagger at the man's throat. The pungent smell of sweat and ale clung to the intruder, souring the air. He could make out the men's features in the moonlight.

"One move and I slit his throat. What do you want?" James growled.

The other man, still on the floor, raised his hands.

"It looks like we're in the wrong room. Let him go and we'll just be off."

"Do you normally go into your own room with your knife drawn? Why are you here? The truth or I slit his throat."

"We heard ye had a purse filled with gold coins." The man he held emitted a squeaky sound.

"Your informant is mistaken. Who told you that?"

"Um-."

James pricked his throat just a little.

"Ouch."

"What did you hear, and who told you?" James growled menacingly.

"Friend of ours in Haver Hamlet told us to follow ye here. Word was ye are lookin' for someone to give money to." Fear overtook the man, causing him to shake.

"Fools. What's your friend's name?"

"I-I don't know." He stumbled over his words.

"Some friend. Your friend lied to you. You go back and tell him to crawl back into his hole. The next man who comes after me will feel the sharp sting of my sword blade. Now both of you get out."

The men clambered out of the door, their feet clattering on the wooden floor. James locked the door and braced a chair against it.

His encounter with the two men disturbed James. Other than asking for directions and renting his room and a stall for his horse, he had not yet spoken with anyone in Updyke Chase. Robert and Thomas would not have divulged his errand. No one else in Haver Hamlet knew he was here. Was someone following him? If people thought he carried a purse of gold coins, he would be a target for thieves. He had better finish his errand and leave.

Soon, he would find evidence of whether Carlos was the mayor's son. If there was none, it would be enough to put Carlos in jail.

CHAPTER TWENTY-SEVEN
MOVE TO HAVER HALL

William tossed and turned all night as his thoughts kept returning to Marguerite. He rose early and went to work in his office while he waited to hear from her. The day she would move to Haver Hall had finally come. He daydreamed about her living there, about what their life together might be like. Being near her muddled his thinking. The smell of her perfume captivated him. When they were together, he wanted nothing more than to press his lips against hers, so soft and inviting. But sitting alone in his office, he had doubts. Marriage was an important step, and he needed to have time to think it through.

His reverie was interrupted when Jeremy escorted a servant from Coeur de Lion to his office. Anticipation of Marguerite's summons caused William's heart to race in his chest, and blood pounded in his ears.

"Sir Throck-Morton, I have a message for you from Mrs. Ellingham."

William frowned, his forehead forming creases. "Tell me, man, what is the message?"

"Come with your wagon. She is ready to depart her house."

"This morning?"

"As soon as possible. Mr. Ellingham was to meet with his solicitor this morning, and she wishes to be gone by the time he returns."

William sprang up and grabbed his doublet and bonnet, then his baldric and sword. He rushed to tell Clive to hitch the horses to the wagon, then saddled his horse. A few minutes later, Clive drove the wagon while Marguerite's servant and William rode ahead of it as they set off for Coeur de Lion.

William felt his stomach tighten, and a cold sweat broke out on his forehead. What if Carlos caught them leaving and demanded to go through Marguerite's things? He did not know what the man's skills were with a sword. William had not practiced with his sword recently and was unsure he could best Carlos. He mused that a refresher session with James would not go amiss.

When they arrived at Coeur de Lion, Marguerite met them wearing her riding clothes, her horse already saddled. William and Marguerite embraced and then moved apart, the smell of her perfume lingering in the air between them.

"Carlos left about an hour ago to see Robert about the ledgers. My trunks are upstairs and ready to go. Hurry." Marguerite stood wringing her hands.

William, Clive, and the servant went upstairs to her bedroom. There they collected the trunks containing all her clothes, jewels, toiletries, and bedding. They hurried down the stairs with the trunks and loaded them onto the wagon.

Marguerite told Prudence and the servant not to divulge her destination to Carlos. He would find out soon enough. She paid the remaining servants' wages for the next week and gave Prudence money to pay for food.

"After this is gone, Mr. Ellingham will pay you. Farewell and best of luck." Marguerite spoke in a voice that was devoid of any feeling.

"God be with you, mistress." Prudence's face settled into a scowl.

Marguerite veiled her face, but William suspected her horse and clothes would betray her identity to the villagers.

William, Marguerite, and Clive departed for Haver Hall. The nervous trio watched for Carlos to appear. They feared he would attack William or find James to arrest them. William held his breath as they traversed the village and passed Robert's office. Carlos was not there. When they made it to the other side of the village without a confrontation, William's breathing returned to normal.

Ellene and Avrill came out to the courtyard to greet their guest. Ellene hugged Marguerite and welcomed her. Avrill greeted her but did not move to make physical contact. William hovered nearby, waiting for Jeremy to appear to help with the trunks.

"William told us about Callum's decision. You are welcome to stay with us until you find something more permanent," Ellene reassured her.

"Thank you for your kindness. I'm so relieved to be here. Carlos appears to lack common sense. He wants to replace the sheep with pigs because he wants ham for breakfast every morning. Only Prudence and three servants remain, and I expect they will leave." Marguerite shook her head and her lips curved downward. "Well, it's no longer my concern."

Ellene patted her hand. "We have a bedroom ready for you, and storage space available for the trunks. Come in."

"Jeremy and Clive, take the trunks to Desiree's bedroom in my wing of the house," William ordered.

A look of shock followed by disapproval crossed Avrill's face, causing her jaw to drop and her eyebrows to knit together. William had not told Avrill he was going to allow Marguerite to use her mother's room. Ellene kept silent, believing he should be the one to tell his daughter why he made that decision.

Jeremy and Clive grabbed the trunks and headed to the house. William and Marguerite clasped hands and followed them. Ellene and Avrill stopped in the Great Hall while the others went up the stairs. From there Ellene and Avrill could hear the creaking of the wooden floor as William, Marguerite, and the servants made their way down the hall. Avrill gritted her teeth and stamped her foot in anger when they were no longer in view.

"Why is he letting her have mama's room? Is he going to marry her?" Anger caused her face to turn red. "Papa promised he is searching for a suitable husband for me. Instead, he visits her each day. Now she'll be in Mama's room."

Ellene weighed her words before speaking. "Although he admitted to having feelings for Marguerite, his plans are still a mystery to me. How do you feel about having a stepmother?"

Avrill redirected her gaze towards her aunt. "I suppose when I'm married and gone, it won't make any difference. But he never mentioned wanting to marry again. I don't know Marguerite well. She is not much older than me." Avrill felt her eyes become wet with emotion.

Putting her arm around Avrill's shoulders, Ellene chewed her lower lip. William's relationship with Marguerite would change her circumstances as well. If William married Marguerite, her days as mistress of Haver Hall would end. His new wife would manage the household. In fact, Ellene would be in the way. Would Marguerite take over planning Avrill's future marriage? Would Ellene no longer be involved?

She reflected on the possibilities her future could hold. Perhaps she could look for a suitable cottage on the estate. She had a sudden vision of James with his kind eyes and broad grin. He still wanted her to marry him. She realized she had grown quite fond of him and appreciated how kindly he treated Avrill. Would he be a loving husband to her? A devoted father to their children? She closed her eyes and shook her head to clear it. Well, no use getting ahead of herself.

"Come, Avrill. I think Bridgette needs us in the kitchen. Marguerite can inform us if she requires our help."

Later that morning, William climbed the stairs to check on their guest. Marguerite stood in the middle of the bedroom, surrounded by scattered trunks standing open. She had a bewildered look on her face.

"William, I'm so relieved to see you. I'm at a loss where to store my things. Would you ask Ellene to come and help me?"

"Of course, right away." It affected William more than he expected to see her in Desiree's bedroom. He stared at her for a minute, then left to look for his sister. He found Ellene and Avrill in the kitchen.

"Ellene, Marguerite requires your help to unpack. She is searching for a spot to put away the things she doesn't need at the present time." William, seeing his daughter's scowl, avoided making eye contact with Avrill.

"Certainly. I'll find out her requirements and direct Sorcha how to help." Ellene inclined her head in agreement, but she hid her annoyance. William was already treating her like a servant. Even worse, so was Marguerite. She glanced at Avrill, wondering if she would volunteer to help. Instead, the girl glared at her father as he ducked his head and hurried from the kitchen.

Ellene collected Sorcha on her way to Marguerite's bedroom.

A wan smile appeared on Marguerite's face as Ellene and Sorcha entered. "Oh, Ellene, I'm overwhelmed. Could you help me unpack?"

"I brought Sorcha to help. She's careful and efficient." There, it put them back into the roles of hostess and guest. At least for now.

Ellene directed Sorcha regarding which storage closet to use for the trunks when Marguerite finished with them. Sorcha brought fresh candles and water for Marguerite to use. Then she removed Desiree's bedding to make room for Marguerite's. Ellene showed Sorcha the guest bedroom to use for storing Desiree's items.

When Ellene returned to the bedroom, Marguerite glanced up and greeted her with a warm smile.

"I'm so grateful to you and William. I couldn't bear to stay in the same house with that hateful man."

"We're thankful we could help. Has William started looking for a cottage that would be suitable for you to live in until he can make more permanent arrangements?" Ellene hoped their guest would not remain long. She felt her affection for the young woman fading.

Marguerite's smile was gone in an instant. "I'm not sure. He hasn't told me yet." She selected another trunk to unpack. "Have you accepted James' proposal of marriage?" She did not look up when she asked.

Ellene's eyes were wide with amazement as she stood still, confronted with the bold question. "Who told you he proposed? James and I are friends. Besides, William and Avrill need me to run the household. I must help Avrill get ready for her marriage."

"But if William were to marry, his wife would take over those duties, wouldn't she? Your role would be … less important." Marguerite peered at Ellene from the corner of her eye.

"Well, he hasn't told me he is planning to marry." Ellene's face grew hot. "Did William tell you that?"

Marguerite's expression brightened with a smile. "Not in so many words. Now that I'm living here, I believe my relationship with William will become more intimate. If you don't want to marry James, William will help you find a husband while he's looking for one for Avrill."

Ellene's mind spun with disbelief at the brazenness of the young woman. She covered her annoyance by grabbing the last armful of Desiree's things from the wardrobe and left the bedroom to find a place in the storage closet. Had William already proposed to Marguerite? Her actions suggested she was sure of her position. Marguerite was unmistakable in her message that Ellene should leave.

That afternoon, Marguerite finished unpacking and strolled outside of the house and into the field. She breathed in the refreshing air and gazed at the plump, juicy fruit on the trees. The sun peeked in and out between scattered puffy white clouds, casting dappled shadows on the lush grass. She murmured in awe at the beauty of the estate, which surpassed Coeur de Lion.

Ellene's pain from Marguerite's remarks had dissipated by then. Sorcha told Ellene where to find their guest. Ellene called to her from the courtyard.

"Marguerite, I'm going to see the vicar, then take a basket of food for Goody Pickwick. It's a short walk, and she wants to meet you. Would you like to come along?"

"Yes, I would. I'll join you in a minute." Marguerite ambled toward the house, a light breeze caressing her cheeks.

"Meet me at the kitchen door. I need to collect the basket." Ellene disappeared into the house.

Marguerite crossed the field to the courtyard and went around the corner of the house. Ellene emerged from the kitchen, the aroma of her basket's contents wafting through the air. Marguerite fell into step with her but remained silent. Ellene felt a wave of uneasiness as the silence between them lingered while they approached the church.

The sanctuary had a dark and musty atmosphere. The air was still heavy with the smell of incense from the recent funeral.

"I like to come in here and soak in the silence for a few minutes. Sometimes Rev. Broun is here, and we talk. I told him we invited you to stay with us." Her eyes searched until she saw him. "Oh, there he is at the altar."

The women made their way to the front pew, where Broun joined them.

"Greetings, Lady Ellene, and Marguerite. What news?"

They told him about the justice's decision to grant the estate to Carlos and Marguerite's move to Haver Hall.

"James won't tell me much about his investigation. I think he believes one of Marguerite's servants is the poisoner, but doesn't want to say so yet," Ellene added. "And he is still looking for the man who attacked her."

"It must be difficult for you, Marguerite. Are you planning to stay at Haver Hall for a while?"

"Yes. Callum says I must find a new home." Tears brimmed in her eyes, and her chin trembled. "William and Ellene are so kind to let me stay with them." She rested her hand on Ellene's arm.

"Lady Ellene, I noticed you and James sat together at the funeral. Is there news?" Broun peered at Ellene.

Ellene's cheeks turned pink, and she let out a sigh. "We are friends. Nothing more, at least on my part."

Marguerite shifted her gaze to her. "Didn't you accept his brooch? It appears to be a love token."

"Did William tell you about his gift? I accepted it as a friend. And I have not worn it yet."

"Let me know when you accept his proposal. It will thrill Avrill because she adores James," Marguerite chuckled, her laughter filled with playful teasing. "She wants to have him as her uncle."

The grin on Ellene's face was far from amiable. "Avrill has many romantic ideas." Had Avrill mentioned James when they were at the Smythes? Perhaps she should warn Avrill to be more circumspect. Then she remembered her errand. "We're taking food to Goody Pickwick. Marguerite will meet her for the first time."

"She's a sweet soul. She struggles with her hearing, but she's got a sharp ear for gossip," Broun said.

The women took their leave and continued along the winding path to Goody's cottage. Along the way, Ellene pointed out some unique features of the estate. When they arrived at the cottage, Goody was inside. Ellene had to pound and shout before Goody opened the door. She greeted Ellene with a shout.

"Oh, it's you, Lady Ellene. You're a welcome sight. I'm getting low on food. And who is this with you?"

Ellene introduced Marguerite and explained her presence at Haver Hall.

"I'm delighted to meet you. Did you poison the mayor?" Goody asked

Marguerite.

Marguerite was speechless, her jaw slack with surprise at the question.

Ellene's answer was swift and decisive. "No. No, she didn't. James will soon discover the person who did it."

"When Eustace was married to Juanita, he visited old master Throck-Morton. Your father, Ellene. I worked in the kitchen then. So, Carlos is alive after we thought him dead, you're saying?" With a pensive expression, Goody's forehead creased in thought.

"That's what he claims, and the justice accepted his evidence." Ellene nodded, trying not to be annoyed that she had already discussed this with Goody.

"But that's impossible. Eustace told us the boy died along with his mother." Goody tightened her lips and swayed her head from side to side.

"Carlos produced a scroll that looks like the original marriage contract between Eustace and Juanita. How could he have gotten it if not from his own mother?" Marguerite raised her hands.

"Forgery. Theft. Did the the justice think of that?" Goody answered promptly.

"Callum examined it and pronounced it to be authentic. He needs more evidence to declare the man is an impostor." Marguerite pressed her lower lip between her teeth.

"That should be easy enough. The boy had a port-wine birthmark on his neck. Big splotch on such a tiny child. Those don't go away, you know." Goody shook her head.

"This is the first I've heard of it. Who else would know about it? If we could have some witnesses testify to that, and Carlos doesn't have a birthmark, it would at least be enough to evict him. He arrived so soon after

Eustace died; maybe he conspired with the killer." Ellene's eyes flashed.

"Few old-timers remain who knew the family," Goody murmured sadly. Then her eyes grew wider as a memory surfaced. "Why, there's a portrait. An artist painted Juanita and Carlos when he was about two or three years old. Eustace was furious with the artist for showing the birthmark and hid the painting in a closet, or so I was told."

"Wait. Is it a portrait of a woman with tawny skin and dark hair and eyes? With a little boy playing at her feet?" Marguerite's eyes sparkled with surprise.

"The very one." Goody nodded.

"But I know where it is. I saw it when I was packing my possessions. If Carlos hasn't destroyed it by now, Ellene and I could retrieve it and give it to James." Marguerite became more animated.

"It would be safer if we went when Carlos wasn't home. That may be difficult since we are so far away and not able to see when he leaves." Ellene was already thinking about how they could do it. "Well, we won't trouble you anymore, Goody. I'll be back in a few days. Come, Marguerite."

Taking the empty basket from Ellene's last trip, the women bid farewell and strolled toward the house.

Chapter Twenty-Eight

THE BANDITS

On Saturday morning, James searched for goldsmith shops in Updyke Chase. Compared to Haver Hamlet, the village had a larger variety of shops to explore. He eventually found one advertising jewelry design. As James entered, the owner looked up from a bench where he was shaping a gold love token. Gray hair cascading from his black coif framed his face, and he wore an apron over his doublet and breeches.

"How can I help you today? A fine love token for your beloved?" He held up his latest project and candlelight glinted off the yellow metal.

"Not today. I'm Sheriff Asher from County Havershire. Are you the owner of this shop?"

"Yes, Obadiah Strand, Master Goldsmith, at your service." He bobbed his head and waited.

"I'm seeking information regarding a man who calls himself Carlos Ellingham. Says he lives in this village and makes a living as a goldsmith. He claims he learned his trade in Cheapside. He has a long and narrow face with gray eyes, slender build, mid to late thirties. Has a burn scar on his wrist."

"Never heard that name around here." First, Obadiah shook his head, then he raised his eyebrows. "I know a man named Rafe Beall who fits the physical description. He was my apprentice for a time. He's no longer allowed in my shop."

"Why, what happened?"

A scowl accompanied his words. "I caught him stealing my gold. Just a little here and there from various items. I always weigh the finished piece to determine how much gold we used when I fix the price. And a pattern developed. My items were always the expected weight. His were always lighter than expected. At first, I thought it was inexperience, so I watched him. Caught him slipping small fragments into a bag. He returned the gold, so I didn't report him to the sheriff. But I ran him off. Haven't seen him around for a while."

"Did you know his mother? Was she Spanish?"

"No, she was as English as you or me. I knew both his parents. They both died of the plague some years back. Moved in with his aunt and uncle in London. Returned with a teenage girl, supposed to be his cousin. He told us the girl left to marry a wealthy man in Haver Hamlet."

"Where does he stay when he's here?"

"He rents a room in a cottage a couple of miles outside the village. Our sheriff can take you there. Has he done something wrong?"

"That's what I'm trying to determine. I need to establish Carlos' identity for an inheritance in Haver Hamlet. Would you agree to appear as a witness at a hearing?"

"Well, I need to see him in person. You say he claims his name is Carlos Ellingham? And you want me to testify otherwise?"

"Yes. I think he is lying to steal an estate."

Obediah looked apprehensive. "I worry about him retaliating against me. I'll testify only if he faces execution."

"That's up to the justice of the peace. Thieves usually just receive a flogging. I hope you'll do it to ensure that justice prevails."

They chatted a while longer. Eventually, Obadiah consented to make the journey to Haver Hamlet and confirm if the man was Rafe. James assured Obadiah he would send his men to provide an escort.

Next, James found the local sheriff and explained his mission. Although skeptical, he agreed to take James to the cottage. The cottage owner agreed to let James and the sheriff enter Rafe's room. The room had only enough width to accommodate a bed, washstand, and trunk. A cheap candlestick rested on the washstand. The window was closed, and the room smelled musty.

James pried open the trunk. Inside, he found shabby clothes, a gray wig, and fake beard. James thought they resembled the hair and beard of the wine dealer who met Eustace at the White Stag Inn. The sheriff gave James permission to take the items to Haver Hamlet for the hearing. Pleased with his progress, James and the sheriff started toward the village. James intended to retrieve his pannier from the inn so he could begin the journey back to Haver Manor.

As they rode, a menacing thunderstorm formed in the distance. Soon, large, heavy raindrops pelted them. Bright flashes of lightning split the sky, illuminating the dark clouds that hung low overhead. The rain hitting the dry ground filled the air with a noticeable earthy fragrance. The horses bucked when lightning struck a nearby tree, startling them. James and the sheriff took shelter in a nearby barn until the storm passed. They arrived at Updyke Chase in the late afternoon, making it impossible for James to travel to Haver Manor that day. James returned his horse to the stable and went to the inn, where he passed the time with some other travelers.

James resigned himself to leaving early the next morning, so he would be back before Thomas looked for him. Then he would show his evidence to Robert. Together, they would approach the justice to let him know Obadiah might expose Carlos as a fraud. Besides fraud, maybe they could charge him with theft as well.

The next morning, the sound of church bells filled the air. People gathered in the local church for Sunday morning services, leaving an empty road to return home. James rose early, collected his horse, and rode out of the village.

As James approached County Havershire, the road took a sharp turn, limiting his visibility of what lay ahead. Preoccupied with his discovery about Carlos being almost certainly Rafe Beall, it startled him when his charger shied. Two men blocked his path, and one came out of the trees behind him.

He drew his sword as the three men set upon him. The bandits had the advantage of surprise. His battle-trained horse offered some help, but it proved insufficient in the end. He pierced one man with his sword, but another came at him from the other side. The youth behind him brought a heavy object down on James' head. James felt the pain, then everything went dark. He fell from his horse onto the side of the road.

Meanwhile, Thomas grew anxious that his cousin had not returned and set out with Rusty and Twig to find him. The trio came upon the highwaymen, two of whom were stripping a man on the road of his money and weapons. A dead man lay nearby in a pool of blood. Four riderless horses milled about. Thomas recognized one horse as James' charger.

"You there, stop." With a resounding shout, Thomas unsheathed his sword, urging his horse forward with a swift kick to its sides. Rusty and Twig followed close behind.

The thieves looked up to see armed men approaching fast. They dropped their plunder and sprinted toward their own mounts. Thomas captured one man, and Rusty captured the other, who turned out to be a boy in his late teens. Handing his captive off to Twig, Thomas jumped off his horse and ran to James, spotting the blood oozing from the back of his head.

"He's unconscious." Thomas pulled off a scarf and wrapped it around James' head to stop the bleeding.

Rusty and Twig tied the bandits' wrists and forced them to sit on the road, then went to help Thomas.

"We must get James on his horse and secure him there. He needs to have Zachary check out his injuries. Get those bandits on their horses. Tie the dead man to his horse and let's go." The unyielding set of his jaw matched the icy look in Thomas' eyes.

When all had mounted, Rusty and Twig led the bandits' horses, and Thomas led James' horse. They had to move at a slow pace to avoid dislodging James. As they approached a fork in the road, one leading to Haver Hamlet and the other to Haver Manor, Thomas halted the procession.

"Take these highwaymen to the jailer and have him lock them up. Leave the dead one with the undertaker. Find Zachary and send him to Haver Manor. I'm taking James there."

Rusty, giving a grunt of affirmation, told his boss, "Consider it done."

The two men headed off with their captives. The bandits grumbled and complained, then offered a bribe to be released. Their captors refused to respond.

In Haver Hamlet, Twig stopped at the jailhouse and summoned the jailer. He emerged from the darkness of the interior, squinting in the sun. Rusty headed off to find Zachary to tend to James.

"Who do ye have here?" The jailer pointed at the captives as he spat on the ground.

"Highwaymen. They attacked the sheriff and knocked him unconscious. Tried to steal his money and weapons. We arrived just in time. Thomas told me to turn them over to you to lock up."

"What about that one there?" The jailer pointed to the dead man.

"Oh, he's ready for the undertaker. No need to fuss about him. Callum will have to determine what to do with his horse. In the meantime, I'll take it to the stable."

"Hey, let us go. He's lying. We never hurt nobody," the older bandit cried out. "We just found the two men motionless on the road. It looked like they killed each other. We decided they wouldn't need their weapons anymore." His eyes darted around as he struggled to loosen the ropes holding his hands.

The youth had a dazed expression and was quivering with fear.

"I know Twig and trust him. Won't hurt to hold ye both until James or Thomas shows up." The jailer frowned.

The jailer and Twig pulled the two from their horses and dragged them into the jail, thrusting them into a cell. Straw smelling of human waste littered the floor. The jailer slammed and locked the cell door. Through a gap in the wall at the roofline, only a sliver of light could enter. A large gray rat dashed across the floor and ducked through an opening in the wall.

"Been meaning to plug that hole. Ye won't mind a little company, will ye?" The jailer guffawed at his joke.

"It might go easier on you if you tell us who hired you. But if the sheriff dies, you'll swing. Why did you attack the sheriff?" Twig demanded.

The youth started crying. "I didn't wanna do it. They made me."

"Who made you, boy? Answer me." Twig grabbed the bars on the door. "If I have to come in there, I'll beat it out of you."

"Shut up, boy. They can't prove anything." The older man's lips pulled back in a snarl, accompanied by a sharp hiss.

"We can prove highway robbery. That's enough to put a noose around your neck." Twig uttered the words through gritted teeth, his jaw tight with rage.

The older of the two gulped. "If I tell you, will you go easy on us?"

"Can't say. But if you don't tell us, we'll beat it out of you." Twig sensed they were weakening.

"A man asked us to follow the sheriff to Updyke Chase. We were to see what he was up to. The man told us the sheriff had a purse full of gold coins. We were just going to rob him."

"What man? Give me a name."

"Ellingham. Carlos Ellingham."

With a sound of disgust, Twig turned towards the jailer.

"Make sure they get minimum rations. Wouldn't want them to starve before they stand trial." Twig handed the jailer a few coins as Rusty returned.

"I sent Zachary to Haver Manor." A grunt escaped Rusty's throat, sounding rough and strained.

"Let's get a drink at the White Stag and head back to Haver Manor. I need to wash a foul taste out of my mouth."

Rusty agreed as they rode off.

Thomas led James and his horse to Haver Manor. As he rode up the lane, the men in the courtyard stopped what they were doing. When they recognized the riders as James and Thomas, they ran to assist.

"What happened?" a man shouted.

"Bandits attacked him. Help get him down and take him to his bedroom. Be careful, they hit him on the head."

Carrying James was hard because of his tall and muscular body. It took several men to transport him into the house and up the stairs.

Agnes emerged from the kitchen clutching a towel. "What's happened to the master?" she gasped.

"He's unconscious and has a head wound. I sent Rusty and Twig to fetch Zachary. Get some cold water and towels." Thomas spoke with a barely concealed anger, the words coming out through clenched teeth.

Agnes scurried back into the kitchen to comply.

"I hope you caught the men who did this," a man commented.

"We did. It looked like James killed one before someone knocked him out. We tied them up and Rusty and Twig took them to the jail."

When they reached James' bedroom, they positioned him on the bed and removed his clothing except for his shirt and breeches. Agnes appeared with the towels and a bucket of cold water. She blotted the wound to wipe away the blood.

After what seemed an eternity, Zachary galloped into the courtyard. He leaped from his horse and ran to the house.

Thomas heard the physician from James' room. "Up here," he called from the stairway.

Zachary rushed up the stairs, taking two at a time, and entered James' bedroom. When he examined the injury, he discovered a lump had formed on the back of his head, but the bleeding ceased.

"Keep cold towels on his head. We need to keep the swelling down. There's not much else I can do." He looked at Thomas. "Somebody needs to stay with him. When he wakes up, try to keep him awake. I'll leave something for his pain and check back tomorrow. Come get me if he gets worse." He gave his head a sorrowful shake before leaving the room.

Agnes entered the room with more cold water. "I heard the physician. I think you should send for Lady Ellene."

Thomas raised his eyebrows. "Why?"

"He's in love with her. Having her here might bring him back."

Thomas stood still, his face an unreadable mask.

"I've tended a wounded man or two in my time. Remind him he has a reason to live. Go on." She swatted at Thomas' arm, and he left the bedroom.

Chapter Twenty-Nine

THE VIGIL

J eremy heard the pounding of a horse's hooves and hurried to the door to see Thomas gallop into the courtyard and leap from his horse.

"Is Lady Ellene here? It's urgent that I speak with her at once," Thomas called as he bounded up the stairs.

"Yes, she's home. Wait here. Sorcha knows where to find her." Jeremy motioned for him to stay in the Great Hall. He hurried upstairs and called for Sorcha. "Do you know where Lady Ellene is? Thomas from Haver Manor is asking for her. He says it's urgent."

"She was helping Mrs. Ellingham the last time I laid eyes on her. Let me fetch her."

Ellene, having heard the voices, emerged from Marguerite's bedroom. "What is it, Jeremy?"

"Thomas from Haver Manor is here, Lady Ellene. Says it's urgent he speaks with you."

"Where is he?" Ellene realized something was amiss because Thomas did not appear at their estate for no reason. She knew he was James' right-hand man.

"In the Great Hall, mistress."

She hurried to the head of the stairs.

"Thomas, what has happened?"

"Lady Ellene, it's James. Bandits attacked him and now he's unconscious. He needs someone to sit with him and keep cool towels on his head. Would you come?"

Ellene turned pale and felt an icy shudder run through her body. When she tried to breathe, a wave of dizziness washed over her. Thomas' words echoed in her mind. James was unconscious. How could that happen? He was a trained fighter and always ready for any trouble.

"Lady Ellene, are you alright?" Sorcha stood behind her.

"Yes." Taking charge, she turned towards the servants. "Sorcha, fetch my cloak and outdoor shoes as fast as you can. Jeremy, tell Clive to saddle my horse."

Marguerite came out of her room, and Avrill appeared at the bottom of the stairs. Thomas acknowledged Avrill, but his attention was on Ellene. Jeremy rushed down the stairs and out the door.

"Ellene, what has happened?" Marguerite called.

"Bandits attacked James. I'm going to help care for him. Tell William where I'll be."

Sorcha appeared with a cloak and shoes. Ellene put on the shoes, grabbed the cloak, and hurried down the stairs. She and Thomas ran into the courtyard, where Clive rushed to bring her horse from the stable. Thomas lifted Ellene up to the saddle, then he mounted his horse. Together, they galloped toward Haver Manor.

Ellene's thoughts were a dizzying maelstrom. What if James was no longer alive when she got there? What if the injury left him paralyzed? She shuddered as she realized how much she took James for granted. While praying for his recovery, she noticed the depth of her emotions towards him.

When they arrived at Haver Manor, the men milled about in the court-yard, and one helped her down from her horse. Thomas accompanied her into the house.

"Where is he?" Ellene's face was wan, and her voice trembled.

"This way." Thomas gestured toward the stairs.

They hurried up the staircase and across the hallway to James' bedroom. Ellene stopped at the open door, stunned, as she gazed upon his still form on the bed. The color had drained from his face, and blood from the wound left a brown stain on the pillow. Agnes stood by his bed and placed a wet towel on his forehead. Ellene never saw him look so vulnerable, and it frightened her. She always thought of him as strong and in control.

"Thank the Lord you are here. Zachary gave orders to use cold towels to keep the swelling down." Agnes, her face full of worry and exhaustion, clasped her hands together at her waist. "Talk to him. Call him back. That's the only way he'll live."

"Of course. Is there something I can read to him? A favorite Bible story? Does he have any books? Please send for the vicar to come and pray for him."

Ellene pulled a chair close to the bed and studied James' face. She reached out and clasped his hand. Rather than the warm, firm grip she expected, it felt cold and limp. "James, it's Ellene. I'm here now. I'll take care of you." She wiped away the tears stinging in her eyes.

Thomas handed her a Bible and a book James had in the room. He and Agnes backed out of the room to leave them alone.

As she opened the Bible, Ellene felt drawn to the Psalms and began reading to him. Agnes or Thomas, from time to time, would bring fresh towels and take away those that were soiled. Agnes presented Ellene with food and ale after a while. She consumed a meager amount of food and drink before she turned back to James. Ellene dipped the towels in cold water and placed them on his forehead, just as she saw Agnes do.

Broun arrived to sit with her. He recited prayers of healing, but refused to recite the last rites. "James is strong. He has a mission on this earth. He will recover, I'm sure of it." The vicar patted Ellene on the shoulder.

Ellene hoped Broun felt as confident as he sounded. He left after some time, promising to pray for James and assuring her of his return the next morning.

When William arrived to find out James' condition, Thomas accompanied him to the bedroom. He explained about James' journey to Updyke Chase to learn more about Carlos.

"If he doesn't recover enough to tell us what he learned, it will be for nothing," Thomas remarked bitterly.

"Is there anything I can do to help?" William could not take his eyes off his friend. It shook him to see James so pale and still.

"All we can do at this point is apply the cold towels and pray. But thank you for coming, William." Ellene grasped her brother's hand.

He gave her a comforting pat on the shoulder before departing for Haver Hall.

When it grew dark, Agnes lit several candles so Ellene could watch for movement and read to him. When she paused to rest her eyes, Ellene noted the room's sparse furnishings. It could benefit from a woman's touch. The blankets were rough wool, and the mattress hard. The plain pitcher and bowl sat on a simple washstand. When Thomas removed James' clothing, he draped it over a chair, creating a pile of fabric. She noticed his clothes had blood stains.

After the sun went down, the evening grew colder, so Ellene wrapped herself in her cloak. Agnes covered James with another blanket and lit a fire to keep the bedroom warm. With the moon's rise, its silvery light overwhelmed the flickering stars. Taking a break, Ellene strolled to a window and looked out. Below, she could see several men standing vigil around a fire in the courtyard.

Ellene's mind spun, her thoughts tumbling over one another. What if James died? What if he lived and proposed to her again? Marguerite's words lingered in her mind, a subtle threat of the possibility of her marriage to William and the impact it would have on Ellene's living conditions. Ellene realized she had powerful feelings for James and would be bereft if he did not recover. But would he be kind to her? Could they make each other happy? She was sure they loved each other. Was that enough?

The sunrise painted the horizon pale pink as Ellene's exhaustion caused her eyelids to droop. She put a fresh towel on James' head, then settled on the far side of the bed. I'll just close my eyes for a few minutes, she thought. Sleep soon overcame her.

The morning light filtered in through the window, casting a soft glow throughout the room. James felt a dull, pulsing sensation in his head. He opened his eyes to see the flickering candles and felt the towel on his forehead, by now almost dry. Satisfied that he was home and in his own bed, he closed his eyes again. What happened? He remembered being attacked on the road on his way back to Haver Manor and killing one man. How did he get here?

He must chastise the person responsible for leaving the candles burning. It not only wasted resources, it might ignite a fire. But something tugged at his mind. The sweet smell of lavender filled the air, and it brought Ellene to his thoughts. Suddenly, he realized he wasn't alone. Another body lay on the bed, accompanied by the audible rhythm of slow, deep breaths. He opened his eyes again. Turning his head to his right made his head spin. He waited for the spinning to stop, then tried again. He must be still dreaming because it looked like a woman. Why would a woman be on his bed? He reached out and touched her shoulder.

At James' touch, Ellene woke with a start and sat up, her hair and clothes disheveled. She looked at James to see his eyes gazing at her. "You're awake. Thanks be to God."

"Ellene?" He whispered. "I have one question."

"What, James?"

"Why are you on my bed?"

She gasped and leaped up, her hand hovering near her lips. "Bandits attacked you, and you've been unconscious since yesterday. Thomas found you and brought you home. Then he came to Haver Hall and asked for my help. I've spent all night placing cold towels on your head to keep the swelling down. I guess I fell asleep. Promise you won't tell anyone. How are you feeling?" She frowned, her forehead creasing with apprehension.

"Bad. I'd feel better if you got back in bed," he teased.

"You are feeling better. Let me get Thomas." She squeezed his hand, relieved to find it firm and warm again.

"Just call out the window. He'll hear."

Ellene went to the window overlooking the courtyard and opened it. Several men bustled around, their voices echoing off the walls. She called to them, "James is awake. Tell Thomas to come quickly."

Twig waved and left to find the steward.

With a slow movement, James sat up and swung his bare feet to the cold floor. Ellene came to his side of the bed to help him. She put another towel in the cold water and placed it on his head. Thomas' footsteps thundered up the stairs as he took them two at a time and burst into the room.

"Twig told me you're awake. How are you feeling? Do you remember what happened?"

"Just that bandits ambushed me. I think I ran one through with my sword. Somebody hit me from behind. That's all I remember. You tell me the rest." James felt the back of his head, causing him to wince, then put the towel back on the wound.

Thomas described his arrival with Rusty and Twig and their successful capture of the bandits. "One man was dead when we found you. The jailer in Haver Hamlet locked the other two up. Their story was Carlos hired them to find out what you were investigating, and he told them you had gold coins they could steal."

"How did he know where I went and when I would come back?"

"We don't know. We thought it best to let you take over the interrogation when you recovered."

Ellene spoke up. "Now that you're awake, I'll go help Agnes with breakfast. James, are you nauseous, or can you eat something?"

James reached out and clasped her hand. "I want you to stay with me, my lady. Let someone else take care of that." Ellene felt her breath catch in her throat at the intensity of the love in his gaze.

A few minutes later, Agnes arrived with a tray piled with bread, honey, and cheese, plus laudanum to reduce his pain. "I brought enough food for you both. Thomas, could you move the table and the other chair over here? You need to send someone to fetch Zachary."

James directed Ellene to one chair, and he sat in the other. Thomas and Agnes left them alone in the bedroom.

James was famished, since it had been a whole day since his last meal. Despite feeling lightheaded, he devoured the food. The laudanum helped dull his headache. Ellene watched him out of the corner of her eye.

"Now that you're awake and moving, I should return home after we eat," she announced.

"No, I need you to stay here with me." He spoke with conviction.

"For how long?" Ellene furrowed her brows.

"Forever." James stared intently and took both of her hands.

His statement struck Ellene speechless, her mouth hanging open in surprise.

"I am asking you to marry me. I need you by my side, Ellene. Say yes."

"James. I—I don't know. I—."

"Do you love me, Ellene? I love you."

Ellene stared at him. She already realized that James was an essential part of her life, and she could not bear to lose him. "Yes, I love you. But I need William's permission to marry."

"I received his permission two months ago."

She made a face, then her cheeks dimpled as she smiled. She resolved to harass her brother for not telling her. "Then yes, I will marry you."

She felt the warmth of his hands against her shoulders as he kissed her lips with a tenderness that made her heart flutter.

CHAPTER THIRTY

RECUPERATING

When William and Rev. Broun arrived that morning to check on James' condition, they found him awake in his bedroom, sitting beside Ellene as they ate breakfast.

"Well, you are looking better this morning. You gave us a scare." Broun's eyes twinkled as he gazed at James.

"I'm glad to see that you're awake. You sustained a nasty blow. We were all worried." William's face lit up with relief.

"Thomas explained to me what happened. I need to go to the village and interrogate the bandits." James' lips twisted into a scowl, and his eyes narrowed.

Ellene realized James was back in work mode. His focus on the bandits gave her time to reflect on their conversation. She meant it when she accepted his marriage proposal. Yet, a wave of uncertainty came over her.

Zachary arrived and examined James, who still had a lump on his head and experienced dizziness when he stood.

"No riding for a day or two. You might black out and fall off your horse. The men in the jail can wait," the physician admonished him.

"But—." James objected.

"James, please don't risk getting injured again." Ellene rested her hand on his.

James gazed at her and relented. "I'll wait. I've been away since Friday morning, so I need to see what's happening here."

The physician left, then Broun prayed for James' continued recovery.

"I had better get back. Are you coming home with me, Ellene?" William gazed at his sister.

Ellene and James looked at each other, conveying a silent understanding between them.

James replied. "I want her to stay with me, at least until tomorrow. We have a lot to discuss. You might as well know your sister agreed to marry me."

"Please don't tell anyone yet." Ellene felt warmth spread across her face as James held her hand in his and pressed a kiss to it.

William's jaw dropped. "But that is marvelous news indeed. Congratulations to you both."

"I told him I need your permission. He claimed you already gave it. Is that true?" Ellene brought her free hand to her hip.

"Indeed, it is." William's face lit up with a smile.

Broun beamed. "I'll keep the information confidential. But I am happy for you both."

James grew serious. "I want you to keep my recovery confidential for now. The person who sent the bandits might believe they succeeded, which could give us a chance to discover more about the plot."

"You have a valid point. The village council is meeting this afternoon. If anyone asks, you're still unconscious and still at home." William nodded.

After everyone left, James noticed Ellene's eyes drooping with exhaustion.

"You need to get some sleep. I'll show you to the bedroom used by the former owner's wife, which will be yours after we marry. I'll go downstairs and meet with Thomas in my office."

His hand rested on her back as they strolled down the hallway to the adjoining bedroom. About the same size as James' bedroom, the fabrics were more delicate, and the furniture embellished with hand-carved floral designs. The bed had a post affixed to each corner, with fabric falling to the floor. Several down-filled pillows were at the head of the bed. Colorful tapestries adorned the walls. Ellene noticed the wardrobe where she could store her clothing. A door led to a short hallway and another door.

"Is that the door to your room?" Ellene glanced at James.

"Yes. Convenient, don't you think?" He gave a roguish wink.

She grinned and closed the door. "This is a lovely room. It looks quite comfortable."

"Good. I want you to be comfortable here."

His muscular arms wrapped around her, pulling her close and kissing her with a fervor that sent shivers down her spine. With reluctance, he released her and closed the door as she lay down on the bed. In the hallway, he felt dizzy and stopped to regain his balance. Then he went down to his office, where Thomas waited.

"Did you find out anything useful in Updyke Chase?" Thomas leaned back in his chair and flicked his blond hair back.

"I believe so. There is a man named Rafe Beall, who lives there and fits Carlos' description. Rafe was born near there and his aunt and uncle in London raised him after his parents died. A goldsmith took him on as an apprentice, but he was discharged when he got caught stealing gold. It appears the man we know as Carlos is not prosperous and not Eustace's son. He also had a young woman with him for a while, possibly a cousin. I found shabby clothes and a gray wig and beard in his room. They resemble the hair and clothes of Harry, the man with the stolen wine. I persuaded the goldsmith to come to Haver Hamlet to tell us if the man is Rafe. I plan to send Rusty and Twig to escort him to Haver Hamlet if Callum agrees to a hearing. But we need some additional proof. Now that we know about him, it should be easier to catch him lying."

"I'll be grateful to see the last of him." Thomas tossed his bangs back off his forehead.

"Keep this confidential for now. I asked Ellene to marry me, and she agreed. I would much rather spend time with her than tracking down criminals. My goal is to train a deputy sheriff to help investigate crimes. Would you be interested in learning to do that?"

Thomas' cool gray eyes gazed at James. "Would it be instead of being your steward?"

"I'm not sure. I rely on you to run Haver Manor when I'm gone. But if you're with me on investigations, I'll need someone else to stay here. I also need to convince the village council to pay for a deputy. Give it some thought. If you decide to remain the full-time steward, can you recommend another man who might show aptitude as a deputy sheriff?"

"Let me think about it." Thomas paused. "I look forward to the day when I can own a holding. I need a house and enough income to support my wife and children. My goal is to prove to William my worthiness to marry Avrill."

Agnes woke Ellene at midday from a deep sleep. Ellene's dark curls escaped from her braid and fell around her shoulders. Agnes found a brush and helped Ellene re-braid her hair. James sought them out since he was hungry, and the trio went back downstairs to eat. After their meal, Ellene noticed James' color seemed off, so she suggested he rest for a while.

"Perhaps a bath after your nap so you can wash the blood out of your hair? And put on clean clothes?"

He still wore his shirt and breeches, which were streaked with blood and dirt and reeked of sweat from his journey.

"Excellent idea. What would I do without you?" James grinned at Ellene.

The afternoon sky was bright and clear, with a light breeze. After his nap and bath, James asked Ellene to take a short walk with him into the field. James carried a blanket to sit on. As they strolled toward his favorite shade tree, they felt a gentle breeze against their skin.

"Oh, James, it's beautiful here. You must be proud of this estate." Ellene's smile revealed her admiration for the peaceful landscape.

"It takes work. I hope to have a son who will inherit it someday."

Ellene bit her lip. She resolved to inform him about her miscarriage.

"Um, James, we need to talk about that. I need to tell you something." She drew in a long breath.

"I'm listening." James' eyebrows rose, curious as he waited for her to speak.

"When I was married to Hunter, I had a miscarriage." A grimace of pain crossed her face.

"Oh, my love, I am so sorry. Why didn't you tell me?" He reached over and clasped her hand.

"The memory is painful. Few people knew. But now I'm worried I won't be able to have a child. Are you disappointed?"

James reached out and drew her close. "There is no shame in having a miscarriage. Some women have several, followed by a healthy baby. We will gratefully welcome however many children God sends us. He may send us all daughters. Who knows? We will face it together." He kissed her hand.

Ellene smiled, though it didn't quite reach her eyes. Was he sincere?

They spread the blanket on the ground, and sat next to each other, his arms around her as she leaned back on his chest. Relieved by James' reaction to her secret, Ellene felt her worries fade. After a few minutes, Ellene could wait no longer to find out his thoughts about the poisoning.

"Who do you think killed Eustace?"

James laughed. "Is this your plan? Get me out here and ply me with questions."

"You invited me, remember? I just thought about what I know, and I'm confused."

"Tell me what you know."

Ellen began ticking items off on her fingers. "Well, Eustace died at the banquet in front of a dozen guests, plus musicians and servants. Whether he ate or drank it, the wolfsbane poisoned him. No one else even got sick, so it had to be something only he consumed, which we narrowed down to wine or honey. It was probably intentional. No one confessed to being near the plants, except the herdsman, who claimed he destroyed them."

"Yet the day after the banquet, I found part of the plant behind the house with leavings from the meal." James chimed in, adding his thoughts to the

223

conversation.

"But somebody not from the estate could have put it there to incriminate the servants. The herdsman reported he saw someone sneaking around the barn on the day the prowler attacked Marguerite. The reason for the man's presence in the barn remains uncertain. It's possible he waited, but their meeting could have been accidental. Was the man a previous visitor, or a potential thief assuming she had left the estate?" Ellene peered at James.

"It could have been the tradesman looking for the barrels he unloaded but did not get paid for. I found a wig and beard in Rafe's room that match those worn by the tradesman. I believe he met with Eustace in the White Stag to sell the wine and then delivered it to the estate. He gave Eustace a bottle to sample. Eustace may have tasted the wine before accepting delivery in the afternoon. It could have contained the poison."

"But wouldn't that have killed him sooner?"

"Probably. Unless Eustace waited until later to drink the wine. The servants don't know when, or even if, he drank it and the bottle disappeared."

"Here's something I found out recently. Marguerite and I visited Goody Pickwick this weekend. She told us there is a portrait of Juanita and Carlos, and Marguerite thinks it is still at the estate. The boy has a birthmark on his neck. If Carlos doesn't have one, that could be evidence to disprove his claim."

"That may be helpful indeed. I'll investigate that when I have a chance."

The couple sat in silence for a few minutes. James reached over and started stroking Ellene's hand.

"What about Andrew Smythe?" Ellene put her finger to her chin.

"I thought we were through talking about the murder. Let's talk about us now." James lifted her hand to his lips. "Like, when do you want to have our wedding?"

"I want to talk about us too, but this is hanging over our plans. Andrew asked about buying the estate soon after Eustace died. And he is in a hurry to be appointed mayor."

"I can't charge a man for being too ambitious. I need more proof he committed a crime." James nuzzled her ear. "How soon can we have our wedding?"

"I've not thought about it yet. There are so many decisions to make. Do you want to invite your father and brothers? Shall we invite the entire village or just the council and a few others? Do you want a banquet? Should we have games?"

"Let's elope."

Ellene's eyebrows arched in disbelief.

"Seriously, all I want is you, me, the vicar, and the required witnesses. Any day will do. We can alert my family later." His gentle kisses tickled her neck, making her squirm with delight.

"That tickles." She let out a giggle. "I want a ceremony with William and Avrill there. I suppose Marguerite, if she and William are to be betrothed. And Thomas and the Smythes."

"Look, Thomas is coming across the field." James sounded annoyed.

"Agnes asks if you are ready to dine or if you want to wait," Thomas called.

James' stomach growled. "I would like to eat now. Lady Ellene, may I help you to your feet?" He stood and reached down to lift her up. "Tell Agnes we are coming."

Thomas nodded and retraced his steps to the house.

James pulled Ellene close. "I love you, Ellene, and I want you to have your wedding ceremony. Remember, we have years ahead of us, God willing. I don't want you to put yourself in danger investigating the crimes. For now, be careful around Marguerite."

"Yes, James, I will be careful. And you be careful as well." Ellene stood on her tiptoes, and they kissed before heading back to the house.

CHAPTER THIRTY-ONE

VILLAGE COUNCIL MEETING

A mischievous smirk played on Carlos' lips, a glint of excitement dancing in his eyes as he mounted his horse. Andrew invited Carlos to meet the council members so he could get better acquainted with them. As Eustace's heir, Carlos believed he had the right to assume the role of mayor of the village. This meeting would give him the opportunity to gauge his opposition for the position.

With a surge of anticipation coursing through him, Carlos set off towards Andrew's sprawling estate. During the short ride, Carlos surveyed the fields and orchards of Coeur de Lion. He already gave notice to his tenants to remove their sheep from his pastures, planning to buy some pigs to raise for food and for sale.

Rural life did not agree with him. The past few days had been unpleasant, with one annoyance after another. The sound of honking in the distance grabbed his attention. Looking around, he noticed a flock of geese flying by. The bothersome birds created a constant disturbance with their noise. They landed in his courtyard, and one chased him into the house. Yesterday a bee stung him when he went out to the garden to look at the plants. He shook his head with annoyance. Maybe he would sell the furniture and silver and buy a townhouse in London.

Upon arriving at the Smythe estate, he dismounted, and the stableman took his horse. The valet greeted him and ushered him to the sitting room, where the councilmen gathered.

Carlos was the last person to arrive. Andrew stood outside the sitting room and greeted him, then motioned for him to enter the room. Forest, Jonathon, Michael, Simon, and William, wearing their chains of office, were already seated on the chairs and benches. Carlos greeted those whom he had already met, then acknowledged the remaining individuals and sprawled in a chair. The valet exited the room and closed the door.

The men eyed each other with suspicion, the flickering candles illuminating their faces, their distrust palpable in the air. William had not shared with them the suspicions Ellene and James had regarding Carlos. He also did not divulge that James was recovering from the assault over the weekend. Andrew introduced the men for Carlos' benefit.

"Forest is a goldsmith, Jonathon is the blacksmith, Michael runs the mill, and Simon is in the mercantile guild. William and I own two of the largest estates in County Havershire." He then turned to Carlos. "What is your occupation, if I may ask?"

"I learned the trade of jewelry design. I have a shop which I plan to sell now that I have inherited my father's estate." The boredom in his tone was clear as he spoke.

"It seems you and Forest have a shared interest." Andrew looked at Forest, who maintained a disinterested expression.

The valet and a maid appeared with refreshments, which they placed on tables along the wall, then closed the door as they exited.

Carlos cleared his throat, and, with a sense of authority, he declared, "Having taken my father's place at Coeur de Lion, it's only natural that you would want to know my intentions." Carlos glanced around the room. Seeing several men nod, he continued. "I asked Robert to petition Her Majesty the Queen to appoint me as the mayor. The role has always been by appointment. Henry VIII appointed my grandfather and father."

"Actually, Edward VI appointed your father," commented William.

"No matter. He was still the monarch. You see my point." Carlos retorted, irritated at the correction.

"You are new to this village." Andrew's smile was empty, lacking the genuine warmth that usually accompanied it. "The residents of the village would prefer the mayor to be someone who has lived here and knows the people and problems. After all, you arrived only a week ago."

The men murmured, some agreeing with Carlos, some with Andrew.

"Perhaps we should settle among ourselves who should be the candidate." Before anyone could voice his opposition, Carlos pulled a bag and some marbles out of his pocket and continued. "I suggest we put six marbles, one of which is black and the others white, in a bag. Pull out a marble but keep it hidden in your hand, then reveal what you have after we select all the marbles. Whoever selects the black marble will have his name submitted to the queen to be the next mayor."

"I disagree. It should be based on who is best qualified to perform the duties." Simon pointed at his chest with his thumb. "I could leave my daughter in charge of my shop whenever I need to convene a meeting. You, Andrew, and William live outside of the village and have estates to tend to."

"If travel distance were an issue, it would have disqualified my father and grandfather," Carlos replied with an air of arrogance. "And my estate is closer to the village than Andrew's."

"If where we live is an issue, William lives even further from the village than Andrew and Carlos," Michael interjected.

"I am content not to be mayor. My estate keeps me busy enough." William shook his head and raised his hands. "Take me out of the running."

"It seems four of you depend on village trade to make a living. There might be an opportunity for corruption because people would expect favors in return for trading with you." As Carlos spoke, his eyes scanned around the table, taking in the reactions of everyone present.

"Now who are you calling corrupt?" Jonathon, his face flushed, sprang up. The loud crash of his chair toppling over echoed through the room as it hit the hardwood floor. His hands balled into fists.

Carlos shrank back as the taller and more muscular man glared at him. "Calm down. I did not accuse you. I said 'might.' Is there something you want to tell us?" Carlos stared at Jonathon. The blacksmith looked taken aback, then he righted his chair before sitting back down.

When the men looked into each other's eyes, the air was thick with tension. After additional squabbling, they agreed to Carlos' suggestion of drawing marbles out of a bag. William abstained from participating, so Carlos selected only five marbles, one of which was black.

Carlos showed the marbles to the others, demonstrated that the bag was empty, and deposited the marbles in the bag. Each man drew a marble from the bag. Carlos drew early in the rotation. When all the men had a marble, they glared at each other. Carlos had each man open his hand. One after another, they revealed a white marble. Carlos, the last to open his hand, revealed the black marble.

"It seems I am to be the new mayor." His lips twitched, but he took care to control his expression. He could see the others were disappointed, and he did not want to provoke a fight. "I'll notify Robert of the decision."

Andrew glared at Carlos and clenched his teeth. William's jaw dropped with surprise. No one else responded. Silently, the men rose and exited the sitting room.

Carlos was the last to leave. After he was well away from the Smythe estate, he grinned from ear to ear and chortled. "No one noticed I kept the black marble concealed in my hand. I shall be the new mayor. Father would be so pleased."

CHAPTER THIRTY-TWO

CHANGE OF FORTUNE

Returning to Haver Hall, Ellene slipped back into her routine, keeping her acceptance of James' proposal secret from Marguerite and Avrill. Ellene and Marguerite gathered in the sitting room in the early afternoon to work on needlepoint.

Ellene made certain no servants were nearby before she whispered to Marguerite. "James has some evidence that Carlos isn't Eustace's son. His real name may be Rafe Beall, and he may have been the man who delivered the stolen wine. I told James about the portrait Goody described. I think it might help James prove the man isn't Carlos." Ellene fixed her gaze on her friend. "I think we should go to the estate to retrieve the portrait and take it to James."

Marguerite grew thoughtful. "I'm not confident we can get Carlos to agree to let us have it. And even if we prove he is a fraud, it won't help me any."

"If he is a fraud, maybe James can prove he is the person who killed Eustace. That would remove suspicions about you and William."

"What suspicions?" She raised her eyebrows, her eyes widening in astonishment.

"Village gossip is that you killed Eustace to be with William."

"No, it's not true. You must believe me."

"I believe you. As for the portrait, Carlos must not be aware of why it's significant. We can tell him it's a gift to you from Eustace, so it belongs to you." Ellene nervously chewed her lips. "It's urgent we find the painting before Carlos destroys or sells it."

"I suppose you are right. All we can do is try." Frowning, Marguerite shrugged her shoulders.

The women agreed to ride to Coeur de Lion that afternoon. Clive saddled their horses while they changed into riding clothes. They decided not to tell William where they were going because they knew he would forbid it.

As they rode, Ellene felt her palms sweating and her stomach churning with worry. The worst Carlos could do was order them to leave, she reasoned.

When the women arrived at the estate, no one came to take their horses.

"Where is the stableman?" Marguerite looked around but saw no one.

Despite the lack of help, they dismounted and fastened the horses to a rail.

"Let's go to the house and see who is there." Ellene's heart pounded, blood drumming in her ears, fearful of Carlos. She saw Marguerite's hands shaking.

The women knocked on the door. Soon Prudence appeared, her gray hair spilling from her coif, as she wiped her hands on her soiled apron. Her jaw dropped as she took in the sight of the two women.

"Mistress, whatever brings you back? And Lady Ellene." The cook looked over her shoulder. "The master is in his office." She made a drinking gesture with her hand. "I'll go tell him you're here."

"No, we don't want to trouble him." Marguerite's tone was light and playful. "I made a silly mistake when I packed. I left a portrait in the closet upstairs, so I came to retrieve it. Could you let us get it? We'll be quick. We don't want to inconvenience Carlos with this minor annoyance." Marguerite's voice was warm and inviting, her lips curving in a friendly smile.

"Oh, come in. But I'd be quick if I were you. He has a temper like his father."

"Of course. We'll be gone in no time."

The women slipped into the house, and Prudence returned to the kitchen. Marguerite found a candle to light the dark room. They tiptoed up the stairs, wincing when the wooden treads creaked. Marguerite opened the closet, and they entered.

Ellene looked around with dismay. They found a lance, a mace, and other weapons from bygone days stowed away in the closet. A former occupant stacked a full suit of armor, rusty from lack of maintenance, into a corner. Children's toys, most likely belonging to Carlos, were in a box in another corner. An open trunk contained a woman's grooming items which must have belonged to Juanita. If there had been gold, silver, or jewelry of any kind, Carlos had already removed it.

"Carlos has been in here. It looks as though he just rummaged through to find anything valuable. What a mess." Marguerite tiptoed, careful not to knock anything over. Then she spotted the carved wooden frame.

"I think I see it." Marguerite pulled the portrait from behind a stack of items and showed it to Ellene. "This is it. I recognize the woman and child from Goody's description."

"I see the birthmark clearly painted on the boy's neck. If we can have Goody testify that this is a likeness of Carlos as a child, and the man claiming to be him doesn't have the mark, that should be evidence he is lying." Ellene's face lit up with a grin. "Surely if this woman was his mother, he would have recognized her in the portrait and retrieved it?"

The women removed the portrait and frame from the closet. Carrying the portrait was awkward.

"How are we going to get this to James?" Marguerite whispered as she stopped in the hallway.

"How are we even going to get it out of the house?"

The women stared at each other. They were not expecting to get this far. Now that they had the portrait, they needed to decide what to do next.

They both jumped when they heard a man's voice coming from the ground floor. The portrait slipped from Marguerite's hands and fell with a thud.

"Mrs. Ellingham, what are you doing here? And Lady Ellene?" Carlos stood at the foot of the stairs, staring up at them, a sword in his hand. He wavered on his feet. He had not combed his hair, and wine stains marred his doublet. Clearly, he was sampling the wine.

"Lady Hunter and I came to collect this portrait. It's mine, and I forgot to take it when I left." Marguerite's face grew hot.

His face reddened in anger. "How did you get into the house?" he asked through clenched teeth.

"Prudence let us in. We didn't want to bother you over such an in-consequential matter. We'll just take the portrait and be on our way." Marguerite spoke in a flippant tone, her hand gesturing as if to brush away the conversation.

"I think you should stay right there."

Carlos stumbled as he made his way up the stairs, scowling. Once on the landing, he waved the sword at them. "I think you are stealing from me. I shall have to tie you up and summon the sheriff." He feigned a look of surprise. "Oh, I hear bandits attacked the sheriff and he may not survive. Whatever shall I do?" He smirked as he waved the sword in their direction, then glared at them. "Why are you stealing that?"

"Eustace gave it to me and I forgot to take it." Marguerite said. "Do you know who it is?"

"No, why should I? I was a child when I left. It's just some woman and her brat. Leave the painting and go to the Great Hall."

"We've done nothing wrong. You're making a mistake," protested El-lene. She did not mention James was recovering and had returned to work.

"Move. Now," he barked.

The women descended the stairs without pause and headed for the front door.

"We'll just be going now. I'll ask Callum to allow me to retrieve the painting. I'm sure he will let me have it." Marguerite's words tumbled out. "Allowing me to take it now would be the most efficient solution for everyone."

Carlos hurried to stand between the women and the door, all the while brandishing his sword.

Ellene had observed James' men training often enough to conclude Carlos was not well-trained in the weapon's use. But even with his lack of skill, it could still be lethal.

"Sit over there. I'll have the valet tie you until I can have you both arrested." Carlos pointed to two chairs.

"Sheriff Asher won't arrest us, you know. He's our friend." Marguerite challenged him, her voice filled with determination.

"I shall be the next mayor of Haver Hamlet. I plan to appoint a sheriff more, shall we say, compliant with my goals?" Carlos boasted, wearing a smirk on his face. He continued to brandish his sword.

Ellene pondered what they should do if the sword injured him. Tend to his wound or run for their horses?

Marguerite stiffened and glared at Carlos. "How dare you accuse me of theft at my house?"

"This isn't your house anymore, is it Mrs. Ellingham?" He jeered at her.

"I have a right to be here. My thirty days isn't up." Marguerite was defiant.

"You forfeited your right to be here when you moved out." Carlos sneered.

Marguerite lunged towards him. Carlos avoided her by taking a quick step back and swung the blade. She ducked, then tripped and fell. Ellene watched in horror and then hurried to help her up.

Carlos waved the sword toward Ellene. "No, stop. She stays there." He looked around for a servant. "Somebody fetch some rope. Do it now. I have a thief who tried to assault me," he shouted.

Tuesday morning came, and although James still had a dull headache, he felt relieved that the dizziness had finally faded away. With Thomas by his side, he set off towards Haver Hamlet, the rhythmic clip-clop of their horses' hooves echoing in the still air.

Their first destination was to fill Robert in on James' journey to Updyke Chase. They found him at work in his office. Thomas positioned himself at the back of the room, watching James and Robert, deep in conversation.

"I heard about the attack by bandits. I'm relieved you have recovered."

"Well, my recovery was in some doubt for a while, but Lady Ellene nursed me to health. The bandits in the jail claimed Carlos had found out about my plans and hired them to keep me from returning. I wonder who could have told him."

"I told no one, I swear." Robert held up his hands.

"Don't worry, I don't suspect you. But someone may have overheard us talking." James paused as he glanced at the open window. He walked over to the window and leaned out, looking in both directions. He noticed the foliage under the window was crushed. He turned back to Robert.

"My journey produced some useful information. I met a man in Updyke Chase who may know Carlos as a man called Rafe Beall. He knew Rafe's parents, and they were not Eustace and Juanita. The man agreed to come and see if it is Rafe Beall, and if so, testify in court as to Rafe's identity."

"So, that should help establish the man is not Carlos." Robert had a glimmer of hope in his eyes.

"Ellene told me about a painting at Coeur de Lion showing Juanita and Carlos. The child had a birthmark. I plan to find it after I talk to the bandits."

"Tell me what you discover. There may be enough information for you to arrest him, then go to the justice of the peace for a hearing," Robert mused, his brows furrowing in thought.

As James and Thomas approached the jail, they could hear the faint sound of inmates shouting from within. The jailer, scratching his ribs and squinting in the sunlight, came out to greet the two men.

"Hello, Sheriff. Good to see ye back in the saddle."

"Good to be back. I believe you are holding the two bandits who attacked me." James dismounted from his horse and pointed to the jail.

"That I am, Sheriff."

"I need to ask them a few questions."

"Where do ye want 'em?"

"Leave them in their cell," James growled.

James and Thomas marched to the cell in the back, gagging at the acrid odor of human waste. The dim light made it difficult to distinguish the features on the inmates' faces. The youth tried to hide behind his companion.

"So, we meet again. Aren't you the two who tried to rob me in my room in Updyke Chase?"

"No, Sheriff, not us." The older man shook his head.

"I see the wound where I held my blade to your neck, you liar. Who hired you to ambush me on the way back to Haver Hamlet?"

"How much is it worth to you?" The man sneered.

"You have no leverage to negotiate. You're facing hanging for being a highwayman."

The sneer vanished, and the man's tongue flickered along his bottom lip. "It was a man called Carlos. He told us you were an assassin, and we'd be protecting him."

"That's odd, because you told me before you were after a purse of gold coins. Which is it?" James clenched his fists.

The prisoners looked at the floor but did not speak.

"How did he find out about my plans?" James continued.

"Somebody overheard you in Haver Hamlet and let him know."

239

"Who was it?"

"He didn't say."

Did Carlos have someone lurking outside Robert's office? Was he listening this morning when James stopped by? James felt a chill run up his spine, but he fought it back.

James questioned them further but learned nothing else of value. He and Thomas left the jailhouse and headed toward Coeur de Lion, intending to arrest Carlos for hiring the bandits to attack him.

Although it had been less than a week since Carlos moved in, the estate already was falling into disrepair. Dirt caked the stairs and weeds overran the courtyard. James listened for the geese and ducks he was used to seeing, but heard only the wind in the trees. No servants came to greet them and take their horses or announce them. Two horses, already saddled, waited for their riders.

"That's Ellene's horse. What would she be doing here?" His eyes widened in alarm and his eyebrows shot up. "Oh, no. I told her not to come here."

"Maybe she came with Marguerite," Thomas suggested. "That's not William's horse."

"Only one way to find out."

Attaching the reins of their horses next to the other horses, they headed to the house and knocked on the front door.

Carlos shouted, "Somebody needs to go to the door and see who's there."

James opened the door to see Carlos standing with his sword hanging at an awkward angle in his left hand. Ellene stood by Marguerite, who was on the floor. Ellene looked at James with relief.

Carlos' face drained of color to see James alive and well. Then his expression changed. "Sheriff, you are just in time. These women broke into my house and tried to steal a painting. Arrest them for burglary."

"No. You drop your weapon. It is you I came to arrest." James grabbed his arm and removed the sword from his grasp.

Ellene helped Marguerite back on her feet. Thomas drew his weapon and circled to the side where he had a better chance of intervening if Carlos tried to attack James.

"I came looking for you, Carlos. Or should I call you Rafe?" He noticed the man's eyes bulge. "There are two men in the Haver Hamlet jail who claim you hired them to kill me." James glared at his adversary.

"I deny that. I don't know who you're talking about," Carlos shouted with defiance in his voice. He maintained eye contact while one hand checked for his dagger.

"They say you hired them to kill me and steal my—how did they put it?—my purse of gold coins. They knocked me out and left me to die. But, as I say, two are in jail, and the third one is in a pauper's grave. And I'm still alive. What do you have to say?"

Carlos flashed his dagger. Swinging the blade, he tried to stab James in the stomach, but Thomas deflected his arm, and the dagger flew across the room. Carlos lost his balance and his body hit the floor with a resounding crash. James bent over and grabbed the front of his doublet.

"Enough tricks. Carlos Ellingham, I arrest you for conspiracy to commit theft and murder. Oh, I met your old master in Updyke Chase. During our conversation, he claimed to have known your family personally, and he revealed that your mother was not, in fact, Ellingham's first wife. So, I'll add the charges of fraud for impersonating Carlos, and theft for selling property under false pretenses. And I found evidence that you stole five barrels of wine, which you tried to sell to Eustace. I'll have quite the list of charges to take to the justice of the peace. In the meantime, you can join your friends in our jail."

"You're making a terrible mistake. My name is Carlos. I'm going to be the mayor of Haver Hamlet and I'm going to fire you."

"Not now. We know who you really are."

James pulled Carlos to his feet, and Thomas tied his hands behind his back.

"Prudence, Carlos will dine at the jail tonight." James called out.

She popped out of the kitchen, her eyes large. James suspected she was listening at the door the whole time.

"Did he kill the master?" Prudence's voice trembled.

"We don't know, but we have evidence he is not Carlos Ellingham. Thomas, take him outside while I talk to the women." James turned his attention to Ellene and Marguerite while Thomas grabbed Carlos by the arm and dragged him through the door.

"Ellene, what brought both of you to this place?" James' furrowed brow and down-turned mouth betrayed his feelings.

Ellene decided the best course of action was to calm him down. The women took turns explaining the purpose of their visit and how Carlos caught them.

"We never dreamed he would threaten us with a sword. He said he would summon you to take us into custody, but thought you were still close to death. We are fortunate you arrived now." Ellene concluded, a look of contrition on her face.

"You are fortunate he didn't stab you. I've never seen such sloppy sword handling. Where is the portrait?"

Marguerite led James up the stairs and pointed to the portrait on the floor. James picked it up and carried it down the stairs, where he propped it up on a chair.

"Now explain what you found in this portrait."

Ellene repeated what Goody told her and pointed to the child with the birthmark.

"If Carlos doesn't have the birthmark, it is more evidence he is lying." Ellene concluded with a satisfied smile. "He did not recognize the woman in the painting, which is more evidence against him."

"Let's go see about the birthmark," James said.

The trio went outside, where Thomas held Carlos. James pulled the doublet and shirt away from Carlos' neck and shoulders. His skin was clear. James held up the painting.

"Tell me about this painting."

"What is there to tell? It was in the priest hide. I never met those people. If I did, I was too young to remember." Carlos had a smug look on his face.

"The woman is Juanita, who you claim is your mother. The boy is her son Carlos. He had a birthmark, but you don't. Care to explain?"

"I told you. I don't know those people. You can't prove that the boy is Carlos."

"I have a witness who knew Juanita and Carlos."

"It's their word against mine."

"We'll see about that." Clearly frustrated, James turned to Ellene and Marguerite. "Well done, ladies. But you put yourselves in danger by being here. Where are you planning to take the portrait?"

Ellene and Marguerite exchanged glances.

"Probably to your office? Or to the justice of the peace?" Ellene volunteered.

James glared at Carlos. "Do you still have a wagon?"

"Yes, in the stable. But I sold the horses."

"You sold the horses?" Marguerite exploded. "James, this man has ruined the estate. He pilfered many things of value in storage upstairs."

"Well, it looks like we'll have to secure the portrait in the house until we can borrow a wagon. Maybe the Smythes have one they can lend. But for now, I need to get this prisoner to the village and in a jail cell." James glanced at Thomas. "Would you and Marguerite take Carlos to the barn and find his horse? I need to talk to Ellene."

"I'm warning you, Sheriff. You're making a mistake." Carlos' face flushed and spittle formed on his lips. "You'll pay for this."

Thomas dragged Carlos toward the barn with Marguerite trailing. James fixed his gaze on Ellene.

"I asked you not to get involved. You should have waited for me to take care of it." As she hesitated to answer, he sighed. He opened his arms, and she stepped forward into his embrace. She felt safe leaning against his warm and muscular chest.

"I'm sorry, James. I didn't think he would do something so stupid as to threaten us with his sword. And we wanted to help you find evidence that he's an impostor. We were afraid he would destroy it before you could retrieve it." She started shaking as the gravity of their situation sunk in.

"You and Marguerite must ride with us to the village to swear out a complaint. I'll send Thomas with you to Haver Hall. It's not possible for me to come with you because I have a lot of paperwork to fill out about this criminal. I'll come see you as soon as I can." He leaned in and softly brushed his lips against hers in a sweet kiss.

Thomas led Carlos, who was on his horse with his hands tied, into the courtyard. Marguerite trailed behind.

"Let's get going," James urged. "The sooner this man is in jail, the better for the rest of us."

The others mounted and the riders broke into a trot going toward the village.

CHAPTER THIRTY-THREE

A NEW TWIST

The next morning, as dawn painted the sky with hues of orange and pink, William, Ellene, and Avrill sat at the dining room table. The fragrance of baked bread permeated the air. Ellene and William chatted about their plans to attend the afternoon hearing regarding Carlos. Ellene would collect Goody so she could testify about the painting they found at Coeur de Lion.

"Where is Marguerite? She is an important witness at the hearing," William fussed, his voice filled with frustration. "Sorcha, go check on Marguerite and tell her we are having breakfast."

Still in her room, Marguerite felt a wave of nausea. The breakfast odors wafting up from downstairs were too much for her. She had just vomited when Sorcha knocked on her bedroom door. When the maid stepped into the room, Marguerite's complexion had drained of color.

"I need you to bring me cold water and a bowl. And clean up the mess on the floor."

"Yes, madame. Do you want some tea or broth as well?"

Marguerite managed a feeble smile. "No, I just need to stay in bed and rest. Give my regrets to William and Ellene."

Sorcha went to the dining room, where she repeated Marguerite's message.

"Should we send for Zachary?" William asked, his voice filled with alarm.

Ellene thought for a minute. "Let me talk to her first. If it's just an upset stomach, she should be better in a day or two. Bridgett could make her an herbal remedy."

"But it could be serious. No, I will send Jeremy to bring the physician." With his mind made up, William summoned Jeremy, who hurried to saddle a horse and ride to Zachary's house.

Ellene had not yet talked with William about his relationship with Marguerite. She peered at him, curious why he showed such concern. The family ate, the air thick with an awkward silence. By the time they finished, Jeremy returned with the physician. Ellene rose from the table to greet him in the Great Hall.

"I'll take you upstairs to see Marguerite. I hope it is nothing serious, but this morning she was sick to her stomach." Ellene ascended the stairway ahead of Zachary, who followed her to the bedroom.

Ellene knocked twice. "Marguerite. Zachary is here. William and I are concerned about your illness."

After a minute's silence, Marguerite called through the door. "Let him come in."

Zachary closed the door behind him while Ellene remained outside. She could hear their voices, but not what was being discussed. After a few minutes, he emerged from the bedroom.

"She wants to see you, Lady Ellene." He nodded and went down the stairs.

Ellene's mouth dropped open as Zachary's statement sunk in. Just those few words and nothing more? She pushed the door open and found Marguerite in bed, still wearing her chemise, tears running down her cheeks.

Ellene rushed to her side. "What is it? What did he say? Are you dying?"

"No." She made a sniffling noise. "He told me—." A hiccup interrupted her breathing.

"What did he tell you?" Ellene scanned her friend's expression, dreading what she might hear.

"He told me I'm pregnant." She dabbed at her eyes with her handkerchief.

Ellene let the implications sink in, then smiled. "Congratulations. It is unfortunate Eustace did not live long enough to see his child."

"It's William's child." Marguerite's voice faltered and shook with each word.

Ellene's smile disappeared as she sank into the nearby chair. William's child? He didn't. Did he?

"Are you sure? It is so close to Eustace's death people will assume it is his child. If you claim it is William's child, they will charge you with adultery. They might subject you to flogging." Ellene chewed on her lips and furrowed her brow.

Marguerite burst into fresh sobbing. "I know. What shall I do?"

"Well, you can't hide the pregnancy for long. William suspects you are seriously ill. Why are you claiming it is not Eustace's child?"

"William will know it is his. Eustace and I have not—well—for more than a year. William and I—." Her voice trailed off. "He hasn't asked me to marry him yet, but I expect he would want to raise the child as his own."

Ellene thought for a minute. "If you claim the baby is William's, people might suspect you poisoned Eustace to marry William. Otherwise, they will assume it is Eustace's baby."

"William and I love each other."

Ellene frowned. "I'll send him up here. You and he must decide what to do. Unless James identifies the actual killer, he can accuse you of killing Eustace so you could marry William." Ellene shook her head. "You are a dear friend. I will support you and my brother, whatever you decide."

William waited for the physician at the foot of the stairs. He called out as Zachary came into view. "How is she? Is it serious?"

"I leave it to her to tell you the diagnosis. But she is not in immediate danger."

Confused, William thanked him for coming. When Ellene returned to the Great Hall to tell him Marguerite wanted to see him, he sprinted upstairs.

Avrill confronted Ellene with questions about their guest. "What did Zachary say? Is her illness contagious? Is she going to recover?"

"Marguerite is not in any danger. She should feel better soon. Your father went to speak with her. In the meantime, we have work to do." Ellene pointed toward the kitchen, and they strolled there together.

After his conversation with Marguerite, William returned to his office and closed the door. Ellene heard his footsteps. Curious as to their decision, she followed him and tapped on the closed door.

"William, do you have a minute?"

"Yes, come in."

She opened the door to observe William sitting at his desk, staring out the window. She noticed him doing that regularly of late.

"Marguerite told me about the baby. She told me it is yours. Is it yours? Did you lay with her while she was married to Eustace?"

"No. She asked me to claim it as mine and marry her as soon as possible. If I do, it may inherit Haver Hall. If I don't, it could inherit Coeur de Lion if Carlos is a fraud."

"What did you and she decide?" Ellene uttered her words in a hushed tone.

William swung around and stared past Ellene for a minute, his expression bleak. Then he locked eyes with her.

"People accusing her of adultery, or even murder, is a possibility if we say the baby is mine. Marguerite is going to tell Callum it is Eustace's child and try to reclaim the estate."

"Regardless of your decision, are you set on marrying her?"

William stared at her, but remained silent.

Ellene sighed and shook her head, her heart heavy with sadness. "I don't understand your reasoning, but I'll support you any way I can."

Later that morning, Ellene made her way to Goody's cottage. They needed Goody to be a witness to the identity of the woman and child in the portrait. She would join Ellene in the carriage for the journey to the White

Stag Inn, where the hearing would be open to the public.

"Goody, are you ready?" Ellene knocked at the door and shouted.

"Who's there?" came the muffled reply.

"Lady Ellene. I'm taking you to the village for the hearing."

The door opened, revealing Goody in her chemise.

"Are you ill? Why aren't you dressed? You are to be a witness at the hearing this afternoon. We're going to the village in the carriage." With patience for the woman, Ellene delivered her explanation.

"Oh, is that today? I had better put on some clothes." Goody's hands fluttered and her eyes darted. "Where are my clothes?"

Ellene pointed to some garments on a chair. "Do you want to wear those?"

"Yes. There they are." She shuffled over to the pile and began pulling out items until she found a skirt, a bodice, and a partlet.

"Do you have a shawl?" Ellene looked around until she spotted a colorful length of cloth. "Is this your shawl?"

"Oh, my dear, you're so helpful. I need my coif."

"You're wearing your coif. Have you eaten this morning?"

Goody pursed her lips. "I think so. I don't feel hungry or thirsty."

"Can you walk with me? We need to go to the house so I can change my clothes before we leave. Would you like a slice of Bridgett's fresh bread?"

Ellene looped her arm through Goody's and guided her to the door. She worried about Goody's mental state. Normally she was up and dressed and busy when Ellene visited. Ellene appreciated the ample time to accompany her to Haver Hall and allow her to rest before their departure for the village.

William decided Marguerite should meet with Robert as soon as possible to inform him about the pregnancy. He convinced her to leave her bedroom and ride with him to Robert's office, then on into Haver Hamlet.

Robert, working at his desk, sprang up in surprise when the valet announced the couple.

"Greetings. What brings you to my office today? I didn't expect to see you until Carlos' hearing this afternoon."

"Marguerite has some important information that bears on who should inherit Coeur de Lion." William nodded towards Marguerite.

Robert, his brow furrowed in confusion, rubbed his chin. "James told me about the portrait and this unsettling idea that Carlos could be an impostor named Rafe."

William and Marguerite looked at each other. William encouraged her to continue.

"May I sit?" Marguerite gestured toward a chair.

"Of course, of course." Robert nodded.

Marguerite lowered herself onto the chair, arranging her skirt before settling in. William stood behind her chair, his hands resting on her shoulders.

"I've been ill recently. This morning William summoned the physician, and it seems—." She stopped and fixed her gaze on the floor.

"It seems what?" Robert was uncertain of what to expect.

She raised her eyes. "It seems I'm pregnant with Eustace's child."

Robert sank into his chair, his mouth hanging open in disbelief.

"Are you sure?" He glanced at William, who had a soft, adoring look on his face as he watched Marguerite.

"Zachary confirmed it. I felt it important that in the interest of the unborn child, especially if it is a boy, I immediately stake his claim to the estate. At least what Carlos hasn't appropriated," she remarked ruefully. "Yesterday, when Ellene and I were at Coeur de Lion, most of the servants were gone. The horses and some of the livestock are gone. It appears Carlos sold the silver plates and candlesticks."

William patted her hand to console her. "She needs your counsel when and how to approach the justice to assert her child's rights."

Robert rubbed his chin. "Carlos is still the heir unless Callum reverses that ruling. In the meantime, I can check to find out when he has an opening on his docket to hear your claim. Zachary must testify regarding your condition, of course."

Marguerite's eyes grew moist as she spoke. She squeezed William's hand and gazed at him. "Oh, William, what shall I do?"

"You must wait for Callum's approval to regain control of the property. You can stay at Haver Hall until then."

Robert's eyes narrowed at their obvious affection for each other. His tone was firm as he inquired, "Is there something between you two that you haven't told me?"

"William and Ellene are dear friends of mine. I don't know what I would do without them." She sniffed into her handkerchief as a blush spread across her neck.

Robert stared at Marguerite, but she did not offer any other explanation. "I suggest we wait until the hearing today is over before we take this to Callum. I understand you are a witness against Carlos at his hearing." Robert pulled a sheet of paper in front of him and started writing.

"Yes, we will go to the White Stag after we leave here." Marguerite nodded.

"I'll see you there in a while, then." Robert was expecting to be called as a witness as well. "Leave it with me. I'll send a message to you when I know the schedule."

William helped Marguerite stand, and they went back to their horses to resume their journey toward the White Stag.

CHAPTER THIRTY-FOUR

JUSTICE OF THE PEACE

A t Haver Manor, James prepared for a long day in Haver Hamlet. His head, still tender from the attack, throbbed with pain when he bumped it, making him wince. He looked at the men already sparring in the courtyard, wishing he was with them. These criminal matters took too much of his time. Today, he planned to attend two important proceedings. First, the two highwaymen would stand trial for robbery and assault. Next would be a hearing to determine if Carlos was indeed Rafe, and whether he committed fraud and theft. He hoped there would be sufficient evidence to indict Carlos for employing the highwaymen.

Thomas, Rusty, and Twig, witnesses to the assault and robbery, waited for him in the courtyard.

When they arrived in Haver Hamlet, the villagers milled around in the streets, eager for the highwaymen's trial. Criminal trials in the village were a spectacle, often ending in flogging or someone being pilloried or put in the stocks. On rare occasions, they hanged the defendant. For serious crimes like murder or treason, they sent the accused to London for trial and punishment. In order to accommodate the spectators, the justice of the peace conducted trials in the White Stag Inn, which was the largest inn in the village.

The four men rode straight to the jail to collect the prisoners. As they dismounted, the jailer appeared, scratching his chest. He squinted as his eyes adjusted to the bright sunlight. Thomas stood beside James, ropes in his hands. Rusty and Twig took their horses to the stable.

"Are ye here to take those worthless thieves to the White Stag for their trial?" The jailer's grin revealed gaps, suggesting multiple missing teeth.

"Yes. We plan to tie them up and march them down the street." James' jaw tightened as he spoke, and his neck turned red.

The jailer led James and Thomas to the bandits' cell. All three prisoners were on high alert as they heard the sheriff and his men approaching. Carlos was in a separate cell facing the bandits. They were grimy, with dirt caked under their nails and a musty smell emanating from their clothes. Thomas went into the cells and dragged them out one by one to have their hands tied in front. Then he tied them in a line with ropes around their necks. When finished, James pointed toward the jail door and he and Thomas marched the three prisoners to the inn.

By the time they arrived, a crowd had formed outside the inn, mocking and jeering. As James brandished his sword, the onlookers took a step back, their eyes widening in response. When the entourage stepped inside the inn, they observed the innkeeper and Bess had moved the tables against the wall while the stools and benches faced the table reserved for the justice. They led the prisoners to a bench close to where the justice would sit. Then they untied the ropes around their necks.

The youth's trembling hands and pale complexion revealed his terror, as he understood the gravity of the charges. The older highwayman sat tall, his eyes filled with defiance. Carlos, seething with frustration, shot a menacing glare at James.

The court clerk started the trial, swore in the jury, and read the charges against the man and youth. James, Thomas, Rusty, and Twig sat near the prisoners. When called upon to give testimony, they recounted the events surrounding the assault and robbery of James. The bandits failed to present an effective defense. With Carlos present, the highwaymen denied accusing him of hiring them. James groaned in frustration. The jury returned a verdict of guilty of all charges.

Callum pulled a black cap out of his robe and placed it on his head. His words hung heavy in the air as he pronounced, "I find you both guilty of the crimes with which you are charged. Because the assault on the victim resulted in him being near death, this court sentences you to hang by the neck until you are dead. I will announce the date when we have the gallows constructed. I conclude this trial."

A collective gasp arose from the onlookers as the prisoners' faces drained of color and they began to tremble. The older bandit shouted at the justice in protest, his words reverberating in the room. The youth pleaded for mercy, but Callum refused to respond.

"Sheriff, remove these two and return them to the jail." Callum waved his hands in dismissal.

Thomas, Rusty, and Twig grabbed the two bandits, dragged them out of the courtroom, and marched them back to the jail. Some of the crowd followed, yelling insults.

"You can't do this. You can't take us back. I'm too young to die," cried the youth, his voice filled with desperation.

"Your companion led you astray, young man. But you planned to leave James to die, so I have no sympathy," Thomas replied. "Shut up and keep moving."

Upon their arrival at the jailhouse, the jailer's snoring was all they could hear. He awoke with a start when he heard voices.

"Brought them back, I see. That must mean they're guilty." He spat on the ground.

"The two highwaymen are to be hung when they erect the gallows. Callum hasn't heard the evidence in the other case yet. At least they can keep you company for a few more days." Thomas' chuckle was devoid of any true amusement.

Thomas shoved the men through the door and down the hall to the cells. After the jailer locked the cell, Thomas returned to the inn. Rusty and Twig left to go back to Haver Manor.

After a brief break, Callum started Carlos' hearing. He scrutinized Carlos and then surveyed the people inside the inn. Carlos' current condition presented a stark contrast to the well-groomed man in stylish clothing who claimed to be the Ellingham heir a few days ago.

"Clerk, are you ready to read the charges against the defendant, Carlos Ellingham?"

"I am, your Honor."

"Proceed."

After he read the charges, the clerk called James to the stand again. Ignoring Carlos' glare, James testified regarding the information he gathered about Rafe Beall in Updyke Chase. He displayed the shabby clothes and gray beard and wig found in Rafe's room, stating they looked like those worn by the man who met Eustace to sell him stolen wine.

The sheriff from County Norcross testified about retrieving the pilfered wine from the Coeur de Lion barn.

Bess described the man who met Eustace to sell the wine, confirming he had gray hair matching the beard and wig. She also described clothes that matched the ones James found. She testified that the man had a burn scar on his wrist. Callum asked her to describe it, then required Carlos to show his wrist, which matched her description.

Another piece of evidence was the portrait. Goody Pickwick identified it as being an accurate likeness of Juanita and Carlos. She pointed out the birthmark on the child's neck. Carlos protested as James pulled back his clothing, showing that he did not have the same birthmark.

Marguerite testified about Eustace switching tradesmen and finding the stolen wine in the barn. She also confirmed finding the portrait in the closet at Coeur de Lion. She described the missing personal property and the reduced herds of livestock after Carlos took possession of the estate. Others testified about buying those items from Carlos.

Ellene, who noted Carlos' inability to identify his mother in the portrait, disputed his claim of being from Cheapside.

During the testimony, Carlos shook his head and made comments, such as "Liar," "Not true," and "That's ridiculous." Callum admonished him to stay silent.

James addressed Callum. "Your Honor, I believe we have presented enough evidence that this man is not Carlos, the son of Eustace Ellingham. I have information that his name is Rafe Beall, and he has unlawfully disposed of property not belonging to him. He also stole wine while presenting himself as a man named Harry."

"Harrumph. Defendant, do you have anything to say?"

Carlos stood, his jaw muscles twitching. "Goody's thoughts are all mixed up. Her mind plays tricks on her. That painting has nothing to do with me or my mother. Mrs. Ellingham broke into my home and tried to steal the painting. This so-called witness in Updyke Chase could not possibly know me. I've never been there. It's a matter of my word against the sheriffs about those clothes belonging to me. I demand to be released."

The justice stroked his chin. "Harrumph. Some of the evidence is still in dispute. I would like the goldsmith in Updyke Chase to testify in person regarding his knowledge of this man's identity. I postpone this hearing until Sheriff Asher can bring the witness to Haver Hamlet. In the meantime, Mr. Ellingham is to remain in the jail." The justice adjourned the hearing and left the inn while Carlos shouted at him.

James sighed with exhaustion. Still recuperating from his injury, he wiped the sweat from his forehead with a trembling hand. "Let's get this man back to the jail, shall we?"

He looked at Thomas, who nodded. Thomas grabbed Carlos by his arm. Carlos seemed like he was going to spit at Thomas but changed his mind after seeing Thomas' expression.

James approached the group from Haver Hall. "I appreciate everyone taking the time to testify. Now I must take this lawbreaker back to jail. I doubt I'll drop by Haver Hall tonight." He grimaced, despite managing a slight smile for Ellene.

"We understand, James. Do what you must do. Be careful and get some rest." Ellene reached out and James clasped her hand. Then he resumed his official demeanor. When he noticed she wore his brooch, his eyes brightened.

"We are going to stay here to eat before we make our journey back. Join us if you have the time." William offered.

"We might do that." James looked at his steward. "Thomas, are we ready?"

At his nod, they marched Carlos back to the jailhouse.

On the way, Carlos protested in a loud voice. "Just let me escape and I'll leave Haver Hamlet and never come back. From what I hear, the mayor had it coming to him." Carlos spun his body to confront James.

"Keep moving. What did you hear?" James jerked Carlos and forced him to keep walking.

"I heard Marguerite and Eustace had a fight before the banquet. He claimed he wasn't the father of her child. He was going to charge her with adultery and turn her out with no money." Carlos looked at James out of the corner of his eye.

"What child? Marguerite doesn't have a child."

"She's pregnant."

"And who did you hear that from?" James had not yet heard Marguerite was pregnant. He tried not to show his interest, but divorce would give Marguerite a motive for murder.

"Prudence. She told the stableman. They've both been protecting Marguerite."

"I'll look into that," James said.

When they arrived at the jail with Carlos, the jailer placed him in his cell separate from the bandits.

Bess and her father moved the furniture back into place to resume serving customers. William, Ellene, Marguerite, and Goody found a table large enough for six. Marguerite nestled up to William and held tight to his arm.

People in the public room gawked at them.

"Why, this is a real treat, Sir William. It's been many a year since I've been to an inn." Goody's face lit up and she looked around the room, trying to take everything in. "I don't recognize a soul."

"Thank you for helping today, Goody. I hope you won't be too tired tomorrow," Ellene fussed.

"Well, I can sleep all day, can't I?" she chuckled.

The group ordered food and ale. Other patrons shouted questions about the trial, but William waved them off.

James and Thomas arrived for their dinner and joined the group. James sat beside Ellene, clasped her hand, and kissed it.

"My, you two look friendly," observed Goody.

Ellene's cheeks gained a rosy hue. A smile spread across James' face. "You have sharp eyes, Goody. You provided valuable testimony today."

Goody's cheeks flushed as all eyes focused on her.

Chapter Thirty-Five

PETITION FOR MARGUERITE

On the following day, Robert contacted Zachary to confirm Marguerite's pregnancy. He then prepared a document asserting her claim to Coeur de Lion and sent it by a messenger to the justice of the peace. Later, after Callum reviewed the document, he summoned Robert to his home.

"Mrs. Ellingham is carrying Eustace's child? That old rogue!" Callum chuckled, his eyebrows raising in disbelief. "That is extraordinary, considering his age and health. Did he know about it?"

"Zachary found out she was pregnant before the banquet and he informed Eustace. According to him, she is about ten weeks along. No one has accused her of being unfaithful. Therefore, it is probable that Eustace, being her husband, is the father." Robert explained.

Callum glanced again at the document. "Harrumph. It seems she has a valid claim. Still, Carlos, if he indeed is the son, has a better claim because he is the elder of the two. If I find him guilty of fraud, however, Marguerite's child would inherit if it's a boy. I would have to appoint a guardian for the boy to manage the property until he comes of age."

"I recommend you appoint Sir William Throck-Morton as the child's guardian. He is Marguerite's guardian and helped with the estate's business dealings until Carlos took over."

"This is a nasty business all around. Harrumph. I'll talk to her on Friday and issue a preliminary decision. You notify Marguerite and Zachary that I need to talk to them."

"Your honor, it seems there is ample evidence the man calling himself Carlos is not the heir. It would seem you could rule now."

"No, I want to hear from the goldsmith in Updyke Chase. I don't want to convict a man based on inaccurate information. I noticed Goody Pickwick's memory was not sharp. The marriage contract looks legitimate. How did he get it if Juanita was not his mother?"

Robert shrugged. It was another of the mysteries with which he and James wrestled.

When Robert returned to his office, he sent a messenger to Marguerite to explain the justice's decision. As he worked on other matters, a knock on his door startled him. His servant escorted Andrew into his office.

"Come in, Andrew. How can I help you?" Robert stood to greet him.

"Just came to see how things are going with Coeur de Lion. Now that the stranger is in jail for impersonating Carlos, I heard the estate might be for sale. I want to make an offer." He pulled a scroll out of his pocket and handed it to Robert.

Robert's eyes widened as his eyebrows arched in surprise. He unrolled the scroll and read the text and numbers, written in precise handwriting. "This seems to be an excellent offer. But some other circumstances exist which prevent me from presenting this to the justice now."

"Of course. I'm not in a hurry." As Andrew looked around the office, a smile played on his lips. "How soon, do you think?"

"Well, there is another claim on the estate."

"What do you mean?" The smile vanished. "Eustace had no other male relatives."

"Marguerite is pregnant with Eustace's child. If it's a boy, he would be the heir. If Callum decides Carlos is a fraud and supports her claim, she plans to move back to the estate." Robert could sense the tension in the air as Andrew's face turned red with anger.

"I can't believe that. Eustace's health was too poor to father a child. Besides, it's the mayor's house. If they expose Carlos as a fraud, they will strip him of his mayoral candidacy, and I have every intention of taking his place. Assuming it is a boy, it will be eighteen years before he will be old enough to take control of the property, if he survives to that age. I offer a fair price. Marguerite would be wise to sell the child's claim and find a new husband." His fingers curled into tight fists as his nails dug into his palms.

"We shall find out the truth in due time." Robert folded his hands on his desk.

Andrew took a deep breath and tried a different approach. "If Marguerite prevails, she will need a guardian for the boy. I'm ready to offer myself for that role."

"William is already acting as Marguerite's guardian."

"I live closer to her estate and am better situated to monitor it. I plan to oppose William being appointed guardian for the child."

"Is there anything else I can help you with today?" Robert leaned back in his chair.

With a curt, "No. Good day," Andrew twirled and rushed toward the door. He did not realize James was in the doorway. James' solid physique propelled Andrew backwards, causing him to stumble. Andrew regained his footing and continued his exit through the door without greeting James.

"Andrew was in a hurry." James stepped into the office, resetting his bonnet as he did so.

Robert's lips tightened into a thin line. "Ordinarily, I wouldn't talk about client matters, but it may bear on your investigation of Eustace's murder." Robert told James about Marguerite's pregnancy and her intent to move back to Coeur de Lion. He then divulged Andrew's offer to purchase the property, and his reaction when he found out about the claim. "Andrew was furious. He wants to buy it because it was the mayor's house, and he plans to be the mayor."

"Interesting. Assassinate the mayor, take his place, and then seize control of the estate. Would Andrew do that, do you think?" James looked thoughtful.

"I hope not. Still, we should consider it as a possible motivate."

"When I took Carlos to jail yesterday, he claimed Prudence told the stableman that Eustace and Marguerite quarreled about the pregnancy, and that Eustace denied it was his child and threatened to throw her out."

"That is a lot of hearsay. We would have to get the cook to testify to Callum. Are you going to question her?"

"Yes, but not right away."

The men were silent as each man reflected on the situation. It occurred to Robert that James had yet to share the reason for his arrival.

"What brings you here today?"

"I want to know if a witnessed letter from the goldsmith in Updyke Chase would be satisfactory to Callum. He's afraid that if it is Rafe, he will seek revenge against him. Otherwise, I need to bring him here. I can send a couple of my men to escort him."

"No, the letter would not be sufficient. The witness must look at the defendant, say that is the man he knows as Rafe, and tell the justice about his history. We have a righteous justice of the peace. He questions some of the testimony, so we need an eyewitness to back it up."

CHAPTER THIRTY-SIX

AVRILL'S DISCONTENT

Avrill, her shoulders slumped, shuffled to her father's office. William was in the village most of the previous day, so this was the first opportunity she had to talk with him in a while. Her thoughts troubled her. What were Aunt Ellene and her father keeping secret? Was he still trying to find her a suitable match? Did her father neglect her because of his obsession with Marguerite? Did he have plans to marry that woman? And what was Marguerite's mysterious illness?

She peered into the office through the open door. William was alone, his quill pen scratching out the words on the page before him.

"Papa, are you busy?" Avrill's words were barely audible.

He looked up to see his daughter's sad expression. "Although I'm busy, I can always find time to talk to you. What's on your mind? Is something bothering you?" William waited for her to speak.

Avrill took her seat in the chair opposite her father. She gazed at her hands, clasped in her lap, and inhaled a deep breath. After a while, she cast her eyes up and met his gaze.

Her voice was full of anxiety as she asked, "Are you planning to marry Marguerite?"

"Why do you ask that, *ma Cherie*?" William's eyes widened in surprise.

"She suggested she plans to marry you and live at Haver Hall. She advised Aunt Ellene to marry and move away. Do you also want Aunt Ellene to leave us? If she does, who can help me get ready for my marriage?"

William cursed under his breath. He stood and walked around his desk and clasped her hands.

"I love you, Avrill. Don't forget that. But someday you will marry and go to live with your husband and his family. It is the right thing to do. If I were to marry Marguerite, it doesn't mean I don't still love you, and Aunt Ellene, and your mother. But I would like to have a wife and more children. Marguerite and I have powerful feelings for each other, but it takes more than feelings to agree to a marriage. Now that Aunt Ellene and James are engaged, she will leave soon. But she will be close by if you need her."

"Is it true Marguerite is pregnant?"

William jerked back, startled. "Where did you hear that?"

Avrill made a face. "Servants hear things and talk about them, Papa."

"Yes, she is carrying her late husband's child."

"So, if you marry her, is her baby going to inherit Haver Hall?"

"Um, no. It must go to my blood relative. I need to marry and raise a son."

He wrapped his arm around her slim shoulders and pulled her in close. "Never fear, *ma Cherie*. In the not-so-distant future, the delightful chaos of a loving family will surround you with children of your own."

She put on a wan smile, but the sadness in her eyes was impossible to miss.

"Have you found someone for me to meet yet?" She studied his eyes, searching for deception. "What do you think about Thomas? If we married and I had a son, could he inherit Haver Hall?"

William wished Desiree was still alive. He felt ill-equipped to talk with Avrill on this subject. "I have several letters from families with sons seeking a wife. I want you to marry into a wealthy family. Thomas is a poor man with few prospects. I have explained this before."

"Yes, but I also want to marry someone I love. Aunt Ellene had an unhappy marriage when she married for money. So did Marguerite. I'd rather not go through that."

"Don't worry, I won't sign anything until you've met him and agree."

"Thomas's lack of wealth doesn't matter to me."

"As I already told you, he cannot support a family. You deserve a wealthy husband, a big house, and servants. Don't worry, Avrill. It will all work out. We just need to pray for the right husband."

"Very well, Papa." She sighed and stood up. "I'm going upstairs for a while if anyone is looking for me."

William planted a kiss on her cheek and stood gazing at her back as she hastened away from the room.

Marguerite stood sideways in the hallway as Avrill brushed past her.

"May I come in?" She fixed her gaze on William.

"Of course. How much did you hear?"

"Most of it."

William's brows furrowed, causing his face to scrunch up in a frown. "I should be the one to tell Avrill and Ellene about our relationship. It is too soon to announce our intention to marry."

"I'm sorry, my love. I'm so happy about us getting married that I spoke too soon. Forgive me?" She closed the door, then put her hands around

William's neck and kissed him on the mouth. He felt dizzy from the scent of her perfume.

"Avrill knows you are pregnant with Eustace's baby." He pulled back and looked to make sure the door was closed. "Be careful, the servants are around to overhear us."

"William, I was wondering, how much are you going to provide for Avrill's dowry? And Ellene's?"

William relaxed, for he felt more comfortable discussing property and finances than relationships. "Avrill inherited her mother's clothes and jewels, and some money. I'll contribute crops, livestock, and some money to the dowry. Ellene inherited from our parents, and her late husband. When her husband died, his family returned most of her dowry. I've been guardian for both and managing their income and investments."

"It sounds like they are financially well off." She brushed her finger along his cheek, her words a gentle purr. "How much property do you own? How much will our son inherit?"

"Do we need to discuss this now? I own a prosperous estate. What is your concern?" William's stomach tightened with unease.

"Are you as rich as Eustace?" The gentle purr disappeared.

"I can't answer that since Robert and I did not complete the audit before Carlos assumed control of the estate." He examined her facial expression. These were uncomfortable questions. He thought she came in for a kiss and a cuddle, but he now realized her mind was on the money. "I can support you and our children comfortably. Does my wealth make a difference?"

"I simply want to clarify your circumstances, that's all." She stepped back. "I just remembered something I need to do. I'll see you later, darling."

She blew a kiss and the smell of her perfume lingered in the air as she scurried out the door.

William pursed his lips, trying to make sense of his conversation with her. Doubt crept in as he wondered if he had been mistaken about Marguerite. Is it possible she singled him out for his wealth?

Tension hung in the air during the evening meal. Marguerite stayed in her bedroom, pleading illness, and Sorcha took food to her. Avrill, usually cheerful, spoke little and pushed her food around her plate. She excused herself early, claiming she had a headache.

"Do you know what Avrill is worried about?" Ellene inquired of her brother.

"Avrill came to my office this afternoon. She voiced her worries about my relationship with Marguerite. She also asked about her marriage prospects. I had to admit I have not arranged for her to meet any eligible young men. She's not happy that I reject Thomas as a suitor. You agree with me, don't you?"

"It's not for me to say. You and Avrill need to do what is best for her. She may lose her fascination with Thomas when she meets other young men. Perhaps you could ask the vicar what he thinks about it."

William shook his head. "Unlike you, I put little store in what he has to say."

That night, Avrill lay on her bed, listening for Ellene to come upstairs. The sound of footsteps in the hallway caught her attention, prompting her to leave her room. She spied her aunt and followed her.

Ellene heard her and turned around, a look of surprise on her face. "Avrill. I thought you would be asleep by now." Ellene reached for her niece to give her a hug.

Avrill swerved to avoid her. Ellene's eyes widened and her eyebrows shot up with surprise.

"What is the matter?"

"Can we talk? I'm so confused." Sadness etched Avrill's face and her lips quivered as if she was about to cry.

"Yes. Certainly. Come to my room." Ellene opened her door and lit the candles in the room. Sorcha had already lit a fire in the fireplace. As the fire crackled and popped, the dancing flames cast a cozy glow. Avrill entered and sat on a chair near the hearth.

"What is troubling you?" Ellene's brow furrowed with concern.

Avrill had every intention of being mature when she confronted her aunt, but she couldn't hold back the tears that rolled down her face.

"Papa told me he may marry Marguerite. He admitted she's pregnant. I don't trust her, Aunt Ellene."

"Well, she is under much strain right now. You need to get to know her better. Still, her child is not a threat to you."

"Papa told me you and James are engaged and you never told me. Papa hates Thomas. Everybody treats me like a child. I don't know what to do."

Ellene handed her a handkerchief and let her cry until she gained her composure.

"I'm sorry I didn't tell you about being engaged to James. We still have much to discuss, and I don't want people to know yet. Your papa wasn't supposed to mention it either. We haven't set our wedding date yet. I will make sure that I don't abandon you before you marry."

"Marguerite's troubles have papa's full attention. He told me he is searching for a husband for me, but there have been no messengers lately. I know Marguerite wants you to leave."

"Oh, don't fret so. You will have many years to be married. Enjoy your freedom while you can. Marriage brings many responsibilities. Your duties will involve ensuring your husband's happiness and raising your children. All while overseeing the household and staff."

Avrill sat thinking for a few minutes, her tears subsiding. "Do you agree with papa that Thomas is too poor?"

"I think Thomas is an honorable man. He works hard and respects you. But you need a husband with a house and substantial income. It may take Thomas years to reach that status. James spent many years in the military before earning Haver Manor. He also waited while he put aside enough to consider marriage and a family." Ellene reached out and squeezed Avrill's hand. "How are the alterations going on your clothes? Has Pernilla finished them?"

A smile appeared on Avrill's face as she talked about the clothes. "They're beautiful. I feel so grownup when I try them on."

After a few minutes, she hugged Ellene and returned to her room.

Ellene sighed. She was remiss in making sure William continued the search. She was also worried James still did not know who poisoned Eustace. He had not yet cleared William and Marguerite. Their infatuation could give James reason to believe they were involved.

Chapter Thirty-Seven

ANOTHER HEIR

An uncomfortable silence filled the carriage as William and Marguerite journeyed to the hearing. The scent of her perfume pervaded the carriage. Her questions about money from the day before still bothered him. Instead of her usual cheerful chatter, she expressed worry about the upcoming hearing concerning her unborn child.

Robert waited for them at Callum's house. A servant escorted them to the sitting room, where the clerk waited. Zachary arrived soon after and sat near William. They watched in silence when the justice entered the room and assumed his seat.

After some preliminary remarks, Callum began asking questions, starting with Zachary.

"Is it your opinion that Marguerite Ellingham, widow of Eustace Ellingham, is with child?"

"I examined her and determined that she is indeed pregnant."

"According to your professional training, how long ago was the child conceived?"

"She appears to be about ten weeks along."

"When did her husband die?"

"About two weeks ago."

"Is it reasonable to conclude that she became pregnant while Eustace was still alive?"

"Certainly."

"And he, therefore, is the father of the child?"

"Yes, it is."

Satisfied, the justice turned his attention to Robert. "Is there any evidence showing Mrs. Ellingham was—um—unfaithful during her marriage?"

Marguerite felt Callum's piercing gaze as his eyebrows drew together in a stern line. She forced her facial muscles to remain in a serene expression, and her body to remain still. She feared any sign of nervousness would cause the justice to probe deeper. William glanced at her and then at the justice.

"No evidence, your honor," Robert stated firmly. James had not yet verified the report that Eustace denied the child was his.

The justice nodded, showing that he had decided on the pleading. "Harrumph. The court finds Eustace Ellingham is the father of Marguerite's unborn child. Despite that, the man claiming to be Carlos Ellingham has a prior claim to inherit Coeur de Lion."

"Your Honor, may I remind the court that there is credible evidence he is an impostor?" Robert spoke with deference.

"I'm waiting for additional evidence in that case. Do you have anything to present?"

"The sheriff assures me he has a witness who can identify the man as an impostor. We expect him to arrive next week for your hearing."

"Harrumph. If the man claiming to be Carlos is telling the truth, he will retain the estate. I'll appoint a guardian for the child. If Carlos loses the case, Marguerite may continue to use the estate for the child's care. According to the entailment, a male child shall assume control when he attains his majority. If it's a girl, I will award her a suitable dowry, but the estate will revert to the Crown." He stared at Robert with intensity. "Who do you propose as the guardian of her child?"

Robert replied, "Your honor, I am executor of the estate. Marguerite's guardian, Sir William Throck-Morton, has graciously agreed to take on the role of guardian to her child."

"Do you confirm that, Sir William?"

William cleared his throat. "Yes, Your Honor."

"Very well. I appoint Sir William Throck-Morton as guardian for Mrs. Ellingham and her unborn child." Callum looked at his paperwork. "Is there any other matter for me to consider today?"

"No, Your Honor," replied the clerk.

"I adjourn the hearing." As Callum stood up to leave, the legs of the chair made a scraping sound against the floor.

Marguerite turned to Robert. "I desire to move back to Coeur de Lion now. William and I need to repair some of the damage Carlos incurred."

"Who inherits is not final yet. If Carlos is indeed the son, his claim is superior to your child's and he will have the right to again occupy the house. If he is an imposter, you may stay there at least until the baby arrives." Robert spoke with caution, emphasizing the potential complications that lay ahead.

William frowned. "I advise against that. I fear it is not safe for you to go back yet. What about the person who poisoned Eustace? And the man who attacked you in the stable? There is a risk, especially for the child."

Marguerite directed her attention to William. "I'll be careful. Your concern is touching, but I'm willing to take that chance. I want to return to Haver Hall now so that I can pack."

James walked into Robert's office after the hearing and saw Robert at his desk, buried under a mountain of paperwork.

"What brings you here today, James? Not another crime, I hope."

"When are the bandits to be executed?" James pulled a chair over and sat, its worn wood creaking beneath him.

"Next week. Behind the jailhouse, the gallows is already being built by the carpenter. The prisoners can listen to the hammers as they await their fate. Callum wants to give them time to confess to any other crimes. So far, they've been silent. Broun met with them yesterday to hear their confession."

"And the trial for Carlos is next week?"

"Yes, when your witness arrives." Robert wrinkled his nose in disgust. He described the results of Marguerite's hearing earlier that day. "Callum did not give Marguerite permission to move back yet. She told William she wants to move back right away, even though her claim is subordinate to Carlos, despite the danger of Eustace's killer returning, and the assailant not being found."

"Interesting. I wonder why she is not afraid to stay there. She even dismissed the men I sent there to guard her."

"There's something else you might find interesting. I noticed William and Marguerite seem quite affectionate."

"I noticed that too. It is even more curious that she became pregnant just before Eustace died, when they have been married for several years." James mulled it over. "If Carlos's statement about Eustace not being the father of Marguerite's child is true, could William be the father? I'm on my way to talk to the servants."

"Let me know when you have something definite I can present to Callum."

James' mind raced as he rode to Coeur de Lion. Gripping the reins, his stomach twisted with dread, fearing what Prudence may tell him about Marguerite.

When he arrived, the cook was in the garden, pulling up carrots and turnips for the evening meal. Hearing the horse's hoofbeats, she straightened up and stretched to ease the tightness in her back. The turnips in her right hand had dirt still clinging to the roots.

"Sheriff, what brings you here? Nobody lives here anymore except us servants. Do you have news about the murder?"

"There was a hearing about Marguerite's baby." He stopped and observed her complexion turn ashen. "So, you knew about her pregnancy?"

"Now, Sheriff, I don't want to get involved in the mistress' affairs." Her eyes darted around the garden.

"I'll take that as a 'yes.' It seems the justice ruled it was Eustace's baby and an heir. Carlos is still being held pending more evidence about his real identity. Marguerite plans to move back here before the hearing next week." He paused. "I need to ask you something. According to a witness, you overheard Eustace and Marguerite arguing about her pregnancy. Is that true?"

Prudence remained silent.

"I'll keep your answer confidential. At least for now. What did Eustace say? This is important."

Her eyes darted, but James blocked her path out of the garden. Her shoulders drooped. "I heard Eustace shout at her. He mentioned Zachary told him about the pregnancy, and he knew it wasn't his child. She denied being pregnant. He warned if she was pregnant, he'd throw her out and disown the child."

"When did it happen?"

"A day or two before the banquet."

"Did you tell anyone about this?"

"Yes. The stableman. I was upset, you see. He and I go back a few years."

"Was she sick in the mornings before she moved to Haver Hall?"

"Yes." Prudence looked at the ground and hung her head. "Now I don't want to get Marguerite in trouble. The master mistreated her. Tried to choke her once."

"Did you ever see other men come to the house when Eustace was in the village?"

The cook looked like she was about to cry. "That Sir William used to visit her. He always claimed he brought a message from his sister. It was odd for him to come when he could have sent a messenger. And the mistress used to go to the barn by herself and stay a while. Came into the house with straw on her clothes."

"Did you ask her about it? Did you see anyone?"

"No, sir, I kept my eyes to myself. It wasn't any of my business."

James let out a slow breath. Going to the barn was not suspicious by itself, but it presented opportunities for her to rendezvous with a man other than Eustace. Could it have been William? He needed to confront

William and Ellene.

Low, gray clouds hung in the sky, and distant thunder echoed in the air. On his way to Haver Hall, James felt a sinking feeling in his stomach. He suspected Ellene would know the truth about Marguerite's pregnancy since they were close friends.

Jeremy greeted James and ushered him into the Great Hall. "Who are you here to see, Sir William or Lady Ellene?"

"I would like to speak to Lady Ellene in private."

James waited in the Great Hall until Jeremy returned with Ellene.

"James, what a pleasant surprise." Her lips curved into a smile, inviting a kiss. When he didn't respond, she stepped back. "What is the matter?"

"I'm here on official business. I need to speak to you. In private."

James saw Ellene's eyes widen with curiosity. "Let's go to the sitting room, shall we? I believe Avrill is in there, but I'll ask her to leave."

They walked in silence to the sitting room where Avrill worked on a needlepoint tapestry. He normally touched Ellene as they walked, but today he kept his hands at his sides.

When Avrill noticed James' presence, a bright smile stretched across her face, radiating happiness. "Hello, James. Or is it Uncle James?"

"Avrill, would you mind leaving this room for a few minutes? James and I need to have a private conversation." Ellene avoided her question.

With a crinkled brow, Avrill made a face that showed her displeasure. "I was about to go upstairs, anyway. How is Thomas?" Avrill put her needlework in a basket and stood to leave.

"He's well. He started helping me with my investigations." Avrill hugged

James, who rewarded her with a kind smile, leaving Ellene in a state of puzzlement.

After he closed the door, James faced Ellene, who waited to find out his mission. She stood, her feet planted, and her hands clasped at her waist.

He could hear his own breathing as he prepared for the critical conversation with Ellene that could change their relationship.

"Ellene, you must be honest with me about Marguerite. Is she pregnant with Eustace's child?"

"Why are you asking me? She told Zachary and Robert that Eustace is the father." Ellene sidestepped the question.

"I have a witness who says Eustace denied it was his child. I believe you share confidences with Marguerite, so I expect you know the truth." Ellene felt the weight of his gaze and glanced away. "You must tell me what you know. Our marriage must be based on us being honest with each other."

Ellene looked into his eyes, struck by their intensity. "I—I can't tell you. I assured her I wouldn't reveal what she told me."

"Would you lie to me to protect your friend?" With a firm grasp on her shoulders, their eyes locked, creating a moment of intense connection. "If she told you Eustace is not the father, you are lying to me when you say he is. I need to know the truth."

"But I promised." Ellene averted her gaze to the floor. "This is hard. You are making me choose between you, who I love, and my brother, who I also love."

James took his hand off one shoulder and lifted her chin with his finger until she again looked into his eyes.

Ellene's shoulders sagged as she released her breath. "You're right. I should not have agreed to cover for her." Then the words tumbled out.

Marguerite told her the child belonged to William. He did not deny it. And they conspired to claim it belonged to Eustace to protect her from charges of adultery, and so the child would be an heir to the estate. They feared if James knew the truth, he would think one of them had killed Eustace so they could marry each other.

"What will you do, James? Are you going to arrest my brother or Marguerite?" Ellene searched his face.

James took a deep breath as he released her. "I need to think this through. Thank you for being honest with me. I couldn't bear it if you weren't." He pulled her close and kissed her forehead. This time, when she turned her face up, he kissed her lips. He then pivoted and left the sitting room.

Ellene stared at the open doorway and listened to his steps in the hallway, heading toward William's office. She hurried after him.

William's door was open. As James approached, Ellene caught up to him and grabbed his arm. James' jaw dropped in surprise as he looked at her.

"I demand to be present when you confront my brother."

He heard the determination in her voice as she spoke, her face expressing her conviction.

"Of course. Come along."

William heard them in the hallway and met them there. "James, I didn't know you were visiting."

"I need to talk with you. Ellene asked to be present."

"It sounds like a serious issue. Come into my office."

The trio entered the office without speaking, and William shut the door. James refused the chair William offered. Ellene twisted her hands together as she stood with her back against a wall.

"I'm here in my official capacity. I want you to know that I'm aware of the scheme Marguerite and you concocted to claim her baby to be her late husband's. You know that is a fraud on the estate."

As he realized James knew the truth, William's face drained of all color. "Yes, she claimed the baby is mine. I told Robert it was Eustace's baby for the sake of protecting her."

James stared at William. "Then you admit to being with her before Eustace's death? According to Zachary, she was already pregnant when he died."

"No, it was after she came here. She's been here about a week."

"Then you couldn't be the father. She is about ten weeks along."

"I'm not the father? Why would she tell me the child is mine?" William's eyes widened in disbelief, and his mouth hung open.

"Why would she lie about it? That's a good question," James said. "If you thought it is yours, why agree to claim Eustace is the father?"

"She can claim the estate for her child," William responded.

"Do you know Zachary told Eustace she was pregnant? He denied the child was his, and threatened to divorce her." James asked in a flat voice.

With wide eyes, Ellene observed her brother with intensity.

"That I don't know." William shook his head, a look of disbelief crossing his face. "Was she trying to trick me into marrying her when she told me it was mine?" His shoulders slumped, and the sparkle was gone from his eyes.

"She's moving back to Coeur de Lion tomorrow. She's upstairs packing." Ellene stared at her brother. Something was amiss with him. "William, why do I feel there's something you're not telling us?"

"Yesterday, she asked about your and Avrill's dowries and how much money would remain in my estate after you both marry, and would I be as rich as Eustace. It seems she didn't like my answers because she abruptly left my office to pack." William hung his head.

"How soon were you planning to marry?" Ellene asked in bewilderment.

"She talked about a double wedding with you and James."

"We haven't fixed a date yet. But it will be before the end of the year. What are your thoughts, James?" Ellene felt a wave of confusion and fear wash over her.

"I can do nothing for now. Wanting a rich husband is not sufficient proof a wife poisoned her previous one. I need more proof to arrest someone. All I have are suspicions. I'll confront her when I have more proof."

CHAPTER THIRTY-EIGHT

RETURN TO COEUR DE LION

Unaware of James' visit, Marguerite stayed up all night packing her trunks. William and Ellene pressed her to stay at Haver Hall until after Carlos' hearing, but she refused. The next morning, William ordered Jeremy and Clive to load her trunks onto the wagon after breakfast. Ellene, Marguerite, and William rode alongside the wagon as they headed to Coeur de Lion.

When they arrived, Prudence met them at the front door. They explained that the justice ruled the baby Marguerite was carrying was Eustace's heir. Although warned by James the previous day, Prudence feigned ignorance and ushered them into the house. Clive and a male servant began carrying the trunks inside. Ellene, William, and Marguerite stood in the Great Hall, looking into the dining room.

Marguerite shook her head as she noticed the missing silver candlesticks, plate, and tapestries. "Did Carlos sell those items? What did he do with the money he received?"

"Carlos spent a lot on food and drink," declared the cook. "The tailor already cut down some of Eustace's clothes to fit him. Not knowing if he would pay, the tailor demanded his fee before starting the work."

"Perhaps we should search his room and see what is there," suggested Ellene.

They went upstairs to the master's bedroom. When they looked in the wardrobe and under the bed, they found some of the missing items in sacks. Carlos hid a purse full of gold and silver coins under the mattress. They piled the items in the middle of the bed.

Marguerite stood with her hands clasped, gazing at the sparkling treasure before her. "Well, he didn't dispose of it all, then. Ellene, could you and Prudence put the candlesticks and plates back where they belong? And William, will you come with me to the office so that I can put the money in the safe?"

William and Marguerite headed to the office while Ellene and Prudence gathered the other items and carried them downstairs to the dining room and Great Hall.

The moment they were alone in the office, William closed the door behind them. Marguerite's perfume filled the room with its intoxicating aroma. He pulled her into an embrace, wanting to test her interest in him.

"My love, are you sure you want to live here? If Carlos returns, he will again claim all the property. Besides, I'll miss seeing you every day." He leaned in to kiss her, but she turned her face away and squirmed out of his embrace. His mouth hung open in surprise.

"What is the matter, my love?" He held out his hands.

"I don't feel well." Her face fell into a deep frown. "Now that Callum declared my baby to be an heir, I think we should wait to get married until after he is born. If we marry before then, people will gossip that we married in haste. Besides, I must keep the estate until the boy reaches his majority.

Marrying you and living here while you live at Haver Hall would create an uncomfortable situation. In the meantime, there is much to do. We should be careful with how we interact with each other. People, especially the servants, love to gossip."

"But you declared your love for me. You talked of a double wedding with Ellene and James. What is different now?" William stretched out his hands.

In place of her usual sweet smile and flirtatious behavior, she seemed unapproachable. "I'm a wealthy woman now. Or at least I will be once Callum awards the estate to my son. Still, I want you to continue to be my guardian. Please, William. I think it is for the best right now."

"As you wish, my love." He reached for her hand. She allowed him to grasp it and kiss it.

William scanned the room and noticed Carlos had ransacked it. He scattered papers everywhere, looking for information about the money. Although Carlos retrieved the ledgers from Robert, William suspected he did not understand the entries. William and Marguerite picked up the papers and stacked them on the desktop.

Because of Marguerite's limited reading abilities, William knew she could not offer him any help. He sat behind the desk, shaking his head. "It'll take a while to sort and organize these documents. You're free to do something else. I'll call when I have some order restored."

"You are my hero, William. I don't know what I would do without you to help me." Marguerite gave him a kiss on the cheek before leaving the room.

William gazed at the door, feeling both regret and relief washing over him. Taking a break from their relationship might be the right decision for him and Marguerite. Was she showing off her beauty to trap him? Did she just want to find another rich husband?

Ellene and Clive returned to Haver Hall while her brother worked to organize the office.

William sought Marguerite after organizing and reviewing the documents. Marguerite was in the sitting room and rose to greet him with a kiss. He felt a sense of betrayal when he understood her actions were an attempt to manipulate him. With a deep breath, he composed himself and assumed his formal demeanor.

"As your guardian, I need to know your financial situation. I know you took property with you when you left. How much money do you have? Which servants need to be hired?" Taking a step back, William scrutinized her expression.

"I need to rehire the herdsman, the stableman, and my lady's maid. Prudence needs an assistant in the kitchen. We need to bring back the tenants' sheep."

"We should head to the office and develop a plan. I suspect your former servants are still in Haver Hamlet. I'll let them know they can return to work."

Marguerite prattled as they strolled down the hall to the office. William sat behind the desk while she glided through the door and settled in the chair opposite him. He made some quick calculations.

"Well, there is enough money for wages for the servants you need. And for food. But you need to be careful how fast you spend it. It needs to last until the harvest brings more money."

She objected, her voice low and husky. "But Eustace was rich. He promised me a new bodice and gown this fall. I need money for that."

"No, there's not enough for a bodice and gown. Eustace was corrupt.

He extorted money from some and didn't pay his debts to others. It made him appear he had more wealth than he did."

"Why can't you do that?" She thrust out her lower lip.

"Because I am honest. Word is getting around about his cheating. Nobody will put up with a return to his corrupt practices."

Marguerite fixed her eyes on William and mumbled, "I never thought I would say this, but I miss Eustace."

She hesitated when she saw the stunned look on William's face. "William, I found some money Eustace hid away, and I took it to prevent Carlos from getting his hands on it. I'll go get it. Maybe that will help with the expenses."

At his nod, she hurried from the room and returned a few minutes later with a purse. "Here, count this."

William's eyes bulged when he poured it onto the desktop and counted it. "Yes, this is a lot of money. There is enough for your bodice and gown."

Marguerite's eyes twinkled with delight, and she beamed. "Oh, wonderful, I shall go see Simon next week and select the fabric." She babbled about having spotted a brocade imported from Italy which would be beautiful in a bodice, gown, and sleeves. A new silk skirt would not go amiss. And slippers to match.

After William left to return to Haver Hall, Marguerite breathed a sigh of relief. If she married William, she would have to endure his miserly ways. She always wondered why Ellene and Avrill opted for simple, unassuming attire. It seems he would not pay for the more beautiful garments she preferred. Still, until a wealthier marriage partner presented himself, she would continue to tease and allure William. Better to have him as a potential suitor than no one at all, especially if she gave birth to a girl.

William located and rehired the herdsman, the stableman, and Marguerite's maid. He also found a servant to help in the kitchen. The maid and kitchen helper set to work cleaning the house. He spent little time with Marguerite, using his other responsibilities as an excuse.

The silence of the house oppressed Marguerite, making her feel isolated and disconnected. She invited Ellene, Avrill, and Molly to spend Wednesday afternoon with her. William escorted Ellene and Avrill to Coeur de Lion. As they were making their way, Avrill broke the silence.

"Papa, why did Marguerite move back to the estate? I thought it belonged to Carlos." Avrill furrowed her brow, looking perplexed.

William told her the details about Carlos and their questions about his claim on the estate. "The justice says Marguerite is pregnant with the mayor's child. It may inherit Coeur de Lion if Carlos is an imposter. So, it seemed logical to her to move back."

"Papa, are you still planning to marry her?"

"We have no plans to marry, *ma Cherie*," he replied tersely.

At the house, the servant led them to the cozy sitting room where Marguerite and Molly talked and giggled. Their conversation came to a halt as the servant entered, announcing Ellene and the Throck-Mortons. William greeted Marguerite but made his excuses for not staying. He bade the women goodbye and continued to the Smythe estate to visit Andrew.

"The house looks much better now." As Ellene took a quick glance around, she recalled the cluttered state that she and William had encountered when Marguerite moved back.

"You're amazing, Marguerite. Trying to run the estate without a husband and while pregnant is a heavy burden," Molly commented.

"William is a godsend. He and Robert sorted out the ledgers, took inventory, and renegotiated the contract with the miller. The harvest will be bountiful this year. I should make a lot of money." A dreamy expression appeared in her eyes.

"Did you return the portrait of Juanita and Carlos to the closet?" Ellene inquired.

"Not yet. The witness from Updyke Chase is coming to testify on Thursday. The justice still needs it as evidence for the trial when he arrives. Hopefully, the justice can find Carlos guilty and sentence him to be flogged and pilloried."

"How much did Carlos sell off?" Molly gave Marguerite a searching look.

Marguerite chuckled and raised her hands. "Well, I don't have a head for figures. William or Robert would have to tell you that."

"William is skilled in handling finances. I will attest to that," Ellene interjected.

The conversation stopped when the servant arrived with the refreshments. She carried a tray with bread, cheese, wine, and an ornate jar filled with honey.

Marguerite's mouth dropped open, and her complexion turned ghostly pale.

"Where did you find that jar?" Marguerite's hands trembled as she shouted.

Ellene leaned back, her eyes widening at her friend's outburst. Molly gasped in surprise and her hand flew to her throat. Avrill glanced at her aunt, wondering how she should react.

"In the pantry, mistress. Prudence pointed it out." The servant's body shook as she shrank away.

"That is my husband's special jar. He declared the honey off limits and no one else may touch it. Give it to me. I'll remove it." Marguerite jumped up, gripped the jar, and rushed from the room. Her footsteps echoed in the hallway as she fled. They heard her go up the stairs and take it to her bedroom.

Ellene rose to follow her, but then stopped. Paralyzed with indecision, the servant wrung her hands in distress.

"What shall I do? I didn't know I wasn't supposed to serve it. The cook told me to." The servant's voice shook with fear.

"It is just a jar of honey. Eustace is no longer around to scold her. What could cause Marguerite's reaction?" Molly speculated, her voice tinged with uncertainty.

"She appeared angry and afraid," commented Avrill.

"I'm not sure what the problem is." Ellene shook her head. She opted not to disclose that she and James had reason to believe that the jar contained poison. "Eustace's jar went missing after the banquet. She seemed frightened."

Ellene moved to the door and looked into the hallway. By that time, Marguerite reappeared from the stairway. She regained her composure, grinning and giggling.

"Silly me. Eustace would have been furious to have his honey served to others. I guess I just reacted out of habit." She directed her attention towards the servant. "I think there are berries in the kitchen. Bring those for our guests." She resumed her seat and waited for Ellene to sit.

"Have you seen the new fabrics at Simon's shop?" Marguerite changed the subject. "William says I may have the new gown Eustace promised me."

The women discussed the newest fabrics and fashionable colors. The mood changed, but Ellene made a mental note to tell James about the incident.

CHAPTER THIRTY-NINE

DECISION ABOUT CARLOS

R usty and Twig escorted Obediah to Haver Hamlet. Obediah stayed at the White Stag Inn after they arrived in the village on Wednesday afternoon. James informed Callum, who then scheduled Carlos' trial for the following day.

On Thursday morning, Thomas headed to the jail to conduct Carlos to the White Stag to resume the trial. Carlos was dirtier and more disheveled than the previous week. Thomas tied the prisoner's wrists and lead him towards the bustling inn.

"You can't do this. If you let me escape, I'll see that you receive a large sum of money." Carlos shifted and pleaded, his voice trembling with fear. "I can give you more than James pays you."

"I'm doing my job. Shut up and keep walking." Thomas jerked his arm.

Carlos dragged his feet, but Thomas grabbed his arm and urged him to walk faster. As before, a jeering crowd of onlookers surrounded the inn. James met them at the entrance. Rows of chairs and benches faced the justice of the peace's table, which was positioned at the end of the room.

James glanced around the public room and noticed fewer people attending this phase of the trial. He hoped the trial would resolve the matter of Carlos and the inheritance. Perhaps the novelty was wearing off. Ellene and William sat near the back. He caught Ellene's eye and nodded, but made no further attempt to communicate with her. Marguerite entered the inn and sat with the siblings in the rear.

The men who formed the jury for the first hearing sat on the side of the room, whispering and pointing.

Obadiah descended the stairs with Rusty and made his way to James' side. James gave the signal for the court clerk to start. The color drained from Carlos' face when he recognized the witness. The clerk announced the justice of the peace, who shuffled into the room and assumed his place behind the table.

"Today we resume the trial of Carlos Ellingham," the court clerk intoned. "He stands accused of impersonating the son of the late Eustace Ellingham, and of committing fraud and theft when he sold various items belonging to the estate."

Callum addressed the clerk. "Call the witness."

The clerk rose and called the goldsmith to come forward. Callum began questioning him.

"State your name, where you live, and occupation."

"Obadiah Strand," he responded. "I live in Updyke Chase. I'm a Master Goldsmith."

Callum's eyes locked with Obediah's as he addressed him, the gravity of their conversation hanging in the air. "Do you recognize the defendant?"

"Yes, Your Honor."

"What is his name?"

"I know him as Rafe Beall. He used to be my apprentice."

"Did you know his father and mother personally?"

"Yes, Your Honor."

"What were their names and where did they live?"

"His mother Maud married Jeremiah Beall. Rafe was born a few miles from Updyke Chase. I've known him all his life."

"Do you know where he lives now?"

"A room in a cottage near Updyke Chase is where he stores his personal effects. He spent a few years in London, then returned with a woman. He told us she was a cousin. She no longer lives there."

"Why is he no longer your apprentice?"

"I caught him stealing gold when he was designing jewelry."

Callum asked other questions pertaining to Carlos' character, then concluded his examination.

"I have no further questions. The witness may resume his seat." He waited as Obadiah returned to sit near James.

Fixing his gaze on the clerk, Callum inquired, "Do you have any additional witnesses in this case?"

"No, Your Honor."

"The defendant will rise."

Carlos stood, a sneer on his face.

"Do you have anything to say in your defense?" The justice's face was devoid of any expression, giving nothing away.

"I deny the charges. I don't know this man, and I've never been to Updyke Chase. My parents were Eustace and Juanita. The portrait is of someone else, not my mother. I object to this miscarriage of justice."

"Do you have any witnesses to prove Juanita was your mother? You have presented us with nothing but a piece of paper. We have no proof

Juanita possessed it. Yet we have one witness who says the mother and boy in the portrait are Juanita and Carlos, but you don't have his birthmark. We have another witness who has known you from birth who says you are not Carlos."

"Your Honor, that is not a picture of me and my mother. The old woman is confused," he protested. "I don't know who this man is. I never worked for him. The sheriff conspires against me." As his eyes widened, they flickered from Callum to James, and then back to Callum, filled with confusion and uncertainty.

"You may sit."

"But Your Honor—,"

"I think the jury has heard enough evidence. Sheriff, see to the defendant."

James stood and started toward Carlos, who stopped talking and sat. James resumed his seat. Callum repeated the charges, then instructed the jury to assess the evidence and render a verdict. After a quick discussion, the jury foreman stood. "We reached a verdict, Your Honor."

Callum fixed his gaze on Carlos. "The defendant will rise."

With a clear look of defiance on his face, Carlos stood in front of the justice. James and Thomas stood nearby, watching him.

"Your Honor, we find he isn't Eustace Ellingham's son Carlos. We declare the defendant guilty of fraud, impersonation, and theft."

The room was abuzz with voices. James stood and shouted for the observers to be silent. The fierce expression on James' face made them halt their conversation.

With calm restored, Callum again focused his attention on the man now known as Rafe Beall.

"Harrumph. Rafe Beall, I sentence you to be flogged in public and put in the pillory for three days. I order you to return the money and other items removed from Coeur de Lion. The inventory prepared by Mr. White after Mayor Ellingham's death will determine what you owe. Sheriff, you may take this man back to the jail to await his punishment." He adjourned the court, then left the room.

James and Thomas dragged Rafe, cursing and protesting, out of the inn. As he passed Marguerite, Rafe shouted, "I'll get you back for this."

Marguerite's face was pale with fear, her wide eyes reflecting her confusion. Others in the room looked bewildered.

"Keep moving," James growled as he jerked Rafe toward the door.

William approached Obediah and thanked him for his testimony, then introduced him to Ellene and Marguerite.

Obadiah peered at Marguerite. "Don't I know you? Aren't you Rafe's cousin from London?"

"No, you are mistaken. I never met the man until he came to Haver Hamlet." Abruptly, she turned to William. "Well, that's resolved. I'll probably never receive restitution for all that he stole, but he will no longer have a claim on Coeur de Lion." Marguerite turned her back to Obediah and rested a hand on William's arm. "Please escort me back to my home now."

"Certainly, immediately," he swallowed nervously.

"William, I'll wait for you in James' office. Stop for me on your way back to Haver Hall." It did not surprise Ellene that her brother gave in to Marguerite once more.

Marguerite bid Ellene goodbye before she and William left the inn. By then, the crowd of onlookers dispersed. As William assisted Marguerite to her carriage, Ellene strolled toward James' office to wait for her brother to return.

Marguerite descended from her carriage and faced William as soon as they reached Coeur de Lion.

"I don't know how to match Robert's inventory with the items still in the house. If you have some free time tomorrow, I would be so grateful for your help." Her words were gentle, and she gazed at him with admiration.

Her gentle words and heady perfume used to entice him to agree to anything. But now he understood that her desire was his money. After he uncovered her lie to trick him, William became more cautious.

"I'll return tomorrow and bring Ellene to help. We won't be able to stay for long. Ellene and I have to redirect our attention to Avrill's marital situation and managing Haver Hall. Lately, your legal matters consumed all my attention, leaving my estate neglected."

"Yes, bring Ellene. I do so enjoy her company." Her voice was not as inviting as before.

As the trio returned to the jail, Rafe's curses and grumbles filled the air. About halfway there, he stumbled into Thomas.

Thomas growled. "You clumsy oaf."

"You're walking too fast. Remember, I'm tied up. I tripped on a rut in the street and lost my balance."

Thomas jerked his arm and steered him toward the jailhouse. "Shut up and keep going."

Rafe continued to grumble as they finished the brief journey. Thomas handed the prisoner over to the jailer, who dragged him back to his cell. The other prisoners hooted at him as the jailer opened the door.

"Hey, how long do I have to stay here?" Rafe demanded.

"Until they drag you out and administer the punishment. I don't know how long," James replied.

Rafe cursed and spat, his eyes flashing with the intensity of a cornered animal. Thomas and the jailer wrapped the rope around the man's wrists, securing him to an iron ring on the wall. The jailer shut and locked the cell door.

While Thomas returned to Haver Manor, James headed for his office. Taking a deep breath, James savored the village air. Although it smelled of animals, smoke, and cooking, it was a vast improvement from the prison's stench. He felt relief as Rafe and the bandits were no longer a threat. Still, he needed to solve Eustace's murder. His thoughts overwhelmed him as he made his way to his office. When he opened the door, his eyes brightened with delight when they landed on Ellene. Her lavender scent filled the room. Their arms wrapped around each other in a comforting embrace.

"What a pleasant surprise. I expected you and William would be on your way back to Haver Hall by now."

"He escorted Marguerite to her house. He plans to stop here so we can return home together. Also, I want to tell you about something that happened yesterday."

Ellene recounted going with Avrill to Coeur de Lion to meet Marguerite and Molly. "But something strange occurred. The servant brought out the jar of honey that belonged to Eustace. Marguerite's voice shook with rage as she yelled at the servant that it belonged to her husband and was not for guests. The servant told me the cook pointed to it in the pantry."

"The pantry? It wasn't there when I searched the kitchen. Go on."

"Marguerite grabbed the jar and fled from the sitting room. I heard her go upstairs, and when she returned, she apologized for being silly about the honey. The sudden appearance of the jar seemed odd."

"Odd indeed. I wonder if Prudence hid the jar. If so, why reveal it now?" James sighed and shook his head in frustration.

"I suspect Marguerite didn't know where it was. The evening Eustace died, William and I took her upstairs, and Zachary gave her something to make her sleep. When I returned to the Great Hall, the servants cleared most of the food away, including the honey."

James gave a slight shrug. "If she knows it is poison, she probably has disposed of it by now. If she killed her husband by poisoning his honey, how do we prove it?"

"Put it out for the rats to eat. If they die, it will be a proof of poison," Ellene offered.

"We might prove her knowledge that the honey contains poison, but not that she put the poison in the honey."

Ellene nodded. "That's true. What do you make of Rafe's last words to Marguerite as he was leaving the inn?"

"Empty posturing, I hope. I don't know why he would blame her. If he survives the brutal flogging and being locked in the pillory, I expect he will flee the village. I don't expect he would dare to return."

While they talked, William arrived in James' office to join Ellene.

"Marguerite asked us to help her with the inventory. Will you have time tomorrow, Ellene?"

"Why does she need your help?" James was curious.

"I discovered she can barely read or write. She needs someone to read the inventory to her and make a list of what is missing."

Frowning, Ellene shifted her gaze to William. "Maybe you should let someone else be her guardian. Or do you want to keep catering to her needs?"

"No, now that I know her actual interest is my wealth, I need to back off. We can help tomorrow and defer to Robert to find someone else to be her guardian next time she asks." The expression on William's face was sorrowful. "Ellene, are you ready to go? Your horse is outside."

"I'm finished here. I'll ride with you as far as Haver Manor." James collected his weapons and bonnet.

William nodded in agreement. "We are glad for your company. When you retrieve your horse, we can be on our way."

During the ride home, the tension in James's shoulders melted away as he felt a momentary respite from the investigations. As they arrived at the lane leading to Haver Manor, they bid each other farewell, and Ellene and William continued their journey.

James and Thomas shared their evening meal in silence. James pleaded exhaustion, then went to his bedroom and changed into his nightshirt. Collapsing onto his bed, his thoughts were about Ellene.

Soon they would be married, and she would be there by his side. He felt frustrated because he hadn't yet solved Eustace's murder. Sleep soon overtook him.

With only the flickering light from the torch in his hand, James navigated through a dark tunnel. Sweat trickled down his face. Pausing near what looked like an exit, he became transfixed by what he saw in front of him. A colossal spider web, with thick strands extending from wall to wall and floor to ceiling, blocked his path. Beneath the web were human bones scattered across the floor. Hearing a noise behind him, he twirled around to see a large black spider advancing toward him. Its fangs dripped venom, and he knew if it bit him, he would die.

James woke with a start, his heart pounding. Without thinking, he snatched up the dagger that lay within arm's reach next to his bed. As he looked around and realized he was in his own bedroom, his heart rate slowed and he settled back onto his bed.

CHAPTER FORTY

MANHUNT

Rafe's nostrils burned from the stench that permeated the cramped cell. He had a plan to escape, but had to wait for the right time to spring it. Among the skills Rafe learned in London was the ability to pick the pockets of unsuspecting victims. When he stumbled into Thomas while en route to the jail, he removed a dagger from Thomas' baldric. The theft had gone unnoticed so far. Inside the jail, the only sounds came from the bandits confined in their cell. The faint light from the moon touched the walls and floor.

With some effort, he freed one hand from the rope securing him to the wall. Then he pulled the dagger from a hidden pocket in his breeches. He freed himself from his restraints by using the thin blade to sever the rope on his other wrist. When he could move about unhampered, he took the next step in his plan.

"Jailer. Jailer." He bellowed in anguish, his groans piercing the silence. "Help me, I think someone poisoned me."

The jailer woke from his sleep. "What's that racket? I don't care if ye are sick. I'll see to ye in the morning."

"Help me now. OOOOHH, my stomach hurts." He shrieked like a banshee.

Cursing, the jailer tumbled out of bed, lit a torch, and stumbled to the cell. He put the torch in the wall bracket and unlocked the door, leaving the keys in the lock. Suddenly, Rafe was silent. The jailer entered the dark cell but could see no one.

"Where are ye? Are ye dead? Rafe, what's going on?"

Rafe darted from the corner to put his dagger at the jailer's throat. "Welcome to my cell. That's right, careful. No sudden moves or I'll slit your throat."

The jailer stumbled as Rafe pushed him to his knees, then hit him on the back of his head with the butt of the dagger. Rafe fled, locking the cell door behind him. The jailer lay on the filthy floor, stunned. The highwaymen shouted to be released too, but Rafe ignored them.

Rafe surveyed the village streets for passersby and was pleased to see they were empty. Every now and again, a gust of wind stirred, rippling through the leaves like a wave. He was familiar with the roads in Haver Hamlet and the moonlight helped him find the road to Coeur de Lion. A snicker escaped him as he imagined Marguerite's expression when she heard about his escape.

As he reached Coeur de Lion, he crept to the back of the house, blending into the shadows. The lock on the back door was easy for him to pick with the thin blade. Carefully, he opened the door, slipped into the kitchen, and tiptoed across the floor. The stillness of the dark house was palpable. He planned to discard his filthy clothes, wash off the grime from the cell, then put on clean clothes. He intended to retrieve what he hid in the master's bedroom and steal a horse. If all went well, he would be long gone before they discovered his escape. He tiptoed up the stairs as he headed to the master's bedroom.

Once in the bedroom, Rafe lit a candle and opened the wardrobe. He needed something inconspicuous for travel. The tailor altered the brocade and velvet clothes to fit him, but they would attract attention. The clothes he brought in his pannier still hung in the wardrobe. He put the candle on a side table and started rummaging for his loot. Assuming the house was empty, he did not worry about how much noise he made.

In her bedroom down the hall, Marguerite tossed and turned, the stifling air making it difficult for her to get comfortable. Her thoughts kept returning to Rafe's trial, the words of Callum's sentence still echoing in her mind. An unfamiliar sound startled her, interrupting her thoughts. She listened with full concentration. It sounded like it came from Eustace's bedroom. She trembled at the thought of her dead husband's ghost returning to haunt her, and she could not shake the feeling of dread.

Marguerite rolled out of bed, wearing only her chemise, and grabbed a shawl to ward off the morning chill. She would peek into the room to verify if it was an intruder. Maybe someone left the window open, and a cat found its way in. She did not know if the servants would come to her rescue if she screamed.

A creaking floorboard in her bedroom made her wince as she made her way across it. She opened the door to reveal the dark corridor connecting the two bedrooms. The musty odor of neglect clung to the short passage as she quietly walked through. A soft glow of light shone from the bottom of the master's bedroom door. How careless of a servant to leave a candle burning. Or was someone stealing his property? Maybe the prowler who attacked her in the barn was in the bedroom. She regretted dismissing

James' guards.

Opening the door, she spotted Rafe by the wardrobe. The squeaking hinges made her cringe. Rafe jumped, then twirled around and saw her standing with her mouth open. He leaped across the room, putting his hand over her mouth, and pinned her to the wall.

"Not a word. If you scream, I'll slit your throat." He raised the blade stolen from Thomas.

She widened her eyes and nodded to show she understood. The reek of his clothes, acquired during his stint in jail, made her stomach churn. He dropped his hand from her mouth and grabbed her by her hair, dragging her over to the bed. He pushed her onto the bed and put his face close to hers.

"So, my poppet, you plan to abandon me to a flogging and the pillory while you live a luxurious life."

"No, no." Her voice faltered, and she stammered, unsure of what to say. "You know I do whatever you tell me to."

"I saw you at the trial, clinging to Sir William, seeking comfort and security. Are you planning to marry him?" He could sense her guilt by observing her expression. "Aha, I'm right. You—you—I rescued you from the London streets and this is how you treat me?"

Rafe stared at her. She grew up with middle-class parents who died when she was in her mid-teens. To survive, she had to work as a prostitute. He invited her to live with him. During one of Eustace's trips to London, Rafe introduced him to Marguerite. Eustace became infatuated with her and married her, believing that because she was young and poor, he could control her. Juanita, who had an affluent family, could rely on them for support. Marguerite and Rafe assumed because of Eustace's poor health, he would die soon, and she would inherit his property. Alas, he lived on, despite the odds against him.

"But what could I do? Your scheme to impersonate Carlos wasn't working. You were wasting the estate's money. I need someone to protect me. William was delighted to take me in."

"You imagine a man in his class would marry you? Bah. Regardless of your looks, he'll investigate your background and find out you're an impostor, like me. He'll reject you and marry a woman of his class who has a dowry."

Marguerite's face was wet with tears. "I'm sorry, Rafe. I don't know what I was thinking. Please forgive me. I'll do what you say, I promise."

Rafe released her hair. "I heard the cook say you're pregnant. Whose baby is it? It had better be mine."

"It is yours, Rafe. I lied, saying it was Eustace's to qualify for the estate. The justice is letting me live here until the baby is born. If the child's a boy, he'll inherit the estate."

"Did you lay with William?"

"Yes, but it meant nothing, I swear. At first, I wanted to entice him to marry me. But much of the property he controls will go to Ellene and Avrill. If I married William, I would not be as rich as I am now."

Rafe glared at her. "I need to leave this country. Now I'm free from that filthy jail, I plan to travel abroad and leave my past behind. You can stay and risk being exposed, or go with me. We can take the gold and silver in this house and live in luxury for many years."

Marguerite searched his face. William had always been gentle and respectful towards her, but if he discovered her background, he might withdraw his offer of marriage. Rafe knew the worst about her and still wanted her to be with him. "I'll go with you. But not in the middle of the night. We need to rise early and pack what we can. We'll be long gone before anyone knows you've escaped."

"Well, I need a bath and some clean clothes. Get a servant to heat the water. Set it up in your room and let me know when it's ready. Don't let anyone know I'm here." He yanked her off the bed and shoved her toward the door.

The oppressive darkness filling the jail cell lingered until after dawn. As the jailer opened his eyes, he felt the cold, hard ground beneath him and inhaled the stench of the filthy straw. Dazed, he rubbed the throbbing lump on his head and remembered what had happened during the night. He stumbled to the cell door, only to find it locked. The jailer called for help, but the villagers dismissed it as a troublesome prisoner and continued with their tasks.

As Thomas prepared for the day ahead, a sense of unease settled in when he discovered that one of his knives had gone missing. He notified James and accompanied him to the village to search for it between the White Stag Inn and the jail. When they arrived in Haver Hamlet, the villagers were just beginning their trek to the market to sell their wares.

Thomas started at the inn and made his way along the street, staring at the dirt road, hoping to see the glint of metal. He worried that someone may have already picked it up.

He heard shouts as he approached the jailhouse. Recognizing the voice, Thomas rushed into the building and found the locked cell holding the jailer. He located the keys to the cell and opened the door. The jailer found it difficult to stand because of the blow to his head. Blood from the wound matted his hair. Thomas guided the jailer, his arm supporting his weight, towards the entrance. He hailed a passerby, directing him to summon the physician. While they waited, the jailer told him how Rafe tricked him the night before.

Thomas' jaw dropped in astonishment. Rafe must have stolen his dagger and used it to escape. "Will you be all right if I leave now? I need to find James and let him know what's happened." Thomas glanced around, hoping to see someone approach who could help him.

The jailer held his head with one hand and waved the other, signaling for Thomas to leave. Thomas ran to James' office, but he was not there. Returning to the street, he noticed James approaching with confident strides. He ran toward James, waving his hands.

"James, he has escaped. Rafe escaped from the jail last night."

"Tell me what happened." James stopped and all the color drained away from his face.

Thomas repeated what he learned from the jailer, and his own conclusion that Rafe stole his missing dagger.

James rubbed his chin. "Probably headed to Coeur de Lion. He's not aware we found his loot. Marguerite may be in danger. We need to get some bloodhounds after his scent, then go to Coeur de Lion and warn her. He should have submitted to the flogging and left the village. This time he'll hang for sure."

They traveled a short distance from the village and arrived at a two-room cottage where bloodhounds milled around the yard. The owner came out to see what they wanted. After hearing about their urgent need for the dogs, he wasted no time in agreeing to provide help.

"I believe you can get Rafe's scent from the jail. Let's go there and tell the jailer you need access to the ropes that restrained him." James' forehead creased in a frown.

The men hurried to the jailhouse with the dogs baying and sniffing, eager to be hunting.

When the jailer saw James, he cringed. "Sheriff, it wasn't my fault. Rafe claimed he was dying. He had a knife on him and knocked me out."

"We can worry about how he escaped later." James explained their mission.

The jailer produced the ropes used to restrain Rafe. The hounds picked up the scent and started toward Coeur de Lion.

"Was he on foot, or did he steal a horse?"

"No information that he stole a horse, Sheriff."

"Even on foot, he has many hours' head start. He may plan to steal a horse from the estate. It's possible that he's in the next county by now." James learned the hard way not to underestimate Rafe. He again thought about resigning. The army trained him to fight battles, not arrest pickpockets.

The bloodhounds sniffed along the ground, noses twitching as they followed Rafe's scent. James organized a posse of men in the village to follow the dogs and find Rafe. He also sent a messenger to warn the residents south of the village in case Rafe headed in that direction.

"We need to warn Marguerite about his escape. He may show up looking for money and a horse. Let's head that way." James wheeled his horse around and set off for Coeur de Lion with Thomas close behind.

CHAPTER FORTY-ONE

KILLER IDENTIFIED

As William and Ellene rode towards Coeur de Lion, the sound of their horses' hooves echoed through the quiet morning, creating a sense of anticipation for the task ahead. An unusual flurry of activity in the village caught their attention as they rode through.

They caught up with a man leading a horse hitched to a cart loaded with goods to trade at the market.

"What is causing all this commotion in the village?" William stopped next to the trader.

The man squinted at William. "That feller pretending to be the mayor's son escaped during the night. Knocked out the jailer. Sheriff's organizing hounds and a posse."

Ellene gasped as her hand rose to clutch her throat. "William, he may try to harm Marguerite. We need to warn her."

"That was my thought. Let's go." William's face was tight with a grim set to his jaw.

The siblings urged their horses to gallop. Along the way, they recognized Prudence and the maid from Coeur de Lion walking along the road toward the village carrying panniers. In a short time, they reached the courtyard at Coeur de Lion.

The stableman was just mounting his horse when they arrived.

"What is happening? We saw two servants heading toward the village."

"This morning the mistress called us all into the Great Hall, reported she's going on a long journey, and sacked the lot of us."

"That's odd. She just returned to her house. We are supposed to help her review the contents today. Where is Marguerite?" William leaped from his horse.

"The mistress is inside."

"What could have happened?" William stroked his beard.

The stableman shrugged his shoulders. "I don't know, Sir William. She didn't say."

"Did she say anything about the man pretending to be Carlos escaping? Maybe she's afraid he'll come here." Ellene's voice trembled with worry.

"Escaped, ye say? Didn't hear about that. When did it happen?"

"Last night, apparently. We found out when we rode through the village. Are you leaving now?" William's voice was tense.

"Yes sir. I collected my belongings and my horse. I won't be back."

"When you get to the village, find the sheriff and let him know we're here. He's there organizing a posse." William's brow furrowed.

The stableman reassured them he would and set off at a trot.

"William, I don't like this at all." Ellene felt a shiver run down her spine.

William uttered a grunt of agreement, and they rushed into the house. Several panniers sat on the floor near the entrance. They could hear two different voices coming from the office. One voice belonged to Marguerite. The other voice was a man.

William threw open the office door to see Marguerite and Rafe hunched over a ledger on the desk. The door to the safe was open, and the safe was empty. Ellene gasped, while William clenched his fists and gritted his teeth in fury.

"What are you doing here, Rafe? You should be in jail waiting for your punishment." William erupted in a fiery rage.

Rafe pulled out a sword before William could reach for his blade. Rafe grabbed Marguerite and put the sword to her throat. Her face twisted in fear.

"Sir William, just stay where you are and put your weapons on the desk. I'll kill her if you don't do as I say."

Color drained from William's face as he unsheathed his knives and put them on the desk. Ellene chose not to reveal the dagger hidden in her skirt pocket. Her breathing was shallow, and her heart raced. She watched Rafe as he spoke, fearful he would injure Marguerite.

"Now, turn around slowly. We're going upstairs to the closet in the hallway."

"What are you going to do to Marguerite?" William gestured.

Rafe released her. Her tinkling laughter echoed off the walls of the room. She grinned at William and Ellene.

"The looks on your faces." More laughter. "It turns out Rafe is my lover. We're going to take the gold and silver from the estate and start a new life in France."

"Why Marguerite? You gazed into my eyes and declared you wanted to spend the rest of your life with me. Were you pretending?"

"Of course. I never loved you, William." She beamed a warm smile in Rafe's direction.

"If you help him escape, they will track you down and put you both in jail." William's eyes widened, and he croaked, "You'll face a flogging and the pillory if you take that risk."

"Brave words from a man about to die. It will take a better man than your sheriff to keep me behind bars. Now move." Rafe brandished his sword in a wide arc, the blade coming close to Ellene's torso.

Ellene and William reversed their direction and headed down the hall and up the stairs towards the closet.

"Marguerite, open the door. You two enter the room. Don't bother trying to escape." Rafe's words came out through clenched teeth.

The siblings paused for a moment. Ellene thought of refusing, but the blade was long and sharp. Rafe could injure or kill them both and dispose of their bodies. Their presence was known only to the stableman, who may not alert James in time. James would be busy searching for Rafe and not stop to look for them. If they obeyed Rafe, they had a chance of catching him unawares. Ellene could see the fear in William's eyes when they exchanged glances. Marguerite opened the door to the dark closet, and the musty smell hit Ellene in the face.

"Marguerite, the least you could do is explain why you are doing this." Ellene confronted the woman she believed was her friend. "You know you can rely on us. We're trying to help you."

"Humph. I don't owe you anything, but I'll tell you, anyway. You both will soon be dead so you can't tell anyone else." Her brow furrowed in anger. "Following the death of my parents, I found myself thrown into the harsh realities of London's streets, resorting to selling my body for survival. Rafe rescued me and arranged my marriage to Eustace. Rafe and I had a tryst in the barn two months ago. I unfortunately became pregnant, and Eustace found out. The day of the banquet, he threatened to send me away without a farthing, so I knew I had to stop him. I found the wolfsbane and mixed it into his honey. He should have died that afternoon before the banquet. If he had, the physician would have ruled it heart failure and James would never have been involved. I hid the remains of the wolfsbane in the waste pile. Apparently not well enough, since James found it."

"Is that why you were upset when the servant brought the jar of honey to the sitting room?" Ellene stared at Marguerite.

"Someone misplaced the jar when they cleaned up after the banquet, so I wasn't able to dispose of it like I planned."

Marguerite's words caused William's face to contort in fear, as if he were watching a poisonous spider crawling towards him. Rafe found some rope in the closet. He passed a piece of rope to Ellene.

"Tie his hands behind his back. Be quick."

Ellene looped the rope around her brother's wrists, but not too tight. Rafe tested the knot and tightened it. "Sit on the floor. Both of you. Back-to-back."

They hesitated, but obeyed when he threatened them with his sword. How could they run, or strike back, from the floor? Rafe held the sword while Marguerite tied Ellene's wrists, then wrapped the rope around the siblings so they couldn't move. To prevent them from making any noise, she gagged them. Ellene, her heart racing, felt sweat trickling down her back. She resolved not to cry because they needed their wits about them.

"Don't make a sound. We'll be here for a while yet, and if I hear you making noise, I'll run you through with my sword." Rafe glowered at them and followed Marguerite into the hallway. He locked the door behind him, leaving them in darkness.

With a violent cough, Ellene expelled the gag from her mouth.

"Wretched man. William, can you talk?" With trembling lips, she whispered, fearful their captors were listening. "I have a dagger in my skirt. I'll try to reach it."

In response, William emitted a brief, gruff sound.

"How did we misjudge Marguerite so badly? I regarded her as a friend, someone I could trust and rely on. There was warmth in her voice whenever she spoke about you, a genuine affection that made me believe she loved you. It appears she was putting on an act, trying to survive." Ellene shook her head, her lips pursed in frustration. Her hand shook as she tugged at her skirt to retrieve the dagger.

Smoke wafted into the room under the door.

"Do you smell the smoke? I think Rafe set fire to the house. He wants to burn us alive." Ellene's voice was frantic.

William squirmed and mumbled.

"I can't imagine they are still here with the house on fire. I prefer to be killed by a sword than by being burned alive."

William kept making noises, like he was trying to talk. In the meantime, Ellene twisted her body until she grasped the hilt of her dagger and removed it from her pocket. The smoke grew thicker, stinging their eyes.

"I can't cut my rope." She wiggled. "I can reach your wrists, though. Hold still."

Ellene felt William's wrists, then the rope. She sawed at the rope until it finally snapped, and William's hands were free. He took the dagger from Ellene, then pulled out his gag and untied the rope that bound them together. Finally, he untied the rope around Ellene's hands and helped her to her feet.

"Quietly now. We need to get out of the house. Maybe we can sneak down the back stair." The urgency and fear in his voice were unmistakable.

With every passing minute, the smoke grew denser and more suffocating. William hurried to the locked door. On the way, he stubbed his toe on a mace. Picking up the mace, he pounded against the door until it shattered, letting in light and smoke from the hallway. He no longer cared about the noise. He had the mace to use against Rafe if it came to that.

The sight of flames licking the ground floor and the first four steps sent a wave of fear through the siblings. They could smell lamp oil which fed the flames. William hurried down the hallway to the back stairs, only to encounter flames and smoke there as well.

"Both stairways are on fire." William coughed as he hurried back to his sister. "We need to get past the fire and get out of the house."

"We may have to go into a bedroom and climb out of a window."

Ellene's thoughts were spinning, and her heart raced. The memory of being in their stable loft when it caught fire flashed through her mind. She had jumped into a haystack and James caught her. Today there were no haystacks for them to dive into, and James was nowhere to be seen. They came to warn Marguerite, but how could they know Marguerite was Rafe's accomplice? If she and William died, it would leave Avrill without her father and her aunt. Would James take Avrill in and find her a husband?

James and Thomas could hear the hounds' baying behind them as they galloped toward Coeur de Lion. They spotted the stableman on the road headed toward the village.

"Sheriff," shouted the stableman. "I've got a message for you."

James and Thomas halted their horses beside him.

"What is it? Have you seen the man who calls himself Carlos today?"

James raised his voice in reply.

"No, Sheriff. But Mrs. Ellingham fired all the servants this morning. Told us she's going on a long journey. Sir William and Lady Ellene arrived at Coeur de Lion a while ago and told me to send you there."

"Thank you, man. We're on our way."

They spurred their horses into a gallop. The men met with a haunting silence upon entering the courtyard. No servants came to greet them and take their horses. They spotted two horses near the barn.

"It looks like Ellene and William are still here." James felt a shiver of dread as his eyebrows shot up. "I fear something isn't right."

"Could they have heard of Rafe's escape and come to Marguerite's rescue?" Thomas wondered.

"No, we were the first to discover it. Still, William mentioned yesterday he was coming to help Marguerite go over the inventory. They probably passed us in the village while we went to find the man with the bloodhounds. Only one way to find out."

They tethered their horses alongside the other two, unsheathed their swords, and ran to the house. The smell of burning fabric and wood filled the air as thick smoke billowed from under the entryway. As they opened the door, the intense heat of the fire at the bottom of the stairs hit them. They both started coughing from the smoke.

James shouted. "Ellene? William? Are you here?" He felt a wave of relief flood his body, followed by a chill of fear when Ellene answered him from upstairs.

"James, thank God you are here. Marguerite and Rafe tried to kill us. We're trapped upstairs. Both the front and back stairs are on fire." Ellene's voice shook with fear.

"We have to climb out a window. There is no other way to escape the fire."

James heard William's shout above the crackling fire. He sprinted outside, his heart pounding, and scanned the windows. Meanwhile, Thomas found a bucket of water in the kitchen and threw it on the fire, to no avail.

James rushed back inside. "There's a tree outside the window of the front bedroom. Can you get to that room?"

"Yes, we can." Ellene's voice still shook.

The siblings made their way through the thick smoke to the bedroom door. With a growing sense of urgency, William cursed when he realized the door was locked, hindering their progress. Coughing, he raised the mace and used it to batter the door until it shattered. William rushed to the window, threw open the wooden shutters, and stuck his head out to assess their means of descent. James stood in the bright sunlight with his eyes fixed on the open window above him. As William turned to face Ellene, his brows furrowed in a frown.

"The tree grows just outside the window. I can lower you to a tree limb. James is beneath the tree to catch you. Then I can climb down myself."

Ellene coughed as smoke wafted into the room and sweat trickled down her back. The flames crept further up the stairs. She realized they had two choices: either they would burn in the fire, or they could go out the window and risk falling from the tree. She made her way to the window.

"Hurry. Hurry." James shouted from the ground. He knew how much she dreaded heights. "You know I'll catch you, Ellene."

Ellene scrambled onto the windowsill, fighting her voluminous skirt, and rotated her body. Her feet dangled as William gripped her wrists. He stretched his arms as far as he could and eased her down. Her feet flailed, trying to find the branch. Blood seeped from her arm after she scraped it on the wall. Keeping her gaze fixed on her brother kept her from panicking.

"Ellene, stop kicking. Move your left foot to your left. There, feel the branch?" James coached from below.

"Yes." Ellene moved her foot to the branch and carefully put her weight on it.

"Now put the other foot on the branch and try to grab a limb for balance."

She moved her other foot to the branch. She dared to look at the tree and noticed a sturdy limb within arm's reach. William held onto one wrist while she reached for the limb with the other hand. He almost fell headfirst out the window and had to release her wrist to catch himself. Gasping with fear, Ellene threw her arms around the trunk.

"Now what?" Ellene pleaded. She swallowed the impulse to burst into tears. She knew she had to get down so William could follow.

"There is another branch below you. Try to lower yourself to it. I can reach you if you get to the lower branch." Beads of sweat cascaded down James' face. He held his arms up and shifted his weight, stirring the pungent scent of sweat into the air.

Ellene, burdened by her billowing skirt, scrambled down to the lower branch, then James grabbed her lower legs and eased her out of the tree. He set Ellene on her feet, pulling her close and pressing his face against her neck as he gave her a fierce hug. She gulped the air and coughed to get the smoke out of her lungs. Tears welled up in her eyes, and she felt the salty drops roll down her cheeks.

William was tall enough that his feet connected with the branch when he lowered himself from the window. He felt the rough bark against his hands as he scrambled down from the tree.

"Not so tight, James. You're suffocating me," Ellene objected.

"Are you hurt?" He loosened his hug, but kept a grip on her arms and studied her face. A layer of black soot from the fire had settled on her cheeks and forehead. He was terrified to think about how he would cope if she had died.

"No, just too much smoke." She had a coughing fit.

"Tell me what happened."

William recounted how they came to be there that morning. Then he explained what they discovered. "Marguerite and Rafe met in London. They arranged for her to marry Eustace. She's pregnant with Rafe's child, and when Eustace found out, he threatened to send her away. Fearing penury, she poisoned Eustace's honey. She expected to inherit his money. Rafe tried to steal the estate when they found out she was not an heir. Rafe stole a dagger and freed himself from the jail, and they agreed to leave together. They bound and gagged us in the upstairs closet and set the house afire."

A sad expression crossed Ellene's face as she shook her head. "She never loved William. She was just after his money."

James moved his eyes away from the siblings and noticed Thomas waiting for his orders regarding what to do next. He heard dogs baying and shouts from the posse as they approached the estate.

"The fire is too intense to put out with only the four of us. The posse and dogs are coming, so maybe they can help. Did Marguerite say where they were going?"

"Yes. To France." There was bitterness in the way William spoke.

"Ellene, I hate to leave you here, but I need to catch those two before they escape." James clenched his jaw. He found himself torn between his desire to safeguard Ellene and his duty to apprehend evildoers.

"Go, go. Capture them before they hurt anyone else. We will be fine." She furrowed her brow. "They were foolish to leave our horses. We'll head back to your office and wait for you there."

"Let's go, Thomas. We need to catch Rafe and Marguerite."

James kissed Ellene and ran to his horse. He and Thomas galloped off to catch the couple. At the end of the lane leading up to the estate, they encountered a family of traders driving a wagon loaded with goods heading toward the village.

"Did you catch sight of a man and woman on horseback on the road? Thin man with a face like a weasel, beautiful woman? Both with panniers?"

"Yes, headed east." The man squinted and pointed east. "They were a few miles up the road. They were in a hurry. Almost ran into the wagon."

"Many thanks," James nodded. He and Thomas galloped toward the east.

Beyond the estate, the road wound past small holdings on the way to the coast. Hoping to intercept them, the men took a shortcut, aware of the many turns ahead. By crossing a field and going down a lane, they got ahead of the couple on the road. Concealed in the vegetation, they awaited their arrival. When the pair approached, James and Thomas sprang onto the road. Thomas brandished his sword and James aimed his firearm.

Rafe and Marguerite startled at the sudden appearance of James and Thomas. They yanked the reins of their horses to avoid a collision. The air filled with the sound of hooves skidding on the dirt road, while the horses snorted in protest.

Marguerite thought fast. "James, I'm so relieved. This man is kidnapping me. He killed my friends and took me as a hostage."

"Is that your story, Rafe?" James stared at the man and waved his weapon.

"No, it was her idea to set fire to the house and kill her friends. I just wanted the money."

"It so happens that your victims are still alive, although the house is in awful shape. I arrest you both for theft and attempted murder. Throw in arson and escaping from prison and you two will probably hang."

Rafe blanched. "No, I won't go back. You'll have to catch me." He spurred his horse into a gallop.

James aimed his firearm and shot at Rafe, who shrieked and fell from the saddle, bleeding from his shoulder. Marguerite, her palms sweaty and her face ghostly pale, sat with her hands held up, her eyes wide with fear. Thomas produced two lengths of rope, which they used to tie the fugitives to their horses.

On the journey to the jail in Haver Hamlet, Marguerite's tears flowed as she hung her head. Rafe drifted in and out of consciousness. James and Thomas rode in silence, each lost in his own thoughts about the capture of the criminals.

Chapter Forty-Two

DETAILS REVEALED

W illiam, James, and Thomas arrived in the courtyard at Haver Hall as the sun sank low on the horizon. Jeremy and Avrill went outside to greet them, and Clive took their horses to the stable. Avrill chatted with Thomas as they made their way into the house. William frowned but did not comment.

Ellene felt relief when they appeared. She moved toward James and they embraced in the Great Hall. He held her close, closing his eyes and inhaling her lavender scent.

"I'm so thankful that is over with," he whispered in her ear. "Now we can spend more time together."

"Were they both convicted?" Ellene noticed his grim countenance.

"Yes. We'll tell you and Avrill about the trials after we eat."

James and Ellene clasped hands as they made their way to the dining room, following the others. Bridgette and Sorcha brought out platters of meat, cheese, vegetables, and fresh bread once everyone was seated around the table. Jeremy brought ale and poured it into their goblets. Ellene observed the men had ravenous appetites.

After everyone satisfied their hunger, Ellene cleared her throat.

"So, both the trials have ended?" she inquired, her eyes searching for confirmation.

William and Thomas looked at James, who hesitated for a moment, exhaled with a long breath, then began speaking.

"Callum held separate trials, first Rafe and then Marguerite. The trial revealed Rafe and Marguerite spun a web of lies about their relationship and their involvement with Eustace."

"What were the charges, Uncle James?" Avrill asked.

"Charges against Rafe included arson, assault on the jailer, attempted murder of your father and aunt, escape from jail, and theft of the gold and silver items from the estate. Rafe's wound became infected and painful. He was just alert enough to defend himself. He admitted to being Harry, the wine dealer, and he assaulted Marguerite by mistake in the barn, thinking she was a servant who caught him snooping. When the jury found Rafe guilty on all counts, Callum put on his black cap and condemned Rafe to death by hanging."

Avrill's hand flew to her mouth in surprise as she exclaimed, "I never met someone before who hanged."

"Fortunately, it's not a common occurrence," William remarked.

"What about Marguerite? What will happen to her?" Ellene recognized the emotional impact their past relationship still had on William.

William hoisted his goblet and gulped. James lifted an eyebrow, then continued.

"The charges against her were like Rafe's, with a few important differences. Since she confessed to poisoning her husband, that was the primary one. Another charge was that she fraudulently claimed Eustace was the father of her baby to gain control of the estate."

William chimed in. "Marguerite claimed during the trial that she feared for her life when Eustace attacked her so she poisoned him before he could kill her. She expressed remorse, of course. She reluctantly admitted that her professed love for me was all an act, a calculated move to liberate herself from Rafe's dominating influence. And she blamed Rafe for everything else."

"Is she to be hanged as well?" Ellene asked.

"No, the penalty for poisoning her husband is to be burned." James said. "Since she's pregnant, Callum delayed her execution. They will hold her in jail until after the baby is born. Rev. Broun volunteered to take the baby and find a Christian home for it."

"There was trouble on the way back to the jailhouse. The villagers were angry that she poisoned Eustace. They watched from the side of the road. Some hissed and jeered and threw rotten vegetables that narrowly missed us. James pulled his sword from its sheath, and the sight of his blade caused them to scatter," Thomas said.

A shiver ran down Ellene's spine, a chilling reminder of the gravity of the situation.

"What about Coeur de Lion? What will happen to it now?"

"That is for Robert and the Crown to sort out."

"My heart goes out to Marguerite. She is young and naïve. Rafe deceived her, and Eustace abused her. She wanted you to rescue her, William, but in the end returned to Rafe." Ellene's words were barely audible as she spoke.

"Don't forget, she is now an adult. She murdered Eustace, and she almost cost us our lives as well. Our offer to help her meant nothing in the end. Pray for her soul, that she repents before her death." There was a bitter edge to William's voice as he spoke.

Several minutes passed in silence until William shattered the stillness.

"James, I'm not sure what to say. I never believed Marguerite could poison her husband. I truly thought she loved me. She beguiled me so I couldn't see clearly." William put his head in his hands, eyes glistening.

"She deceived both of us. I considered her a close friend." Ellene reached out and squeezed her brother's hand. "Avrill told me she didn't trust her, but I thought she just was jealous because you paid Marguerite so much attention."

"Marguerite was more open around me because she expected me to be gone soon enough. To her, I'm still a child. I think I saw a side of her you and Papa never saw." Avrill spoke with solemnity.

"Well, I'm relieved it's over. Right now, I'm eager to get on with our lives." James' warm hand enveloped Ellene's. "Now that we have solved the mysteries and sentenced the criminals, shall we arrange a wedding?" James looked at the siblings.

"Agreed." Ellene and William replied enthusiastically.

A messenger arrived at Robert's office and handed him a letter. He was stunned to discover Queen Elizabeth's seal on it. His knees buckled, and he sank into his chair. A message from the queen demanded prompt attention. He broke the seal, then unfolded the parchment. The signature at the bottom was William Cecil, the queen's secretary. He scanned the letter, then read it again more slowly.

To my loyal subject, Robert White, Esquire

Regarding the demise of Eustace Ellingham, former Mayor of Haver Hamlet and Owner of Coeur de Lion:

Until Her Majesty the Queen appoints the new Mayor of Haver Hamlet, the Office of the Mayor shall remain unoccupied.

According to the entailments, ownership of the Coeur de Lion estate has reverted to Her Majesty the Queen. It shall remain in her possession until she deems it fit to bestow upon a loyal subject of the realm.

The position of Estate Administrator shall be retained by Robert White, Esquire, until the new Owner assumes possession. The Estate Administrator possesses the jurisdiction to use the estate funds for repairing the fire damage sustained in the house and other repairs as necessary.

Quarterly, the Estate Administrator is required to submit an accounting of income and expenses for Coeur de Lion to the Treasury until the new Owner takes possession.

Robert set the letter down on his oak desk, shifting the pile of papers nearby. He rubbed his chin as he pondered its impact on Haver Hamlet. He thought Andrew would not be pleased to hear the news as it would stall, or perhaps end, his ambition to become the mayor.

EPILOGUE

A week later, James and Ellene sat facing William in his office. William glanced at the two scrolls in front of him, their surfaces covered in dense, meticulous handwriting. He had paper and pen close at hand on his desk. Sunlight from the windows behind him bathed the room in its warm glow.

William beamed at his sister and James. "I know you want to discuss Ellene's dowry before you marry. Here is the marriage contract from her union with Lord Hunter, showing those dowry terms." He pointed to one scroll. "Hunter's heirs returned some of the property to her after he died, but not all. In addition, she received a bequest from his estate. This is a copy of his will." He pointed to the other scroll.

Ellene, wearing James' brooch, squirmed in her seat, trying to get comfortable. Customs dictated wealthy families exchange property before marriage. It could be rings or other pieces of jewelry, money, livestock, sometimes real estate. Still, this discussion of her dowry made her feel like she was chattel. As if her brother was having to increase her attractiveness to James by adding material goods.

James leaned forward and took the scrolls, then scrutinized them while settling back in his chair. As they discussed the terms, the men's voices filled the room with a low hum. William took notes on what they discussed. The faint scent of ink and parchment lingered in the air. Quills scratching on paper provided a rhythmic backdrop to their negotiations.

She studied the two men she loved as they traded information. James struggled to keep his features neutral, yet a momentary flash of emotion escaped. It disappeared before she could discern what it meant. She may have erred by joining them during the meeting, but her curiosity got the best of her.

Her parents arranged her previous marriage when she was not much older than Avrill. She was too grief stricken when her husband died to pay attention to her inheritance. Intrigued, she now wanted to learn more. As William enumerated the livestock, personal, and real property belonging to her, she realized she was a wealthy woman. Maybe her wealth would enable James to resign from his position as sheriff and devote his full attention to his estate.

After settling the dowry, James proposed the terms of their marriage contract, discussing the arrangement of her inheritance if he were to pass away before her.

"I also agree to be Avrill's guardian if you were to become incapacitated or die before she is married." James pointed to that paragraph in his contract.

After Marguerite and Rafe tried to kill them, Ellene convinced William to provide a guardian for his daughter in the event he died before Avrill could marry. Because of the special bond James and Avrill shared, he agreed without hesitation.

When the men declared they were finished, James pulled Ellene close, wrapping his arm around her shoulder.

"I love Ellene and want to do what's best for her. I think we can tell Robert to draw up the documents for us to sign. We can ask the vicar to publish the marriage banns this weekend. In just a month's time, we'll become husband and wife. I'll have a banquet before then to announce our betrothal."

Ellene's breath caught in her throat. A month? Married so soon? Did she make the right decision? She realized that signing the papers would bind her forever, even if she later regretted it. James noticed her eyes widen and her color fading away.

James and William stood, then James helped her to her feet.

"Will you walk with me, Ellene? We can talk awhile."

"Yes, let's walk." She gave him an awkward smile, and he grasped her hand.

The only sound that accompanied them was the gentle rustle of the grass as they left the house and ventured into the field. They paused in the shade of an enormous tree. For a few minutes, they stood listening to the birds' warble and the leaves whisper in the wind. James' eyes lingered on Ellene, taking in every detail on her face.

"Ellene, what's troubling you? It looked like you were frightened when I mentioned our wedding. I'd hoped you'd be just as thrilled about our marriage as I am." He gazed into her eyes, feeling the electricity between them.

"When you and William haggled about the dowry, I felt diminished somehow. You're not just after me for my money, are you?"

"Ellene, Ellene. My love for you is deep and timeless. I don't view you as property. I'd still want to marry you if all you had was what you're wearing. But it turns out that you're a woman of wealth. I intend to be a faithful husband and a careful guardian. Please believe what I'm telling you."

"The thought of the marriage taking place in just a month makes me nervous. There is much to do. It will be a major change for both of us."

"Yes, but we'll help each other adjust."

Ellene gazed into his eyes, which expressed a gentle, loving concern. When they first met, their interactions were combative. He dismissed her opinions as ignorant. But now he treated her with patience and respect. He could have ended their relationship after discovering that she had withheld information about Marguerite, but he did not.

"I love you." James leaned over and pressed his lips against hers. She kissed him back, and they fell into each other's arms.

"I love you, too," she murmured, her voice trembling with emotion. "I want to marry you." She felt an overwhelming sense of security in his powerful embrace.

"That's what I wanted to hear."

Thank you for reading my books about Lady Ellene and Sheriff James. It will help me continue writing if you leave a review on the site where you purchased the book.

ABOUT THE AUTHOR

R. M. Shepherd's works explore the lives of women who challenge the norms imposed by society. Her novels take place in England, Scotland, and France during the Tudor era (sixteenth century).

This novel is the second in a series set in County Havershire. Lady Ellene and Sheriff James constantly clash and disagree. The mayor's death by poison forces them to work together to find the killer. As they delve deeper, they discover a complex web of lies that put several lives in jeopardy. *The Purloined Dagger*, the first book in the series, introduces Ellene and James as they seek to unravel the mystery of a stolen family heirloom, in a captivating locked-room mystery scenario.

A trilogy penned by Shepherd brings to life the intriguing tale of Marjory Bowes Knox and her husband, the controversial Scottish preacher John Knox, set amidst the years of the English and Scottish Protestant revolutions. The books, *A Pearl to Cherish*, *In the Shadowy Vale*, and *Led Forth from the Shadows*, all explored the themes of faith, hope, and love.

A resident of Galveston County on the Texas Gulf Coast on the Texas Gulf Coast, Shepherd enjoys crocheting, knitting, and reading. She is married and lives near her family.

Other Works by R. M. Shepherd

Fiction:

The Purloined Dagger (2020)

A Pearl to Cherish: Book One Marjory Trilogy 2nd ed. (2021)

In the Shadowy Vale: Book Two Marjory Trilogy (2021)

Led Forth from the Shadows: Book Three Marjory Trilogy (2022)

Non-Fiction:

Sacred Narratives: The Literary Craft of the Bible (2025)

John Knox: Sounding God's Trumpet (2018)

He Strikes at the Root (2016)

These books are available in digital and paperback formats online.

Short Stories:

"A Hurricane Like No Other" in *Hurricane Harvey: A Storm Like No Other*

"Gracie's Boat Ride" in *Hurricane Harvey: A Storm Like No Other*

Please visit the author on social media:

Website: www.shepherdrm.com

Facebook: R. M. Shepherd

Email: shepherdrm@gmail.com

Amazon author page: R-M-Shepherd

Goodreads: R. M. Shepherd